Robert Muchamore was born in 1972. His books have sold millions of copies around the world, and he regularly tops the bestseller charts.

He has won numerous awards for his writing, including the Red House Children's Book Award. For more information on Robert and his work, visit www.cherubcampus.com

Praise for CHERUB and *Henderson's Boys*:

'These are the best books ever!' Jack, 12

'So good I forced my friends to read it, and they're glad I did!' Helen, 14

'The CHERUB books are so cool, they have everything I ever wanted!' Josh, 13

'Never get tired of recommending CHERUB/*Henderson's Boys* to reluctant readers, because it never fails!' Cat, children's librarian

'My son could never see the point of reading a book until he read *The Recruit*. I want to thank you from the bottom of my heart for igniting the fire.' Donna

BY ROBERT MUCHAMORE

The Henderson's Boys series:
1. The Escape
2. Eagle Day
3. Secret Army
4. Grey Wolves
5. The Prisoner
6. One Shot Kill
7. Scorched Earth

The CHERUB series:
1. The Recruit
2. Class A
3. Maximum Security
4. The Killing
5. Divine Madness
6. Man vs Beast
7. The Fall
8. Mad Dogs
Dark Sun
9. The Sleepwalker
10. The General
11. Brigands M.C.
12. Shadow Wave

CHERUB series 2:
1. People's Republic
2. Guardian Angel
3. Black Friday
4. Lone Wolf

Don't miss Robert's breathtaking new series:

Rock War
The Audition (ebook)
Boot Camp (coming soon)

LONE WOLF

Robert Muchamore

Hodder
Children's
Books

a division of Hachette Children's Books

HODDER CHILDREN'S BOOKS

First published in Great Britain in 2014 by Hodder Children's Books

This paperback edition published in 2015

ISBN 978 1 444 91411 5
Export edition: 978 1 444 92856 3

Typeset in Goudy by Avon DataSet Ltd, Bidford-on-Avon, Warwickshire

Hodder Children's Books
An imprint of Hachette Children's Group
Carmelite House
50 Victoria Embankment,
London EC4Y 0DZ

An Hachette UK Company
www.hachette.co.uk

WHAT IS CHERUB?

CHERUB is a branch of British Intelligence. Its agents are aged between ten and seventeen years. Cherubs are mainly orphans who have been taken out of care homes and trained to work undercover. They live on CHERUB campus, a secret facility hidden in the English countryside.

WHAT USE ARE KIDS?

Quite a lot. Nobody realises kids do undercover missions, which means they can get away with all kinds of stuff that adults can't.

Key qualities for CHERUB recruits include high levels of intelligence and physical endurance, along with the ability to work under stress and think for oneself. The three hundred kids who live on CHERUB campus are recruited between the ages of six and twelve and allowed to work undercover from age ten, provided they make it through a gruelling hundred-day basic training programme.

CHERUB T-SHIRTS

Cherubs are ranked according to the colour of the T-shirts they wear on campus. ORANGE is for visitors. RED is for kids who live on CHERUB campus but are too young to qualify as agents. BLUE is for kids in basic training. A GREY T-shirt means you're qualified for missions. NAVY is a reward for outstanding performance on a single mission. The BLACK T-shirt is the ultimate recognition for outstanding achievement over a number of missions, while the WHITE T-shirt is worn by retired CHERUB agents and some staff.

PART ONE
December 2012

1. CASH

Kentish Town, north London

There was ice on the pavement from snowfall a few days earlier and the wind had a sting that made Craig Willow pull his Spurs scarf over his ears. He was a big man, with a boxer's flattened nose, but two decades past glory days in the ring.

The street was all Victorian houses. Most had been refurbished by posh types, but number sixteen was shabby, with a tumbledown garage and ancient sash windows faded to the dull green of something you might hack up after a dose of flu.

Craig pulled a front-door key out of grubby tracksuit bottoms. The place had been used as student accommodation until a few summers earlier. The hallway had pre-pay gas and electric meters, pigeonholes for mail and a long-disconnected payphone.

There was no heat, but it was still warmer than outside. Craig pulled off sheepskin gloves and gave numb fingers a rub before banging his fist on a metal door. Someone sped downstairs on the other side and spoke with a tetchy Welsh accent.

'That you, Craig?'

Craig sounded irritated. 'Nah, it's Father bloody Christmas come a week early. You can see me on the CCTV.'

'Hagar says you've got to say the password. Nobody gets in or out without it.'

'OK,' Craig said, taking a big breath and tightening his fists. 'The password is, *Open the door you little knob head, or I'll stick your skull through the wall.*'

After a pause, bolts started clanking inside the heavily reinforced door. When it swung open, Craig advanced three steps and gently cuffed the skinny teenager on the other side.

'Password,' Craig snorted. 'You're going the right way about getting a slap.'

But Jake didn't take the threat seriously. 'Boss's son,' he teased, as he led Craig up steps covered with frayed carpet. 'You'll probably have to call me sir, some day.'

'You're Hagar's *step*son,' Craig corrected. 'When he loses interest in your mother he'll ditch you like week-old bread.'

The conversation dropped because they'd rounded the top of the stairs and stepped into a large room. There were blackout blinds at all the windows. At one end was a pair of long desks, and an electronic money counting machine. The other end of the room was a chill-out area, with wrecked couches and a big-screen TV showing Sky Sports with the sound muted.

The two men in the room were touching fifty and seemed intimidated by Craig's bulk.

'What's been happening?' Craig demanded.

'Three hundred and sixteen thousand,' the taller of the two men said, as he pointed to a large safe. 'Vacuum-wrapped into 10K blocks. The other safe's got two hundred and twelve. And there's eighteen KGs of cocaine in the sports bag.'

Craig's brow shot up and one of the men took a frightened half-step backwards.

'Are you messing with my head?' Craig blurted angrily. 'Who said to send drugs to the count house? Why didn't someone call me?'

Jake answered. 'Piece of business went bad. It were an emergency, like. Hagar said it's a lot of merchandise and this was the safest place.'

Craig shook his head with contempt. It was a basic rule of drug dealing that spanned millionaire kingpins to kids hustling £10 bags on the street: you always keep money and merchandise separate. 'Any pick-ups scheduled?' he asked.

'It's just you and Jake on guard, unless something changes.'

'OK then,' Craig said, looking at the money counters. 'Get yourselves home to them wives and not a peep to anyone about our eighteen packets of powder.'

'A couple of crews came up short,' one of the oldies

said, pointing to a notebook on the table. 'Archway firm, as usual. It's all in the ledger.'

'A few swings of my old baseball bat usually loosens their pockets,' Craig said, relishing the prospect of some violence.

Jake gormlessly mimed the gesture of a swinging baseball bat as the two cash counters headed for home. Once they were through the steel door at the bottom of the stairs, Craig made sure they'd cleared the building on a security camera before going down and putting the bolts back across the steel door.

When he got back up, he was again irritated by the bulging sports bag filled with eighteen kilos of cocaine under one of the desks. Apart from a few assault charges, Craig had always stayed out of trouble with the law and had never been to prison. Getting busted guarding a house full of illicit money would mean a three- to five-year prison sentence. A house full of drugs *and* money would up the sentence to ten years and the thought sat uncomfortably as he dumped his jacket on the couch.

Jake shouted from the kitchen. 'There's a City match on Sky in a bit. I did a run to Sainsbury's earlier. What do you fancy? There's microwave curry, hot dogs, or I could do bacon, egg and chips.'

Craig made a grunting sound before speaking. 'I'll look in the fridge in a second. I've gotta go upstairs for a shit.'

'I could start cooking,' Jake said.

Craig tutted. 'We're on guard for the next twelve

hours, kid. What difference will waiting for me to take a crap make?'

Craig grabbed a copy of the *Sun* off a coffee table before heading to the bathroom on the top floor. The toilet was rank and the only cleaning product was an empty bottle of Toilet Duck which he lobbed into the bathtub in frustration.

'I'm sick of dirty scumbags never cleaning up after themselves around here,' Craig roared, as he pulled down his tracksuit bottoms and settled on to the toilet.

'You say something, boss?' Jake shouted up.

'Never bloody mind,' Craig said. Then, to himself as he shook his head, 'Twelve hours stuck here with that dumbass . . .'

It was a regular bathroom, apart from the LCD screen which flicked between images from eight different CCTV cameras. They showed everything from the count room and stairs, to the unoccupied lower floors, the back garden and the street out front. There was also a controller which enabled you to pan and zoom each camera.

As Craig aimed a huge fart into the toilet bowl, he was disturbed by a rustling sound behind his head. Thinking it was a mouse or cockroach, he rolled up his newspaper to take a swipe. But instead of an insect he saw that a gloved hand had punched through the plaster wall behind him.

Before Craig could do any more than turn his head, a needle stabbed the flab between his shoulder blades and the hand injected a syringe filled with a fast-acting sedative. As he slumped forwards on the toilet with jeans around his ankles, a woman in a hockey mask began quickly but quietly knocking out chunks of plaster.

Within a minute, the fist-sized hole was big enough for the woman to clamber through. To make it she had to shove Craig's chubby, unconscious body off the toilet. As the woman – who was named Kirsten – knelt down and placed two fingers on his neck to check for a pulse, her thirteen-year-old niece Fay stepped through the hole.

'Is he OK?' Fay asked.

Kirsten and her niece were of similar height and dressed identically in hockey masks, black jeans, hooded fleeces and black Converse All Stars. All of their gear was covered in plaster dust.

'He'll come around in a few hours with a nasty headache and a lot of explaining to do,' Kirsten said. 'Don't forget the bags.'

As Fay knelt on the toilet lid and reached through the hole into the house next door, Kirsten pulled out the handgun holstered around her waist and took the bolt off the door.

'If anything goes wrong, you run like mad,' Kirsten said. 'Although I can't see Jake giving us too many problems.'

Fay nodded as her aunt opened the door and began creeping downstairs. The teenager watched from the landing above as Kirsten surprised Jake in the kitchen.

'On your knees or I'll blow your head off,' Kirsten yelled.

Fay grabbed the backpacks and hurried downstairs, by which time Jake had been marched through to the count room, and made to kneel with his hands on his head.

'Get the brace,' Kirsten ordered, as she kept her gun aimed at Jake's head.

Then Kirsten looked at Jake. 'You know how to open the safes?'

'They're on a time lock,' Jake said, shaking his head frantically. 'Can't open 'em before ten in the morning now.'

Kirsten laughed. 'That's funny, 'cos we patched a link into your CCTV cables. I've been watching this count room for two weeks and I've seen you opening that safe up at all times. Day and night.'

As Kirsten said this, Jake's posture deflated and Fay pulled a bizarre set of rubber underwear out of her backpack.

'You ever been to Texas, Jake?' Kirsten asked.

'No,' Jake said warily.

'Folks grow big out there,' Kirsten began. 'My girl over there is holding genuine Texas Department of Corrections-issue electrified underwear. When they get some real big-assed, hundred and fifty-kilo guy and need to keep him under control, they make him wear one of those. You switch it on for a couple of ticks and it blasts him with enough electricity to make him sob like a pussycat.'

'How long until the morning shift arrives?' Fay asked, following a script she'd practised with her aunt.

'Eleven and a half hours,' Kirsten announced. 'These suits take one or two blasts to break the biggest, meanest men on earth. Now, young Jake, I'm gonna shoot you with a tranquilliser and you'll wake up wearing that underwear. Then I'll have *all* night to zap your tiny little balls. Or, you can be a sensible boy and go open those two safes right now.'

Jake raised one finger and flipped Kirsten off. 'I'm not scared by a couple of chicks,' he spat.

Fay instantly responded by whipping out an extendible baton and smashing Jake in the back of the neck. As he sprawled across sticky carpet, the thirteen-year-old planted the heel of her trainer between Jake's shoulder blades, then expertly grabbed his arm and yanked it up behind his back.

'Jesus, nooooo,' Jake screamed.

'Eleven hours,' Kirsten said, her eyes narrow slits through the hockey mask. 'We may be chicks, but we like to play rough.'

'Stop it,' Jake moaned breathlessly.

'Will you open the safes?' Fay asked.

'If you leave my arm alone.'

Fay let go and allowed Jake to crawl towards the twin safes. As the first one popped open Fay began loading the wodges of vacuum-packed notes into a nylon bag.

'Five hundred and twenty-eight grand in cash,' Kirsten said. 'Plus eighteen kilos of cocaine, which we can offload for another eight hundred.'

'One point three million,' Fay said, as she cracked a smile. 'Not a bad night's work.'

Once the bags were packed, Kirsten jabbed Jake with enough sedative to take him offline for a few hours.

They drove away in Jake's Vauxhall Astra, abandoning it behind St Pancras Station. Once they'd stripped off their black clothes, they picked a taxi off the station rank and took a short ride to a flat in St John's Wood.

2. APARTMENT

Fay cut a striking figure, running along Regent's Park's Outer Circle amidst lawns crisp with morning frost. She was slim, but not skinny. Hazelnut hair and bright green eyes. The thirteen-year-old moved quickly, on battered Asics trainers that had pounded this route a hundred times before. At the end of two laps, she stopped her runner's watch. She was a minute outside her best time, but that wasn't bad considering the stress of the night before.

St John's Wood is one of central London's top neighbourhoods. Luxurious apartment blocks house bankers and wealthy artists, while houses are the preserve of multimillionaire CEOs and pop stars. There's a heavy foreign contingent, which was one of the reasons why Fay could run around the park on a weekday without anyone stopping to ask why she wasn't in school.

Fay stopped in a patisserie to buy croissants and a walnut loaf, before a doorman opened her path into the smart lobby of the apartment building they'd lived in for the past few months. The open-plan twelfth-floor apartment had large windows with a beautiful view over the park.

Kirsten greeted her niece with a smile, but spoke stiffly. 'Do your stretches *properly*, then take your shower.'

Fay dumped the bread on a kitchen cabinet and stepped out of her trainers.

'I'll make you hot chocolate,' Kirsten said. 'Then you need to hit the maths books.'

After dumping her sweaty running gear into a laundry basket, Fay stepped under a hot shower. Her cheeks and fingers were numb from being out in the cold. Her body was toned and quite muscular, but bore a few bruises from regular kickboxing sessions with her aunt.

'Don't take all day in there,' Kirsten shouted.

Fay peered through the steamed-up shower door to make sure the bolt was across, and decided to take as long as she liked.

After dressing in T-shirt and tracksuit bottoms, Fay came out expecting a rebuke from her aunt. Instead she found walnut bread, cheese and diced apple, set out on the dining-table alongside hot chocolate with marshmallows and a three-centimetre stack of stapled printouts.

'What are these, Auntie?' Fay asked, though she could

see that they were from school websites.

'We got lucky, hitting the safe-house when there were drugs *and* money inside,' Kirsten said.

Fay nodded thoughtfully as she stabbed a cube of Cheddar with her fork. 'Hagar will be paranoid that it was an inside job. Which should take the heat off us.'

'Hopefully,' Kirsten agreed. 'We'll launder the cash through our usual route. I have a contact in Manchester who'll give us a fair price for the cocaine. And that puts us over the edge.'

'Over what edge?'

'I've got a couple of jobs in the planning stage which I might as well work through,' Kirsten explained. 'But I can handle them alone.'

Fay's jaw dropped. 'We've worked together since my mum died.'

Kirsten tapped the pile of printouts. 'Those are some of the best fee-paying schools in the country. Or at least the best ones with places for a thirteen-year-old with a patchy school record.'

'You've home-schooled me well enough,' Fay said. 'I don't see why I need some fancy school.'

'Sweetie, I know how much explosive it takes to blow a safe open. I even know guys who'll sell me a few sticks of dynamite. But that doesn't mean I can teach you GCSE chemistry. Plus there's the social side. You can't spend all your life with a thirty-six-year-old auntie. You need to mix with people your own age.'

Fay picked out one of the school pages at random

and scowled at lines of confident-looking kids in a school playground.

'Mum sent me to school when I was little,' Fay said stiffly. 'Other kids pissed me off.'

But Fay had only done a few terms of primary school, and though she was too hardnosed to admit it, the idea of being in a room full of strange kids scared her. 'I'm a lone wolf,' she shouted, as she flicked the mound of printouts on to the floor and stood up. 'When Mum died, you swore *you'd* look after me.'

Kirsten didn't rise to her niece's anger and began calmly picking the papers off the floor. 'This *is* looking after you,' she said, as she calmly placed the papers down in front of Fay. 'Your mum and me were teenagers. We grew up in care homes and began by knocking over street dealers for twenty quid. Then we started with the bigger dealers. Then we started sniffing out cash houses and major drug hauls. Now there's two million in clean cash, which neither of us will be able to spend if we wind up in prison.'

'What'll *you* do all day?' Fay asked. 'I can't see you sitting on your arse watching *Antiques Hunt*.'

Kirsten shrugged. 'I could set up a kickboxing academy. I could buy a café, learn Japanese, take up golf, try the banjo . . .'

Fay snorted. 'What about the thrill of the chase?'

'Luck always runs out, Fay. If we're lucky the cops'll get us and we'll go to prison. But if a dealer catches up, they'll torture and kill us.'

'You're *so* melodramatic,' Fay said.

'Your mother thought she'd live forever and Hagar got her.'

'I don't see why I've got to go to some stupid school,' Fay shouted, as she held up one of the leaflets. 'Look at 'em. Little ladies in pleated skirts and knee socks.'

'If you don't pick one, I will,' Kirsten said. 'Like it or lump it, you're gonna go to school.'

'I'll flunk the entrance exam.'

'Then I'll send you to the local comprehensive. This isn't up for debate, Fay. We've made all the money we need and you're going to school.'

*

Two mornings later, Fay lay on her bed in a pink robe. She'd done the same two laps around the Outer Circle, only this time followed up with an hour-long kickboxing session with her aunt. The room had plenty of wardrobe space, but they moved every few months, so Fay habitually lived out of a pair of wheeled suitcases, whose contents had sprawled out like some multicoloured floor fungus.

Kirsten knocked and came in without waiting. 'Manchester,' she said abruptly. 'Get dressed.'

'Right now?' Fay asked.

'Buyer's all lined up. Sixteen kilos at forty-five thousand per kilo.'

Fay looked confused. 'I thought we stole eighteen.'

'And word's on the street that eighteen got stolen from Hagar, so I'll shift sixteen now and keep a couple back for a rainy day.'

Fay looked excited. As the teenager grabbed jeans

and a T-shirt off the floor, Kirsten was pleased to see the stack of school website printouts looking well thumbed. Fay had also added comments in the margin such as *dorky uniform* and *middle of nowhere*. Kirsten laughed when she saw a picture of a boy with *FIT* written across his school jumper in red biro.

'The four on top are my favourites,' Fay said.

Kirsten laughed. 'All *mixed* schools I see.'

'Well, if you're *forcing* me to go to school, I might as well go where they have some boys.'

'All-girls schools are kind of creepy,' Kirsten agreed. 'And I'm glad you're warming to the idea.'

'So what's the next step?' Fay asked.

'I'll call admissions and see what the situation is,' Kirsten said. 'If they have spaces, it might be possible to get you in after Christmas.'

Fay gulped. 'That's just over three weeks. I *thought* you were talking about September, when the new school year starts.'

'I'd rather you bedded in to school life before you start your GCSEs.'

Fay smiled. 'If I get a good report, can we rob someone during the school holidays?'

Kirsten laughed. 'Fay. You scare me.'

'Why?'

'I rob drug dealers to make money,' Kirsten said. 'You're just like your mother was. You want to rob places for the hell of it.'

3. MAGAZINES

Kirsten drove from London to Manchester in a silver Mercedes wagon, hired using a driving licence and credit card in the name Tamara Cole. Fay spent the journey in the back seat reading a book about a man who sailed around the world. She liked the idea of being all alone in a tiny boat, with waves crashing around it.

'I want to do a sailing course,' Fay announced, as the silver Merc eased past a coachload of pensioners.

'If you do well at your new school,' Kirsten said.

Fay seemed satisfied with the answer and delved back into her book.

Their destination was the Belfont. It was one of Manchester's newest hotels, with a swanky black marble lobby where the air had a slight jasmine scent and illumination so moody that you could barely see a hand in front of your face.

The sixteen kilos of cocaine had travelled in a wheeled aluminium case, and Kirsten had to shoo off a top-hatted doorman eager to help with her luggage. Kirsten asked for directions to a meeting room called The Windermere and got directed to the ninth floor.

After backing away from reception, Kirsten looked at Fay and spoke in a whisper.

'They won't like having a kid in the meeting, so you wait here. They'll want to check every brick for purity before handing over the cash, so I'll be gone for at least forty minutes. Don't wander off.'

Fay didn't look too happy. 'All right if I go to the Starbucks across the street and grab a Frappuccino?'

The green Starbucks roundel was visible in the street opposite the lobby and Kirsten nodded.

'But don't go any further than that. Once we're sorted, we'll find somewhere nice for a late lunch and shopping, OK?'

Fay wasn't a big shopper, but she wanted some new running shoes, and wondered if she'd be able to find any more books on sailing.

As Kirsten waited for the lift up to the ninth floor, Fay exited the hotel lobby through a revolving door and crossed a side street. It was still cold out, so after a short queue she ordered a hot chocolate topped with whipped cream. The Starbucks seats looked comfier than the ones in the hotel lobby so she settled into an armchair close to the counter and fished her book out of a little linen shoulder bag.

Her aunt seemed confident that she'd sell the drugs

they'd stolen from Hagar, but they'd never dealt with this Manchester-based crew before. So even though it was a good book, Fay found it hard to focus with her aunt involved in a seven-hundred-grand drug deal across the street.

She had the hot chocolate up to her lips when a woman kicked her outstretched leg. Instead of saying sorry, she glowered at Fay.

'Can't you mind where you're putting them legs?'

'How about *you* look where you're walking?' Fay spat back irritably.

The woman didn't reply. She just grabbed a cardboard rack with six coffees slotted into it. As she headed for the door, Fay noticed how the woman was all bulked out around her waist, and wearing black shoes like a cop would wear.

Fay took another sip and decided she was being paranoid, but then something else hit her: the woman had spoken with a London accent. So there was a woman from London wearing cop shoes, with her waist bulked out like she had cuffs and equipment. And she was buying six drinks, like there was a whole bunch of them . . .

Am I imagining things?

Sometimes when you're nervous you see things that aren't really there. If Fay had been certain she'd have called her aunt straight away, but she wasn't, so she burned her mouth downing the hot chocolate and stuffed her book back in the linen bag as she headed for the door.

The woman with the six drinks was already across the street and pushing her way through the Belfont's revolving front door. From the rear Fay caught the unmistakable silver glint of a set of handcuffs poking out the bottom of a nylon body warmer.

Fay immediately grabbed her mobile and dialled her aunt.

'Come on,' Fay mouthed, breath curling in front of her face as she reached the hotel's revolving doors. She tried to see what the cop was doing inside but the lobby was too dark. Finally there was a click in her ear.

'Hello, you've reached Tamara Cole. I'm not currently available to take your call. If you'd like to leave a message wait for the beep.'

Fay grunted with frustration and left a message as she pushed through the revolving door. 'Auntie, I just saw a cop heading into the hotel. Leave everything and get the hell out of there.'

As Fay got into the lobby she peered through the oh-so-trendy gloom and saw the cop with the drinks disappear behind a set of closing lift doors. Fay ran to the lifts and pressed the up button. While she waited, she tapped out a text message:

Cops everywhere. Bail now!!!!!

Fay had a horrible queasy feeling as she stepped into the lift. She thought about going to the eighth floor and taking the stairs for the last floor, but she was desperate to give her aunt every possible chance so she decided to risk going straight for the ninth.

The elevator opened into a broad corridor with

grandly named meeting rooms off either side. Fay took a step out and immediately saw a commotion. The Windermere was a double-doored conference room at the end of the hallway. Several armed cops stood about and there was a haze of gun smoke and cocaine powder in the air. At least three men lay handcuffed on the carpet, and another was spread-eagled over a long table getting patted down.

Fay's phone made a *ding-doing* sound. She had a message from her aunt.

DON'T come upstairs

A senior-looking cop was shouting: 'How did you let her get out? I want everyone looking for her.'

Fay stepped back into the lift and pressed G, followed by the *close door* button. It felt like the doors took about a week, but she was soon trundling back down to the lobby, tapping out a text message to her aunt.

Where RU?

All was calm in the lobby. Fay took a deep breath and walked quickly, but not so fast that she'd arouse suspicion. Her heart skipped when she passed a uniformed officer coming through the revolving door into the hotel as she headed out.

Fay didn't know the area and couldn't think of anything she could do to help her aunt. The only logical thing seemed to be to put as much distance between herself and the hotel as possible and then arrange to meet up with her aunt later on, provided she got away. If Kirsten didn't get away then god knows what she'd do.

Fay realised that she was trembling as she crossed the street. Another text from her aunt buzzed in her pocket.

Turn your phone off. Cops might use it to track you.

Fay stopped walking, intending to text straight back. But she got a weird feeling like there was something creeping up on her, and when she looked behind she saw two bulky cops.

'You've not done anything,' one of them said. 'We want to ask some questions about your aunt.'

'My arse,' Fay said, before breaking into a sprint.

She almost ran straight into the path of an oldie on a Motability scooter. Once she'd regained her balance, Fay ran fifty metres on from the Starbucks and turned into a busy shopping street. The pavements were rammed with pre-Christmas shoppers so she cut on to tram tracks.

After a few hundred metres, Fay took a glance back and saw that one of the cops had dropped back more than seventy metres, while the other had given up completely. The only trouble was, a tram was turning into her path, with the driver frantically ringing a bell for her to get out of the way.

As Fay hopped back on to the pavement, she landed awkwardly on a tram track and stumbled head first into a crowd of shoppers.

'Grab hold of her!' the chasing cop shouted.

Fay scraped her knee on the pavement as she hit the ground, alongside a black woman and a tangle of Primark and M&S bags.

'Sorry,' Fay gasped.

The woman was furious because some mugs had broken.

'Keep hold of her,' the cop shouted, as the crowd parted to let him through.

A man grabbed Fay around the waist and tried to scoop her up, but she managed to catch him in the ribs with the point of her elbow. Somehow she got running again. The shopping street was rammed, so she set off across a pedestrianised square with a Christmas tree at its centre.

There was no sign of the cop, but Fay was still in a strange town with no idea where she was and no idea whether her aunt had been busted. After a final sprint, she found herself on the far side of the square and reckoned she'd stand out less if she slowed to a brisk stroll.

Once she was walking again, Fay reached into her bag and checked her phone, but there hadn't been any more messages from her aunt. She cut into a dingy-looking alleyway filled with barber shops, kebab houses and places that unlocked mobile phones. Her hand was still in the bag when a uniformed female cop appeared at the opposite end of the alleyway. She spun around, only to see that the original guy who'd been following her was closing in from behind.

'Stay still and I won't hurt you,' the woman shouted, as she pulled out a baton.

Fay's left hand rummaged inside her bag until she felt the handle of a small pocket knife. She figured that her best chance was to charge the smaller female cop, so she unfolded the blade and made a run.

Seeing nothing but a slim thirteen-year-old, the female officer made herself broad and took a clumsy swing with her extendable baton. Fay used her kickboxing training and spun away from the blow, then launched a backwards kick.

The policewoman's body armour made this blow less effective than Fay had hoped, but it was enough to knock the officer off balance and send her slamming backwards into the aluminium shutters of a balti house.

The male officer had now caught up and he swung the baton at Fay's arm in an attempt to knock the knife out of her hand. But Fay saw the move coming. She stepped back, then lunged with the knife as the officer overbalanced.

The tip of the blade caught the officer's throat, before making a sweeping cut up his right cheek. Fay jumped back as the cop stumbled forwards coughing blood. If he died, she was screwed. If her aunt had been arrested, she was screwed. It was almost as bad as when they'd found her mum, tied up and tortured by one of the dealers they'd ripped off.

But at least I'm a good runner.

4. HIDE

Fay kept seeing the knife and the blood. She'd been running for ages, half expecting a helicopter overhead or squad cars to come and scoop her up. But she'd made it a couple of kilometres out of the town centre, to an area dominated by shabby low-rise housing.

Fay ducked between a side wall and an overgrown hedge. Her trainers squelched over frosty bin bags until she settled on a short row of steps leading to a boarded-up front door.

She checked her Samsung for messages, and there was nothing since the text from Aunt Kirsten: Turn your phone off. Cops might use it to track you.

She'd left the phone on, hoping for more information, but now she held the power off button until the screen went black. There was a lot to think about. *How had they been set up? Had Kirsten got away? Was the cop dead? Where to go now?*

Fay realised there was no point losing her head thinking about the big picture. Right now she had to focus on getting as much distance as possible between herself and the scene of the crime. She started forming a plan, which began by taking a tissue out of her jacket, moistening it on a frosty handrail and using it to wipe her bloody knife.

After dumping the stained tissue and shaking off frozen fingers, she pulled a Velcro wallet from the back of her jeans. She had twenty-five pounds, plus a cash card which the police would trace in seconds if she dared to use it.

Fay reckoned the best strategy would be to go back to her home turf in north London. The police might know about the apartment in St John's Wood, but Kirsten had a flat and a couple of lock-ups in less salubrious neighbourhoods and it was also where Kirsten would head if she'd got away.

The problem was, the police would have CCTV from the hotel showing what Fay looked like and what she was wearing, and they'd doubtless have people on lookout at the train stations. If it had been summer Fay would have considered spending a night or two in the boarded-up house until the pressure died down, but it was December and she'd freeze.

Fay decided she needed to get a change of clothes, more money and if possible a smartphone. Her first thought was to mug someone, but she'd only get clothes by ripping them off a victim so she decided to go for a burglary.

The area looked rough, but you can learn a lot about a house from the exterior. Net curtains and neat front gardens mean old people, who'll probably be at home and won't have the right kind of clothes or a smartphone. A people carrier in the drive means a family with kids and barred windows mean they've been burgled before.

Fay had almost lost hope when she found a house with old-fashioned sash windows and recycling bins stuffed with takeout pizza boxes and cheap supermarket-brand beer cans. It *had* to be students.

Fay peeked through the letterbox and saw bikes in the hallway. Then she crept around the side to a large window, which gave her a vista over a filthy kitchen with a week's worth of washing-up in the sink.

She gave the back door a tug, just in case it had been left open. Unfortunately it wasn't that easy, but the small window alongside was big enough to get through. After a furtive glance, she took a step backwards and gave the window a kick before ducking down.

When she was sure that nobody inside had heard, Fay put her arm carefully between the shards of jagged glass and reached across to the inside handle of the back door. Glass crunched underfoot as she stepped into the kitchen. The warm air was a relief but there was a god-awful smell, like old curry mixed with rotting vegetables.

A sign on the fridge read, *Abandon hope ye who enter here*. Fay braved the warning and was pleasantly surprised to find a bottle of freshly squeezed orange juice well inside its sell-by date. She gulped it as she walked down the hallway.

At the bottom of the stairs she was alarmed by a gentle thumping sound. The bass line became something vaguely recognisable as she crept upstairs. After passing a bathroom that was better not thought about, and the closed door which was the source of the music, Fay checked out the other two bedrooms on the floor.

One belonged to a guy who'd left his stinking rugby gear all over the place and whose idea of interior decoration was to hang a bright yellow Norwich City flag across his window. The third first-floor bedroom looked a lot more promising.

Its owner was female. Judging by the clothes strewn about she was a borderline Goth, similar height and shoe size to Fay but a much heavier build. Fay undressed quickly, swapping her blood-spattered jacket and jeans for a black puffa jacket, black leather boots and striped black and green leggings.

She swept a ten-pound note and a fiver's worth of change off a small desk. Unfortunately, people take their smartphones with them when they go out, but there was a laptop on the desk, and Fay was delighted when she tapped the space bar and it came to life without demanding a password.

After opening the web browser and noting that the laptop's owner was called Chloe, Fay typed the name of the street she was on into Google Maps to work out where she was. Then she looked at the train routes back to London. Travelling from Manchester Piccadilly in the centre of town was too risky, but she worked out that she could get a bus from a nearby street to

Stockport and pick up a London train from there.

The bad news was that she now had about forty pounds, and the ticket to London was sixty-five. Dressed in her baggy Goth gear, Fay headed up to the second floor. This floor comprised a single room carved into the loft space.

The occupants seemed to be a couple and Fay started going through the drawers looking for money. She found a few euros and a dead mouse between the wardrobes, but the problem was, students don't have lots of money, and they take the money they do have with them when they go out.

Fay was back on the stairs when she heard the first-floor toilet flush. She doubled back, but the guy who'd been listening to music in his room eyeballed her halfway down the stairs.

'Who are you?' the lad asked. This was a shared house, so his north-west accent sounded more curious than alarmed.

'I'm friends with Chloe,' Fay said airily. 'She gave me the key and said to wait for her. We're studying together.'

Fay emphasised this by making a writing gesture.

'Studying what exactly?'

'Our subject,' Fay stuttered.

'You'll have a tough time. She dropped out and works behind the till in Tesco's. Now tell us who you are and why you're sneaking around our house?'

As the lad said this, he moved up the stairs and tried to grab Fay's arm. He was well-built, so Fay's only advantage was surprise. She let the hand grip her shoulder, but countered with a vicious palm under the chin. As the student stumbled back, Fay launched one of her newly acquired black boots at his stomach. Then she jumped down the stairs and knocked him cold with a knee to the face.

'That'll teach you to ask awkward bloody questions,' Fay said, as she crouched down and started going through the student's pockets.

She found ten pounds in his jeans, but hit the jackpot when she got into his room and found a wallet containing fifty. That gave her enough to get back to London and grab something to eat along the way. There was also an iPhone, but it asked for a pin code when she turned it on, so she left it behind.

5. EUSTON

Fay expected cops every time someone came into the carriage, every time the train stopped and when she arrived at London Euston. It was 8 p.m., bitter cold and sleety. After scoffing a quick Burger King she took a bus to Islington.

The studio apartment Kirsten owned there was at the top of a six-storey block. The lift was out and Fay got called a 'skinny slut' by random kids hanging out on the stairs. Once she was in, she switched the boiler on. She found a bin liner and placed the knife in it, along with everything she'd worn that day.

After a shower Fay towelled off and opened a wardrobe. There were spare clothes, though she'd grown since they'd been left here so she ended up wearing some of her aunt's gear instead. Once she was dressed, Fay pulled an armchair out of a corner, rolled back the carpet and lifted a floorboard.

She felt slightly more secure when she saw the cache. There was twenty thousand in cash, two small bricks of cocaine, mobile phones and a selection of weapons and body armour, including two automatic pistols and a compact machine gun.

Fay took out a knife and a couple of hundred in cash. The only place to sleep was a sofa bed, so Fay unfurled it and hunted around until she found a duvet and pillows in a cupboard off the hallway. As she lay in bed, part of her was tempted to turn her mobile on to see if there was any message from her aunt, but she knew it would give her location away.

Instead she burrowed under the duvet feeling scared, trying not to see the knife slashing the cop's face and hoping that her aunt was going to turn up with some sort of plan.

*

Fay woke early, but had nothing to do except hide. It was a grim December morning and the flat felt lonely so she reached out with her big toe and switched on an ancient portable TV. The signal kept breaking up, but Fay sat with her head poking out of the duvet watching a cosy interview with a bunch of kids from some new reality show, followed by Carol the weather girl.

Then the seven o'clock headlines gave her a ten-thousand-volt shock.

'*Manchester police are hunting a girl of thirteen who left a police officer in a critical condition after a major drug deal went wrong.*'

Fay saw herself up on screen. The first image was blurry CCTV footage from the lobby of the Belfont hotel. The second was a full-resolution photograph, taken when she'd visited France the previous summer. The cops could only have got it by searching the apartment in St John's Wood.

The TV cut to a clip from a police press conference:

'Following lengthy surveillance work, Manchester Police in conjunction with the Metropolitan Police staged an operation to break up a large drug deal. Several Manchester gang members and a London-based female were arrested. Sixteen kilos of cocaine and a large quantity of cash were also seized.

'One of the suspects is believed to have brought her thirteen-year-old niece with her. When police tried to apprehend the girl, she assaulted two officers, leaving one in a serious but stable condition. I can't emphasise strongly enough that this young teenager is extremely dangerous. So I must ask the public not to approach her, but to inform the police as quickly as possible if you think you've seen her.'

The TV cut back to a correspondent standing outside the Belfont hotel.

'Within the last few hours it's become clear that a girl fitting the police description robbed a house in the Ardwick area of Manchester; following this, CCTV shows her boarding a train from Stockport to London.'

As Fay sat up in bed, a dry heave rose from her stomach. Her aunt had been busted, the cop was on the critical list and her picture was on every TV screen in the country.

'You are *so* screwed,' she told herself.

The flat was a refuge, at least. Fay had money and weapons, but when she padded through to the kitchen she realised that there was no food. She remembered passing a convenience store the night before and she reckoned it was best to go out while it was dark and the streets were quiet.

The lifts were still out of order, so she buried her head in one of her aunt's hoodies as she walked down six floors and crossed the street to Dinesh's Food & Wine. She moved quickly, filling a basket with fruit, chocolate bars, microwave rice and enough tinned stuff to last her a week.

At the counter she felt sick, because her face was staring off half the morning newspapers. She wondered whether she'd have been better off going hungry for a day and hoping that her face dropped out of the news.

Back in the flat, Fay started thinking long term. She had money and weapons. All she'd ever known was robbing drug dealers and she reckoned she could keep that up on her own. Maybe the heat would die down after a week or so. She'd be able to move around more freely. But realistically, could she live on the run, or was she just delaying an inevitable arrest and the consequences of what she'd done?

Fay needed something to take her mind off things, but the apartment didn't offer much. She made beans on toast, then she lay on the sofa bed, obsessively watching News 24. Every half-hour it was the same story about the cop in a critical condition and the correspondent standing outside the Belfont hotel getting colder but saying more or less the same thing.

Sometimes Fay got upset, thinking about her aunt in prison. Sometimes she worried about the cop, knowing that the consequences would be a lot more severe if he died. Just after ten she started crying. She picked up her phone and thought about turning it on and telling the cops to come and get her.

Then the front door exploded.

'Police!'

A blast of CS gas came down the hallway. Fay moved instinctively towards a sliding glass door that led out on to a balcony. As she threw the door open she breathed a mix that was half air, half gas, and felt a burning sensation in her lungs.

Freezing puddles soaked Fay's socked feet as she scrambled out on to the balcony. Cops were coming into the apartment, clad head to toe in black body armour and gas masks. She looked up, but the building's flat roof was out of reach. She looked down at the chance of death, splattered over the street six floors below. The idea of jumping had a certain appeal, but one of the cops reached on to the balcony and grabbed her hoodie.

He pulled her inside so hard that her neck clicked. The air inside the apartment was full of CS gas, and Fay retched and choked as she was 'accidentally' slammed against the apartment wall before a big boot kicked her legs away.

Fay's head caught the corner of the TV stand as a burly cop slammed her hard against the floor. The officer then ripped her arms behind her back and locked on a set of plasticuffs.

'Fay Hoyt, you are under arrest on suspicion of attempted murder. You do not have to say anything, but anything you do say may be taken down and used in evidence against you.'

The CS gas made Fay's eyes stream as the cop shoved her towards the apartment door.

'We don't like people who attack our fellow officers,' the cop growled. 'You are in deep, deep shit.'

PART TWO
June 2014

6. RANK

CHERUB campus

'Dammit, team Sharma!' Instructor Speaks shouted, as he leaned into a changing room stained with the residue from thousands of paintball battles. 'I've seen one-legged pensioners move faster than you. If you're not dressed, equipped and lined up for inspection within two minutes, you can run five laps around the training compound.'

There were two teams of four on the training exercise. Fifteen-year-old Ryan Sharma had been dragged out of bed ninety minutes earlier. He'd been given ten minutes to dress and eat breakfast, before being made to run out to the campus obstacle course. After three gruelling circuits over climbing nets, narrow poles and rope swings, his black CHERUB shirt was a soggy sheet of sweat that clung to his skin.

Ryan's team mates were his three siblings: twelve-year-old twins Leon and Daniel, and nine-year-old Theo.

'We're gonna boil running around in this lot,' Leon moaned, as he zipped a padded overall over his running kit and started pushing his feet back into his boots.

While Leon complained, Theo was having a meltdown because the zip on his overall was stuck. 'This is so bogus,' he shouted.

Ryan already had his boots and face mask on and instinctively moved to help his youngest brother.

'Calm down,' Ryan said firmly. 'How will you make it through a hundred days' basic training, if you get flustered over a little zip?'

'You're such a wuss, Theo,' Leon added unhelpfully.

Ryan gave Leon a look of contempt as he stepped in front of Theo and put a hand on his shoulder. 'Let me try.'

'It's totally stuck,' Theo blurted, as he tugged the zip with all his might.

'You're trying to force it,' Ryan said. 'You'll just break it.'

Instructor Speaks shouted through the doorway. 'Thirty seconds.'

Ryan went down on one knee. He took hold of the long zip running up the front of Theo's overall and ran it back and forth a couple of times before successfully whizzing it all the way up to his chin.

'There,' Ryan said, as his little brother smiled gratefully. 'Panicking won't get you anywhere, will it?'

Warm sunshine hit the four dark-haired brothers as

they stepped out of the changing room dressed in matching army-green overalls, thick gloves and black paintball helmets.

'Ahh, finally,' Instructor Speaks said, as he made a clap with his giant black hands.

The Sharma brothers' rival team had already assembled on the tarmac ramp leading up to the paintball range. Its four members were all friends of Ryan: fifteen-year-old Fu Ning, his sometime girlfriend Grace Vuillamy and his two best mates Max Black and Alfie DuBoisson.

'Gonna flatten you!' Alfie threatened.

'We may be younger and smaller, but we've got it where it counts,' Daniel shouted, as he tapped his head. 'Brainpower.'

'Your team consists of two chubby chicks and a pair of cock heads,' Leon added.

Ning and Grace both reared up.

'Say that to my face and see what you get,' Grace shouted.

Mr Speaks puffed out his muscular chest and cracked some knuckles. 'This banter is all *very* entertaining, but I want to keep those hearts pumping, so listen good because I'm not going to repeat myself.

'Spread around the paintball range you will find eight paintball guns, eight compressed air cylinders to make the guns work, and eight hoppers containing a hundred and fifty paintballs. You may also find shields and other equipment that will assist your efforts to get hold of these items.'

'It's like the Hunger Games,' Theo said quietly.

'The object of the game is to find and assemble the guns and shoot the four members of the opposite team. If you are hit by a paintball, you're dead and must leave the compound.

'If neither team wins within three hours, the game will be declared a draw and I'll make you all run around campus holding large sandbags over your heads. Usual safety rules apply. No low blows, or eye gouging. Additionally, with paintballs zipping around, keep your helmets on at all times and don't do anything to remove another person's helmet.

'Your individual performances will be assessed. Anyone not showing initiative or working hard throughout will be referred to the training department for a one-on-one refresher training course with yours truly. Any questions?'

Max Black raised his hand and Mr Speaks pointed at him.

'Three laps of the training compound after the exercise for you,' Speaks spat.

Max was incredulous. 'What?'

'I explained everything that needs explaining,' Speaks shouted. 'If you need to ask a question, it means you weren't listening.'

Max swore quietly inside his mask, but knew he'd only get more punishment laps if he argued.

'The time is now eleven minutes past nine,' Mr Speaks shouted. 'So you have until eleven minutes past twelve. Get moving!'

Mr Speaks opened the paintball compound gate and the two teams jogged through. A black bin bag stood on the grass about a hundred metres inside. Ryan caught sight of it first and broke into a sprint, but soon found Max and Alfie from the rival team charging up behind.

Ryan grabbed the bag and instantly saw it was too light to contain paintball stuff. Max got a hand on it and ripped the plastic open. A bunch of brightly coloured ropes and climbing gear spilled out over the grass. Ryan bent down to scoop some of it up, but immediately got tackled by bulky fourteen-year-old Alfie.

'Give it up, prom queen,' Alfie ordered, as Ryan clutched a bunch of ropes to his chest. He wasn't sure how useful the ropes were likely to be, but he was determined to keep hold of some.

Ryan glanced over his shoulder, hoping that one of the twins would come and give him a hand. But apparently Grace and Ning had taken exception to being called chubby and - unable to tell which twin was which - had decided to go after both of them.

After a tussle, Ryan found himself flat on the ground with Alfie sitting across his chest and Max holding a bunch of ropes.

'Why don't we tie him up?' Max asked. 'Then we'll just have his three little brothers to deal with.'

'No tying up,' Ryan protested.

'Says who?' Max asked, as he prepared a large loop to hook around Ryan's ankles.

Alfie nodded. 'We got the standard lecture about low blows and head shots, but I never heard nothing about tying up.'

Ryan bucked frantically. 'Damn your big fat arse, Alfie.'

Alfie smirked. 'Shut it or I'll grunt on you.'

'Exterminate!' Theo shouted, as he jumped out from behind a tree holding a plastic dustbin lid.

When he got close, he spun to avoid Alfie and barged into Max who was much skinnier. Theo was less than two thirds of Max's weight, but he had enough momentum to knock him sideways.

As soon as Ryan had room to move, he brought his knees up.

'Ooof!' Alfie moaned, as Ryan's kneecap connected with his balls. 'Low blow!'

With Theo driving him sideways, and Ryan bucking underneath, Max wound up in a heap in the grass. Alfie tried getting his arms around Theo's waist, but only got whacked with the dustbin lid for his trouble.

Ryan started scrambling forwards, crawling at first but finding his feet. Max grabbed Ryan's boot and managed to unlace it but he was soon up and running.

'You saved my butt,' Ryan told his little brother as he scrambled off. Theo looked extremely proud of himself.

Alfie was still groaning and holding his balls, and Max didn't fancy his chances going after Ryan and Theo on his own. So the two brothers made it over a couple of hundred metres of clear ground before diving into a copse of trees.

'Did you see what happened to Leon and Daniel?' Ryan asked.

'I saw the girls going after them.'

Ryan nodded. 'I don't fancy their chances, especially against Ning.'

'It's bogus,' Theo complained. 'The other team are all fifteen – well, Alfie's fourteen but he's enormous.'

'Life's not fair,' Ryan said. 'That's what they're trying to teach us.'

'So what now?' Theo asked. 'Shall we try to help the twins?'

Ryan shook his head. 'Even if we caught up with them, our chances aren't good. I say we stick together, cover as much ground as we can. The other team is bigger and stronger, and the only way to even up the odds is by getting our hands on a gun and some ammo before they do.'

7. LAUNDRY

Idris Secure Training Centre

'It's not difficult,' Chloe Cohen said, as she ambled into the laundry room, dressed in an England rugby shirt, Adidas tracksuit bottoms and a pair of flip-flops.

Chloe's fourteen years had been a succession of abuse and disaster, that had finally got her locked up after she'd got high and burned down a house owned by her stepdad. Her companion Izzy was thirteen, but seemed more like eleven. She was doing time after stealing chemicals from her school science lab and brewing poison tea for her parents and older sister.

As Izzy put a plastic laundry basket down on the floor in front of a washing machine, Chloe dipped a scoop into a giant box of powder.

'Open the drawer on the front.'

Izzy opened the drawer and Chloe tipped in the

powder, with a few sprinkles hitting the floor.

'Clothes in,' Chloe said. 'Close the door and set to thirty-degree wash. Push start.'

Izzy stepped back from the machine nervously, then turned to Chloe and gave a relieved smile when it started gurgling.

'Takes an hour,' Chloe said. 'I'll come back and show you how to do the dryers when it's done.'

'Hello, hello!' Fay Hoyt said.

Now fifteen, Fay wore battered jeans and a black T-shirt that stretched over muscular shoulders. Chloe backed up towards one of the machines and Izzy detected her angst and did the same.

'Is this the new girl?' Fay asked, looking down her nose as she took a step nearer to Izzy. 'Got on the six o'clock news for trying to poison her whole family?'

Chloe narrowed her eyes. 'Well, *you* tried to kill a cop.'

'I tried to get away,' Fay said. 'If I'd tried to *kill* Constable Shitface, he'd be dead.'

'You act so tough,' Chloe spat. 'But I'm not scared of you.'

Fay laughed, then threw a punch. It stopped well short of Chloe's cheek, but she jumped backwards, making Fay howl with laughter.

'Nah. You're not scared of me at all, are you?'

As Fay moved in again, Chloe made a clumsy lunge. Fay snatched Chloe's flying wrist and bent back her fingers, while using her other hand to slap her face. Chloe sprawled backwards over a washing machine before Fay pulled her up and shoved her head first towards the dryers.

'Stay where you are or I'll kick your head in,' Fay warned, before turning towards Izzy.

The petite thirteen-year-old had backed into a corner stacked with powder boxes. Fay pointed at the floor tiles in front of her and growled.

'Get here.'

Izzy was trembling.

'Don't make me come and get you.'

'Leave her alone,' Chloe shouted. 'You're twice her size.'

Izzy was still too scared to move forward, so Fay stepped up, grabbed Izzy around the back of the neck and pushed her head against the top of a washing machine. Then she wound Izzy's long red hair around her wrist and pulled it painfully tight.

'What have you got?' Fay asked.

'What?'

Fay smiled. 'If I go to your room and you give me something nice, we'll be best friends and I won't have to hurt you.'

'Clothes?' Izzy suggested.

'Bonehead,' Fay spat. 'I'm not going to fit in your stupid midget clothes, am I, you stupid midget?'

'Don't give her anything,' Chloe shouted. 'She's a psycho! She won't stop.'

'Let's go to your room and see,' Fay said.

Fay moved towards the door, dragging Izzy by her hair. The hallway outside was painted custard yellow and had prison-style doors off either side. At least one girl saw what was going on, but kept her head down as Izzy was manhandled halfway down the corridor to the cell she shared with Chloe.

'You'd *better* have something decent,' Fay shouted.

Izzy looked desperately around her room and pointed at a novelty bedside clock, shaped like the dinosaur from *Toy Story*. Fay immediately knocked the clock off the bedside table and kicked it, while simultaneously keeping her grip on Izzy's hair.

'Just this once I'm gonna let you off,' Fay announced. 'But keep your trap shut and you'd better have something to give me next time I see you.'

As Fay unwound Izzy's hair the cell door opened and two burly women charged in.

'No, no, no!' one of them shouted.

'This isn't on, young lady!'

Fay looked around and saw a couple of school books on the window ledge. 'She went in my room and stole my books,' Fay shouted.

As soon as Fay had been prised off, Izzy started sobbing. The two guards expertly grabbed Fay under the arms and put her in a restraining hold before marching her out of the cell. Chloe was right outside, wearing a smirk.

'I know you grassed me up,' Fay shouted. 'You wait! You just wait.'

Chloe boldly gave Fay the finger before dashing into the cell to comfort little Izzy.

'Hey, don't cry,' Chloe said soothingly. 'Fay's a nasty

bitch, but the good news is they're kicking her back out on the street in two weeks' time.'

*

Thirty-five minutes into the exercise, Ryan and Theo had found guns and ammo, as well as an equipment pack containing binoculars, water bottles and a collapsible shovel. Theo stood in the fork of a tree using the binoculars, while Ryan covered from the ground.

'It's Grace,' Theo whispered excitedly. 'No weapon.'

Ryan smiled. 'Are you sure?'

'Less than fifty metres,' Theo said, as he jumped down quietly.

'You cover my back, I'll try and take her out,' Ryan said.

As Theo crouched down with his gun poised, Ryan set off at a steady pace, placing his boots carefully to avoid making any kind of noise. Paintball guns aren't particularly accurate, so when he got to within twenty metres he went down on his knees and kept crawling. When he was ten metres away, Grace glanced at her watch and started to walk.

Ryan bobbed up and took a shot, but he somehow managed to completely miss. Grace heard the paint spattering a nearby tree trunk and started to run. Ryan knew that moving out of cover into an open chase risked being led into an enemy trap, but he decided that chasing an unarmed opponent was too good an opportunity to give up.

Grace charged out on to open ground, with a vista of CHERUB campus' main building half a kilometre away. As Grace vaulted a log, she caught the tip of her boot and fell flat on her face. Ryan quickly closed to within five metres and shot Grace as she lay on the ground.

'Ryan's got me!' Grace shouted, hoping to alert her team mates to his location.

In the background Ryan heard the distinct clatter of paintball pellets.

'Theo?' he gasped.

He spun around and saw flashes moving through the branches in the direction he'd just come from. A paintball whizzed over his head and he dived for cover behind a tree trunk. Part of him wanted to charge out and help save Theo, but that would be suicidal until he had some idea of where everyone was shooting from.

After twenty seconds crouching, Ryan caught his friend Alfie's emergence from the clearing with paint splattered across his helmet and arms raised in surrender. The clatter of paintball ammo was still going and Ryan began a cautious walk towards the noise.

He thought he was still at least twenty metres from the action when his friend Max darted out from between two trees. Ryan took aim from five metres and this time he made his first shot count.

Max was a pretty laid-back character and took being killed with good grace. 'Nice shooting,' he said. 'Suppose I'd better go and run my punishment circuits.'

'Is Theo still alive?' Ryan asked.

But Theo came out of the trees and answered for himself. 'Naturally,' he said, wearing the cocky smile of someone who'd got one over on a bigger kid.

'Any sign of Leon or Daniel?' Ryan asked.

Max laughed. 'Grace and Ning tied them up and we dealt with them as soon as we found our first gun.'

'So that just leaves Ning alive on the other team,' Theo said, as he gave his brother a wary smile. 'Two against one, in our favour.'

8. PREDATOR

A secure training centre is as hard to break out of as an adult prison, but in most other respects Idris was far less strict. Guards were known by their first names. Wendy, the head of Fay's wing, sat at a desk with the slogan *Every Child Matters* painted on the wall behind.

'Well, Fay, what have you got to say for yourself?'

Fay sat across the desk from the uniformed officer and pursed her lips like she was about to say something important. But she didn't.

'A new inmate. Physically small, facing a difficult period of adjustment. You march into the laundry room. You assault her room-mate, Chloe, then you assault Izzy and drag her back to her cell demanding money with menaces.'

Fay shrugged. 'If you say so.'

'I can understand why some girls in here lash out.

They have emotional problems. They have eating disorders, substance problems or a history of abuse. Many of them have basic educational difficulties. But you're an exceptionally bright young lady. You should do well in your GCSEs. You're athletic. The only reason you won't get into a good university is if you let yourself down.'

Fay cleared her throat. 'When I was ten years old, I came back from the shop and found my mum hacked to pieces by a drug dealer. Last year my aunt Kirsten got suffocated in prison while she was awaiting trial. Murdered by another drug dealer. Those were the only two people I cared about. And the only two people who've ever cared about me.'

'People here care,' Wendy said.

Fay snorted. 'You'll be glad to see the back of me.'

'Fay, you've discussed this in group counselling – at least until you refused to attend any more sessions. We've given you techniques for dealing with your past and coping with strong emotions.'

Fay laughed. 'I stopped going because therapy is all bullshit. My aunt Kirsten is the only one who understood.'

'Understood what?'

'That I like it.'

'Like what?'

'I like the life,' Fay said, finally raising her voice above a dull monotone. 'The shiver that goes down your back when you're about to rip someone off. The look of fear on someone's face when you put a knife to their throat.

Running away, knowing that you're dead if you're not fast enough. Once you've lived the life, it's hard to knuckle down to that history essay, or get excited about the next plot twist in *EastEnders*.'

Wendy cleared her throat awkwardly. 'And you replicate that thrill by bullying some poor girl like Izzy?'

Fay laughed. 'First off, that *poor* girl is a crazy loon who tried to poison half her family. Second, the world is full of sheep. Millions and millions of 'em, living their dreary little lives. Then there's a few wolves, and their job is to eat a couple of sheep once in a while.'

'So you're a wolf?' Wendy asked.

'Absolutely.'

'And it doesn't matter if wolves hurt sheep?'

Fay laughed. 'Not to the wolf it doesn't.'

'So when you get out of here in a couple of weeks' time, what do you plan to do?'

Fay shrugged. 'Oh, I'm gonna straighten right up. Get my exams, go to university. Marry a guy called Connor. We'll have a Labradoodle called Scotty, three kids, a Ford C-Max and a little cottage in Suffolk for the weekends.'

Wendy shook her head and spoke firmly. 'Well, I very much hope that you do find stability before you mess your life up. But after this afternoon's incident you'll be going into segregation for five days and I'll provide you with a copy of this institution's anti-bullying policy.'

Fay rolled her eyes. 'I'm sure it's a gripping read.'

*

The campus paintball range wasn't huge, but it was big enough that two groups moving stealthily could go a long time without bumping into each other.

For almost an hour, Ryan and Theo crept around, searching for Ning as the sun rose and sweat bristled under their masks and overalls. They found several sites where Ning's team had unearthed bags of equipment, but no trace of Ning herself.

'I bet she's gone way up in a tree or something,' Theo said.

'Hope not,' Ryan said forlornly. 'Speaks said we'll all get punished if neither side wins and I don't fancy more running in this heat.'

'What if I try luring her out?' Theo suggested. 'I'll move out in the open. When Ning shoots me, you'll shoot her and be the last man standing.'

Ryan shrugged. 'That's not a *great* plan, but it's better than anything else we've got.'

The obvious spot was the open ground right at the front by the main gates. Ryan was irritated when he saw Leon, Daniel, Alfie and Grace sat outside the changing hut with their overalls off and bottles of ice-cold water in their hands. It felt like they were being rewarded for getting knocked out.

But Ryan didn't have long for this thought, because there was the clap of a paintball the minute Theo stepped into the open. The shot had come from a long way off and missed by several metres.

'Can't shoot straight!' Theo taunted, as he sprinted across the open grass and dived into a bunker.

Ryan was anxious: if Theo was too bold, he'd get himself killed before there was a chance for him to close on the position where the shots were coming from. Fortunately, some assistance came from Leon on the outside.

'She's between the two big oak trees.'

This remark caused outrage from the two members of Ning's team, who immediately began shouting information.

'Ning,' Alfie shouted. 'Theo's in the first bunker up near the gate. Ryan's gone into the trees, trying to flank you.'

'Just come out and have a shoot-up,' Daniel said irritably. 'We'll all get nuked by Mr Speaks if nobody wins.'

As Theo crouched in the bunker, dodging occasional wild shots from Ning, Ryan had ducked into the trees and closed on Ning's position. After a minute he was close enough to the two big oak trees to see where Ning was hiding.

Ryan dropped to a crawl as more shouts came from outside the fence.

'Theo's out of the bunker!'

Just as Ryan thought he was about to best Ning, he was startled by a rustling in the leaves behind. He swung around and took a quick-but-wild shot. Ning had taken up a position behind tree less than four metres away.

Ryan crawled on his belly, keeping an eye out for any movement. When he got to within two metres, Ning sprang out from behind the tree and took a couple of shots. Ryan rolled out of the way, but his return shots were as bad as Ning's.

But he could hear Ning running and – with the fact that they'd all get punished if neither team won – he decided that it would be best to chase after her. Over several hundred metres Ryan and Ning traded shots, several of which missed by only a few centimetres.

Eventually Ning found herself in the lowest part of the paintball range, which would run with a small stream after heavy rain. She dived against the embankment and waited, but it had all gone silent. After a couple of minutes with no sign of any noise, Ning crept back up the shallow embankment, using the paintball splats on leaves and branches as a reminder of her route.

She was surprised to see a leg sticking out from beside a tree root. Ning instantly shot it, but grew concerned when there was no movement.

'Ryan?'

Ning crouched in the grass and rolled Ryan on to his back.

'Ryan, are you OK?'

Ryan raised a hand to his head and spoke slowly. 'I think I bumped my head on something while I was running.'

As Ning leaned further forwards to give Ryan an arm up, Theo jumped out from a position a few metres away and shot Ning square in the visor, leaving her half blind.

'Dead meat!' Theo shouted excitedly.

But Ning had other concerns. 'Ryan hit his head on a branch. I think he's got concussion.'

Ryan cracked a big smile and shrugged. 'Me head's fine, I don't know what she's on about.'

Ning shot back to her feet and threw her gun down furiously. 'You . . . You, utter, utter . . . Lying, cheating . . .'

But there was something infectious about Theo's victory smile, and Ning started to laugh.

'I'll get you two back for this,' Ning said, as she walked towards the gates with her arms raised. 'I don't know how or when, but some fine day, when you least expect it . . .'

9. SEGREGATION

Wendy the guard opened a barred gate and offered a handshake to the policeman on the other side.

'Detective Constable Schaeffer,' Wendy said, shaking the officer's hand. He was a tall man, with curly brown hair and a bulbous nose, but his most distinctive feature was the long scar Fay Hoyt had left down his cheek. 'Welcome to Idris STC.'

Wendy led the officer a few metres to her office, and noted that he was holding a brown paper McDonald's bag.

'So the injuries Fay inflicted, is there anything beyond the scarring?' Wendy asked.

'Some nerve damage,' Schaeffer said. 'My cheek feels numb a lot of the time. It's worst when you try to eat and end up with food dribbling down your face.'

'You harbour no resentment towards her?'

Schaeffer shook his head. 'I'm not Fay's number one fan. But I regularly deal with people a lot less pleasant than her.'

Wendy slid a piece of paper across the desk. 'This form gives you our consent to interview Fay. However, as Fay is a minor and there is no other adult present, nothing can be recorded or used in evidence and you must leave the room if she requests it.'

'I know the score,' Schaeffer nodded. 'This isn't about anything Fay's done in the past. I'm hoping to offer her a path to redemption, and a way of avenging the death of her aunt.'

Wendy smiled wryly as she grabbed a worksheet off the desk and held it up. 'As I warned when you phoned to request the interview, Fay's never been very cooperative. For the last three days she's been confined to our segregation room after a bullying incident. Anyone who bullies is required to complete a series of anti-bullying worksheets. Here's an example of Fay's answers:

'Question four. *If I see another inmate being bullied, what should I do?* Fay's answer, *Grind up some glass and put it in their breakfast cereal.* Question nine, *If your room-mate bullies or intimidates you during the night, what is your best response?* Fay's answer, *Wait till they fall asleep, then slit their guts open before plaiting their entrails to make an attractive skipping rope.*'

'Quite an imagination,' Schaeffer said.

'So now you've signed the form, would you like to meet the beast?'

Wendy led Schaeffer to the isolation room, which

was located directly opposite her office.

'Iso rules are harsh,' Wendy explained. 'Fay gets one set of clothes, school books and personal hygiene items only. There's no TV or radio and you're only allowed out of the room to exercise for one hour after the other girls have been locked down for the night.'

As she finished speaking, Wendy knocked on the door.

'Fay, Detective Constable Schaeffer is here to see you.'

'What's he brought for me?' Fay asked.

'McFlurry,' Schaeffer said.

'In that case you can come in.'

Fay hadn't showered in the three days she'd been in isolation, but she'd kept herself busy with a routine of sit-ups, squats and push-ups. Combined with hot weather, the resulting BO was pretty toxic.

'Nice scar. How'd you get that?' Fay asked, before breaking into wild laughter.

'Show some respect,' Wendy said.

'Kinda sexy, I reckon,' Fay said, ignoring the guard. 'Do you pull a lot of chicks?'

Schaeffer held out the McDonald's bag and Fay snatched it.

'McFlurry!' she blurted happily. 'Did you get Crunchie like I asked? If it's not Crunchie you're not getting another word out of me.'

Fay dipped the plastic spoon into the McFlurry and nodded happily when she crunched honeycomb.

'So good!' she said, squealing girlishly. 'Why don't you sit down?'

Schaeffer settled on the end of Fay's bed.

'Here's a question,' Fay said. 'You must be at least forty. But you're still Detective Constable Schaeffer. So does that mean you're a rubbish cop?'

Schaeffer cleared his throat before explaining. 'A lot of officers prefer action to paperwork. When you get promoted, you tend to spend a lot more time sitting at a desk.'

'So you're an ack-shonnnn man!' Fay said as she scoffed more of the McFlurry. 'I'm not usually this hyper, but I haven't had a conversation in three days. Apart from the boring cow who walks me around outside after lights out.'

'It must be very hard for a girl with your potential to be stuck in a little room,' Schaeffer said.

'You're actually lucky I got my butt locked in iso,' Fay said. 'I thought it would be funny if I made you come here, buy me a McFlurry and then gave you the silent treatment.'

Wendy raised one eyebrow and looked at Schaeffer as she backed out. 'Good luck, I'm just across the hall if you need me.'

'You wanna shag me, constable?' Fay said, trying but failing to shock the experienced officer. 'Bit of under-age naughtiness?'

'You don't like me and I don't like you,' Schaeffer began. 'But we do have an enemy in common.'

'I don't have enemies, I love everyone.'

Schaeffer looked surprised. 'Even Erasto Ali Anwar?'

'Never heard of him,' Fay said.

'Born Somalia circa 1983. Based in the Kentish Town area of north London. Believed to control large heroin and cocaine operations in the London boroughs of Islington, Camden, Haringey and Hackney. On the street, he's simply known as Hagar.'

Fay nodded, and looked slightly curious. 'I never knew the man's real name.'

'Hagar and his crew are believed to be responsible for the 2009 torture and execution of Melanie Hoyt, your mother, and the 2012 prison slaying of Kirsten Hoyt, your aunt.'

'I know that much,' Fay said.

'Your mother and aunt ripped off Hagar more than a dozen times, along with a bunch of other north London drug dealers. To commit those robberies, they had to know everything. Hagar's habits, his hangouts, his women, who his sidekicks are, what he liked to do on his days off. You lived in that world and knew everything there was to know about Hagar.'

Fay gently shook her head. '*Knew*,' she said. 'Past tense. Things move fast.'

'If I put you in a car and drove you around those neighbourhoods, I bet you could point out things and faces that would generate a dozen leads.'

'Hagar's been running the show for twenty years,' Fay said. 'If you want him, go get him.'

'Hagar's also extremely careful,' Schaeffer explained. 'He rarely goes near cash or drugs, he gets other people to fetch and carry and dole out punishment beatings. We've locked up a dozen of Hagar's lieutenants, but it's been hard to pin anything on the man himself.'

Fay snorted. 'Plus half the cops in north London take backhanders to turn a blind eye.'

'I find that hard to believe,' Schaeffer said, assuming that Fay was trying to shock him again. 'But if you've got any evidence of corrupt police officers, I'd be very happy to hear about it.'

Fay was irritated by Schaeffer's calm demeanour and tried to think of something that might annoy him.

'Do you think about me every time you look in the mirror?' Fay asked. 'You must really hate me.'

'Do you want me to hate you?' Schaeffer asked.

'I don't care what you think,' Fay said.

'I think you do,' Schaeffer said. 'Not because you're the badass you try and make yourself out to be, but because me thinking about you would mean that someone in the world cared that you existed. Your mum and your aunt are dead. You've got no real connection with anyone, and bullying and acting crazy are the only ways you know you'll get attention.

'In a couple of weeks' time you'll be released into a foster-home or a care facility. It probably won't be very nice. But if you keep things straight you'll gradually make friends, pass your exams and start to lead a normal teenage life.'

'Who the hell are you?' Fay screamed, as she stood up and placed her hands on her hips. 'Don't act like you know everything about me.'

'You're angry about what happened to your aunt and your mother,' Schaeffer said. 'I'm offering you a chance to take a walk around your old haunts, look at some photos in our suspect books and give us everything you know about Hagar and his crew. And maybe, just maybe, you'll give us a sliver of information that will help us put some or all of them behind bars.'

'I don't want Hagar in prison, I want him to die,' Fay said. 'Preferably in the most painful way imaginable.'

Schaeffer shrugged. 'I'm afraid we live in a society of laws. I can't offer barbaric punishments, but if Hagar goes down, it will be for a very long time.'

'I'll sort Hagar out,' Fay said, as she finished the McFlurry.

'Oh come on,' Schaeffer said, smiling slightly. 'You're a fifteen-year-old girl.'

'And I'm no grass.'

'You're seriously telling me that you don't want to spend a few hours helping the police arrest the people who killed your aunt and mother?'

Fay scowled. 'I fight my own battles.'

'Your aunt and mother were both older and more experienced than you are and Hagar got them in the end. His crew are probably more powerful now than when you went inside eighteen months ago. So I *really* hope you're not foolish enough to mess with them.'

Fay shook her head. 'I'd like you to leave now.'

Schaeffer took a business card out of his jacket. He held it out, but Fay refused to take it.

'I'll leave it on the window ledge,' Schaeffer said. 'Please give me a call before you try anything stupid.'

10. CONTROL

After years of leaks and repairs, CHERUB campus' high-tech mission control building was finally free of *out of order* signs and drip buckets. Ryan Sharma was crunching along the gravel path leading to its main entrance when he heard someone jogging across the surrounding lawn towards him. Upon seeing that it was Ning, he threw down the backpack looped over his shoulder and dropped into a fighting stance.

'Nervous, are we?' Ning teased, raising her hands into a surrender gesture as she slowed up and stepped on to the gravel. 'Don't worry. I'm not gonna get you back right now.'

'How about a free punch?' Ryan offered. 'Anywhere but my balls or nose.'

Ning grinned. 'It's way more fun keeping you in suspense.'

'Playing dead wasn't even my idea,' Ryan said. 'Theo thought of it.'

Ning laughed. 'Oh you're *nice*, blaming your nine-year-old brother. And I wouldn't get Theo back, he's too cute!'

'Cute but deadly,' Ryan said. 'He starts basic training soon and I reckon he'll ace it.'

'Got my e-mail from the training department,' Ning said. 'I passed the exercise with no faults, so no extra training for me.'

Ryan looked a little nervous. 'When did that come through?'

'I just came out of French and it was on my e-mail.'

Ryan immediately pulled out his iPhone and opened the e-mail app. There was a new message from Mr Speaks in the training department and he read aloud nervously:

'*Performed reasonably . . . Fitness acceptable . . . Worked well with others . . . No requirement for remedial training.* Ahh, thank *god* for that!'

'Nice one,' Ning said. 'So you're heading for mission control?'

Ryan nodded. 'Usually that's exciting, but it's only James Adams.'

'I'm seeing James too,' Ning said, looking confused. 'I thought he seemed OK when we did advanced driving.'

'Yeah,' Ryan agreed. 'James is a decent guy, but he's only just been promoted to mission controller. If we were being lined up for some big glamorous mission, it'd be John Jones or Ewart Asker sending for us rather than the new guy.'

'So I'm not likely to get my black shirt out of this one?' Ning said, still sounding cheerful. 'I fancy a mission. I've been on campus for over four months.'

They'd reached the mission control building's main door. Ning was ahead and stared into an iris scanner. After a couple of whirring sounds, the main door popped open and a little screen flashed up, *Proceed to room 7A.*

Ryan didn't bother with the scanner, and just sneaked through behind Ning.

'Come in,' James said, after Ning knocked.

James was twenty-two, well-muscled, fair-haired, and currently experimenting with a slightly dodgy beard. The office was a decent size, with a big leather couch and floor-to-ceiling windows looking out over woodland. However, Ning looked around at empty shelves and bookcases.

'Only got this office last week,' James explained. 'I expect I'll have it stuffed with mounds of files and crap in no time.'

'So you're a full mission controller now?' Ryan asked.

James nodded. 'And I was a CHERUB agent myself, so I know *exactly* what you're thinking: I'm the newest mission controller, so all I'm gonna have to offer are boring routine missions.'

Ning and Ryan both shook their heads.

'Thought never crossed my mind,' Ryan said, though he struggled to keep a straight face.

'The mission I've cobbled together is fairly low-key, but if it pays off it could turn into something quite juicy,' James began. 'What do you two know about cocaine?'

'Goes well sprinkled on toast,' Ryan answered, before Ning gave a more serious answer.

'Drug. White powder. People snort it and it gives them a rush.'

James nodded. 'But if you go into a bar or a club and buy fifty quid's worth of cocaine, the chances are you're not actually buying much cocaine at all. Most of what you get is junk that's been mixed with the cocaine to make selling it more profitable.

'Cocaine starts off as coca leaves, almost always grown in South America. The leaves are processed in a rural lab and you end up with pure white powder. This gets vacuum packed into bricks and smuggled to Britain in near hundred per cent pure form. Then it gets thinned out by mixing with another white powder – typically lactose, baking powder, lidocaine, even chalk dust. This is called cutting.

'Everyone cuts the cocaine. By the time a top-level dealer gets it from an international smuggler, the cocaine is cut to about forty to fifty per cent purity. A mid-level dealer will then cut it to around thirty per cent purity and the street-level dealer adds more crap so that your regular buyer-on-the-street ends up with a gram that contains less than twenty per cent cocaine.

'Some of the cocaine sold at street level is of such poor quality that police have busted dealers and had to release them because the quantity of cocaine in their product is so low that it's not even illegal.'

'Is the stuff they cut the cocaine with harmful?' Ning asked.

James nodded. 'It's not great to be snorting chalk dust and baby laxatives up your nose, and it's even worse for people who inject. Some say the impurities cause more health problems than the drugs themselves.

'Now, the reason you two are standing here is that a few years ago, a rather clever police officer in Germany started thinking about the purity of cocaine. He started a database logging the purity of the drugs seized in every cocaine bust in Germany. Then he started investigating the areas where the cocaine was purest. Any idea why?'

Ryan nodded. 'The cocaine gets cut at every stage. So if you find high purity cocaine, the chances are you're getting close to the top-level dealers who smuggle it into the country.'

James smiled. 'Spot on.'

'But why don't they just dilute the cocaine more if they're selling it on the street?' Ning asked. 'Like from a hundred per cent purity to twenty per cent purity in one go?'

'They can cover their tracks that way and I'm sure many do,' James said. 'But the point is, there are areas where high purity cocaine is sold on the street, and experience in Germany and other countries shows us that investigating areas where purity is high often leads to a large-scale drug importer.'

Ryan and Ning both liked the sound of bringing down a large-scale drug smuggler.

'So where are these high purity drugs being sold?' Ryan asked.

'You'll be based in Kentish Town in north London,' James explained. 'The street cocaine there is consistently around twenty-five per cent pure.'

Ning looked confused. 'Twenty-five per cent is good?'

James nodded. 'For street cocaine, twenty-five per cent is about as good as it gets. It's also consistently cut with two parts lactose and one part lidocaine. The lidocaine is an anaesthetic, which creates numbness, making you think the cocaine is stronger than it really is. The fact that the same chemicals have been detected in dozens of drug seizures indicates that all the cocaine comes from a single, large-scale cutting operation.

'The trade in cocaine and heroin in that part of London is dominated by a man named Erasto Ali Anwar, more commonly known as Hagar. Kentish Town is his base, but he has a network that sells cocaine and heroin through the London boroughs of Islington, Camden, Hackney and Haringey, and also in nightclubs in central London.

'According to the Kentish Town drug squad, Hagar uses teenaged boys for quite a lot of small-scale dealing and grunt work. Many of these lads are members of a youth club run by a charity known as The Hangout.

'Ryan, if you accept the mission, your job will be standard CHERUB stuff. You'll attend a local school and spend time at The Hangout youth club. Hopefully, within a few weeks, you'll be able to work yourself into a position where Hagar's crew take an interest in you.

Once you're inside the organisation, your job will be to find out everything you can.'

Ryan spoke. 'You said Hagar dealt in cocaine *and* heroin. Am I interested in both?'

'The same rules on purity apply to heroin, and police are using the same techniques to track it down. Analysis shows that the heroin sold by Hagar's gang is of poor to average quality, so it's unlikely they're close to the original smuggling source.'

'Fair enough,' Ryan said.

'So are you up for the job?' James asked.

Ryan nodded. 'Sure, it sounds like a decent mission.'

'So what about me?' Ning asked. 'If Hagar's gang only recruits boys, where do I fit in?'

'I've got something different lined up for you,' James said, as he cracked a slight smile. 'It's a long shot, but if it works out it has the potential to smash Hagar's operation wide open.'

11. BEDS

Officer Wendy opened the isolation cell and found Fay sitting on the end of her bed, glowering.

'Are you ready to behave?' Wendy asked.

'Will you miss me when I'm gone?' Fay asked back.

Wendy snorted as Fay tucked her school books under her arm and headed for the door. Fay made a short walk to her room, dialled a three-digit combination into her locker and grabbed a towel and clean clothes before heading off for her first shower in five days.

She came back in a bathrobe, and this time there was a Chinese girl sitting on the right-hand bed, doing homework.

'You're in the wrong cell,' Fay said firmly. 'Where's Amber?'

Ning shrugged. 'Amber got moved to a lower security unit, pending release.'

'You what?' Fay shouted. 'Amber's my roomie.'

'I'm your roomie now,' Ning said, as Fay peeled off her bathrobe and grabbed a bra and T-shirt out of a drawer.

Ning went back to concentrating on her textbook, but as Fay pulled on a clean pair of jeans, she noticed that there were no pillows on her bed, while Ning had a mound of four propped behind her back.

'Who said you could touch my pillows?' Fay demanded. 'Give.'

Ning smiled. 'I'm using them.'

Fay wasn't used to girls giving her backchat. 'Pardon me?'

'Oh, are you deaf?' Ning said cheerfully, before shouting: 'I SAID I CAN'T GIVE THE PILLOWS BACK BECAUSE I'M USING THEM.'

Fay now stood over Ning's bed with her fists bunched. 'Give me my pillows,' Fay said. 'Or I'll smash your dopey head through the wall.'

Ning tutted. 'You really *are* an ill-mannered little girl,' she said.

Fay couldn't take any more. She leaned in to throw a punch, expecting Ning to be squealing and handing back pillows a few moments later. But Fay was surprised to find that Ning intercepted her fist, then kicked up with both feet, booting Fay in the stomach.

As Fay doubled over, Ning stood and tried to wrench Fay's arm behind her back. But Fay managed to straighten up quickly and threw a wild punch which caught Ning in the kidneys.

'So you know how to fight?' Ning said, as she stepped forward aiming a barrage of punches.

Fay was forced to retreat until she'd backed up to the metal lockers. Ning landed several heavy punches before Fay stumbled out of the corner fighting for breath. As Ning turned to face Fay's new position, Fay launched a vicious kick that knocked Ning back into the lockers.

Ning knew that Fay had kickboxing skills, but hadn't anticipated that she was this good. Ning fought pain from the kick as she charged forward. Fay was tall and had greater reach, while Ning was broad and came forward like a battering ram.

After a speedy exchange of kicks and slaps, Ning grabbed Fay's hair and threw her across a bed. Then Ning sat across Fay's back and dug her elbow painfully between her shoulder blades. A guard named Gladys had heard the commotion and came charging in.

'What the *hell* is going on?' she shouted.

Ning immediately jumped off Fay's back. 'Nothing, miss.'

Fay groaned as she rolled over, but managed a smile for the guard. 'Just a little roughhousing,' she confirmed.

The guard pointed accusingly. 'I'm gonna be keeping my eye on you two,' she warned.

Ning moved towards her bed as the guard backed out. Fay scowled and rubbed a hand that had been grazed somewhere along the way. After a minute, Ning picked up two pillows and threw them across at Fay's bed.

'There,' Ning said. 'Where'd you learn kickboxing?'

Fay stood up and plumped the pillows before answering grudgingly. 'My auntie taught me. You?'

It's best to keep the number of lies you have to remember to a minimum, so Ning had worked out a back-story that was close to the truth.

'Grew up in China,' Ning said. 'I got picked for a sports academy, did a lot of boxing and martial arts.'

'You're the first girl in here I've not flattened. I'm Fay, by the way.'

'I'm Ning.'

Ning reached between the beds and Fay gave a wary smile as they bumped fists.

'So how'd you end up in Idris?' Fay asked.

'I was in a care home,' Ning explained. 'Broke curfew, came in drunk. Attacked the night supervisor. Smashed up his office and broke both his arms.'

Fay laughed. 'Subtle! So how long have you got?'

'Thirty days,' Ning said. 'But I served most of that in a low security unit, until I got in a fight. I'm just here for seven days. You?'

'Eighteen months for slashing a cop, but only a week left now.'

'A cop,' Ning said. 'Impressive.'

'Breaking both arms is good though,' Fay said. 'I feel sorry for whoever has to wipe his arse until they're out of plaster.'

Ning dropped a line she'd carefully prepared to have an effect on Fay. 'At least you're going out to family and stuff.'

Fay sounded irritated. 'What do *you* know?'

'Sorry,' Ning said. 'I just assumed. I've got nobody on the outside. Dad's in prison in China and my mum died. So it'll be another crummy Islington care home.'

'Islington?' Fay said. 'Whereabouts?'

'Tufnell Park.'

'I've lived near there most of my life,' Fay said. 'I'm just like you: no family. Mum died a long ways, then my aunt got killed.'

'Pisser,' Ning said.

Fay smiled like she'd thought of something funny. 'You know, Ning, it's a pity you didn't get here a few months earlier, because if we'd worked together we could have *owned* this place!'

*

Ryan's hands gripped James Adams' waist as the mission controller opened the throttle of his 865cc Triumph Bonneville and rode under a bridge at close to seventy miles per hour. James zoomed past a red double-decker and blasted over a pedestrian crossing, before taking a right into a side street and slicing between a people carrier and the kerb.

After cutting the throttle, James took a lazy right-hand turn and pulled through gates in front of a brick-built, three-storey council block. Once the bike was stopped on a little paved patio, Ryan hopped off and gasped with relief as he pulled off his helmet.

'Enjoy the ride?' James asked chirpily, as he looked at his watch. 'Ninety-five minutes from campus. You'd never get *close* to that in a car.'

Ryan trembled with a mixture of fear and rage. 'You're insane!' he yelled.

James grinned. 'Four years in the saddle and no accidents, mate. *Slow down, James, I feel sick, James, mind the lollipop lady, James.* You're worse than my girlfriend, Kerry. She won't ride with me any more.'

'*I'm* not riding with you any more,' Ryan said.

James shrugged. 'Fine, but the journey back to campus is a bus, three trains and a taxi. Now let's see what the relocation team has done for us.'

Ryan's hands still trembled as he put the key in the front door. It was a two-bed, ground-floor flat on the edge of the Pemberton estate. The rooms were small, but the whole place had been refurbished to a decent standard.

Ryan found a small bedroom and saw that the relocation team had already put his clothes in the wardrobe, while his mission equipment stood in a flight case at the end of the bed.

'They got our shopping from Waitrose,' James said, as he shoved a ready meal in the microwave and pressed *start*. 'Dead posh. You hungry?'

'I think it'll take my guts about a week to settle after the bike ride,' Ryan said.

James shook his head with contempt as Ryan stepped up to the kitchen sink and opened the slats of a Venetian blind. There was a tiny paved back garden, followed by a view downhill of several more low-rise blocks set around a courtyard.

At the centre of the courtyard was a concrete play

area and a large, corrugated metal building with a giant blue and red logo along the side which read *The Hangout – Youth Centre.*

12. FLOOD

James cooked up bacon and mushroom omelettes for breakfast. Ryan wolfed it down in his underwear, before heading back to his room to put on the black and yellow tie and green blazer of St Thomas' Boys school.

'Remember what we talked about in the briefing,' James said. 'To get in with the drug dealers you've got to create the impression of being tough and rebellious. But not so crazy that people think you're unstable.'

'I know,' Ryan said.

'And the photographs?' James asked.

James had been through all this the day before on campus and Ryan sounded mildly irritated. 'God, James! I've studied the pictures we got from Kentish Town Police, so I know which kids to try hanging out with.'

This part of north London wasn't known for great schools and St Thomas' was the worst of a bad bunch.

The main building was an old Victorian schoolhouse, the air in the lobby fouled by a putrid aroma coming out of the boys' toilets.

The woman on reception directed Ryan to an office on the second floor. The head of Year Ten was a lanky IT teacher called Mr Kite.

'Welcome to St Thomas',' he said, as he firmly shook Ryan's hand. 'Now, how about we get off on the right foot by tucking that shirt in?'

Ryan grudgingly tucked his shirt in, before sitting through a boring lecture on the difficulties he'd face catching up with the GCSE programme, and how the school had a family ethos and didn't tolerate bullying or racism.

Once the spiel was out of the way, the bell for first lesson was long gone and Ryan managed to arrive at his science class twenty minutes late. He charged into the room noisily and went straight for a seat near the back.

'Young man, what are you doing?' a bearded teacher asked.

Ryan looked down between his legs. 'Sitting on a stool,' he said sarcastically, making a couple of other kids laugh.

'Well, you don't roll into my lesson twenty minutes late and sit down. Especially when I have no clue who you are.'

Everyone in the class watched Ryan as he strolled to the front of the room and showed the teacher a timetable. There were two kids he recognised from surveillance photos in the room.

The teacher pointed out a name on Ryan's timetable. 'Science, *Miss Dingwall*. Do I look like Miss Dingwall to you?'

Ryan grinned. 'I don't know, I've never met Miss Dingwall.'

The teacher stroked his beard.

'Some women are pretty hairy,' Ryan said, which made the classroom erupt with laughter.

The teacher chose to ignore the quip and pointed to the right. 'Two classrooms down.'

'All right,' Ryan said sourly, as he headed for the exit. 'No need to get snotty.'

'I don't like your attitude,' the teacher shouted. 'You're lucky I don't report you to your head of year.'

Ryan sauntered out, walked down a hallway and then crashed noisily into Miss Dingwall's classroom.

'Oh right, you must be the new student,' she said, in a posh accent. 'You're a little late and we're just about to start an experiment, OK? So if you can quickly copy the diagram on the board, I'll come over and help you set up, yaah?'

'Yaah!' Ryan said.

Ryan immediately recognised three kids from surveillance pictures, but only one had an empty bench next to him. He was a chubby half-Somali, half-English kid called Abdi.

'Miss, I haven't got a workbook,' Ryan said.

But Miss Dingwall had been expecting a new student and was already coming across the room with a workbook, a textbook and several printed worksheets.

As she worked with Ryan, helping him set up the equipment for an experiment, the rest of the class grew so rowdy that she was forced to return to the front and yell at everyone to settle down.

Ryan looked across at Abdi. 'I'm Ryan,' he said.

Abdi scowled and looked Ryan in the eyes. 'And why should I give a shit?' he asked.

*

Fay and Ning chatted through the night, from little stuff like what films and music they liked to big things like what they planned to do when they got out of Idris.

'Everyone says I'm just a kid,' Fay complained. 'But I'm not gonna let the people who killed my aunt and mum get away with it.'

'I admire your determination,' Ning said. 'But you'd be taking on an entire organisation. Maybe you *should* ride with that cop you were talking about.'

Fay tutted. 'I'm not a snitch.'

It was gone 3 a.m. when the two girls stopped talking and went to sleep. As a result the pair were tired and grumpy when a guard named Sarah woke them up for school.

Lessons were compulsory in the STC, but each teacher had to struggle with fifteen kids who varied wildly in age and ability and often didn't have English as their first language. Fay and Ning's teacher didn't seem bothered that the pair settled on cushions at the back of the classroom and dozed off.

When school ended at 2 p.m., all the girls headed back to the accommodation block.

'There's only ever Wendy plus one other guard on duty,' Fay said. 'You wanna have some fun?'

Ning looked intrigued, but sounded wary. 'Nothing that gets my sentence extended.'

'Agreed,' Fay said. 'But there's only one segregation cell and I'll bet you five pounds that I can get put in there before you.'

Ning smirked and put her hands on her hips. 'Are you saying you're more of a badass than me?'

'I'm not saying,' Fay said. 'I *know* I'm more of a badass than you.'

Once they got back from the education block, most girls started going to their rooms, while a few changed clothes to go join a netball match outside. Fay cut into the laundry room and dived on top of a washing machine.

She tried reaching down the back, but her arms weren't long enough and she looked back at Ning.

'Don't just stand there, give us a hand,' Fay said, as she started dragging one of the machines away from the wall.

When they'd pulled the machine back half a metre, Fay jumped into the gap behind and wrenched the water hose out of the back. As water began to spew, Fay reached around and pulled the pipes out of the machines on either side.

'Tip all the powder,' Fay said.

There were two giant boxes open and the girls each threw the powder in all directions as water began puddling on the floor.

'Anarchy!' Fay yelled, as she backed out and headed for their cell.

The pair sat on their beds, waiting for someone to report their sabotage to a guard. It felt like ages, but it was little Izzy who saw the water pouring down the corridor. She ran back to Wendy's office.

'Miss, there's water flooding the laundry room!'

Fay and Ning peeked out of their room as Wendy frantically yelled for the second guard, Sarah, to come running. As the guard splashed down a hallway running with an increasing torrent of water, Wendy dispatched Izzy to go find the facility's maintenance person.

'I'm not sure how to shut it off,' Wendy shouted. 'There must be a stopcock somewhere.'

As soon as she was sure that the two guards were inside the laundry room, Fay led Ning across the hallway and into Wendy's office.

Fay immediately opened the filing cabinet and began chucking out files and throwing them across the floor. Ning realised she had to join in and yanked out the desk drawers, scattering their contents.

A bunch of girls had started gathering in the hallway to watch the running water and a couple joined the fun, grabbing the folders and files from Wendy's desk and throwing them out into the damp corridor. Fay and Ning were both laughing, but also a little bit scared.

Ning thought they'd accomplished what they needed to, but Fay had one final target. She stormed back into the hallway and sploshed her way down to Izzy and Chloe's room. Izzy had run to get maintenance, but

Chloe stood in her doorway and had rolled up a towel to try stopping the flood from getting into her room.

'Grass bitch,' Fay shouted, as she gave Chloe a two-handed shove into the cell.

Chloe screamed as Fay kicked her hard in the thigh, then sent her sprawling backwards over her bed. Ning's instinct was to defend Chloe, but her mission was to get close to Fay and she had to find a way to break up the fight without jeopardising their friendship.

'This is what you get if you screw me over,' Fay shouted, as she lined up a punch.

As Chloe braced for a punch on the nose, Ning snatched Fay's arm.

'You'll get done for assault,' Ning shouted. 'The cow's not worth it.'

Fay growled, but seemed to take Ning's point.

'You're lucky,' Fay shouted, firing a ball of spit in Chloe's face as she backed up.

'Let's get back to our cell,' Ning said.

As the pair stepped back into the corridor, four huge, black-clad figures charged in up at the end by the laundry room. Izzy tried saying something to one of the men, but only got splattered against the wall before getting an almighty shove.

'Lockdown, back in your cells!' the men shouted.

Several girls screamed as the helmeted men shoved them back towards their cells. A girl who fell found a size-twelve boot planted in her stomach before she was picked up and shoved backwards while a man screamed, 'What did I tell you?' right in her face.

Fay and Ning scrambled back to their cell ahead of the onslaught. Ning was worried about what was happening to the other girls, but Fay just lay back on her bed, studying her blood-smeared fist.

'This is what life's all about,' she roared. And then she started laughing.

13. ASSEMBLY

Ryan could smell James cooking bacon in the kitchen, but the aroma made him queasy and he wished he didn't have to get up for his third day at St Thomas' school.

'I'm making your breakfast,' James said, when he burst in a couple of minutes later. 'You might at least have the decency to get up and eat it.'

Ryan emerged from under his duvet. He wasn't exactly tearful, but James could tell he was upset.

'What's the matter?'

James seemed like a decent bloke, but Ryan wasn't sure he was the kind of person you could really talk to, so he just said, 'It's nothing.'

'It's clearly *something*,' James said, as he sat on the end of Ryan's bed. 'If you don't want to talk to me, I can set up a call with one of the counsellors on campus.'

'No,' Ryan gasped, worried that a call back to campus

would get put on to his mission record. 'It's just . . .'

James smiled as Ryan tailed off. 'Bloody hell, Ryan, I don't bite.'

'It's just . . . I'm so shit at making friends with people.'

James frowned. 'You're a black shirt, so you must have done something right.'

'I got my black shirt from one big mission,' Ryan said. 'And at the start of that I had to make friends with this guy Ethan. I got it so wrong that I almost got the poor kid killed. Now I'm on this mission and I'm *still* useless.'

James thought for a couple of seconds. 'We're trying to find a major source of high purity cocaine. Nobody is expecting instant results.'

'You don't get it,' Ryan moaned. 'Agents like Ning waltz in and make friends with people really easily, but I always fail.'

'I was always pretty good at that stuff,' James admitted. 'It's mostly about being relaxed, not trying too hard and having a bit of luck.'

Ryan put his hands over his head. 'But I'm *so* crap. I tried talking to this kid called Abdi who's in my form and he blanks me. I've tried speaking to a few other kids on our target list and none of them want anything to do with me.'

'If you're anxious you probably come across as trying too hard,' James said. 'But I might be able to set something up that'll help.'

'Like what?'

'Is there a place where the kids you're targeting spend time?'

'The Hangout,' Ryan said.

James shook his head. 'I mean near the school, during lunch break, or at the end of the day.'

Ryan nodded. 'There's a little swing park. Quite a few of the target kids hang there at lunchtime.'

'OK,' James said, as he stroked his beard thoughtfully. 'I'll have a think. You keep your phone switched on this morning because I'll probably need to talk to you.'

*

Fay got another three days in segregation for beating up Chloe, but emerged looking cheerful because her sentence wouldn't outlast the week.

'Ningy!' Fay said exuberantly, when she got back to her cell. 'Ningy, Ning, Ningo, bingo!'

Ning raised one eyebrow and smiled wryly. 'You can cut that out.'

The two girls hugged like old friends and made high-pitched *squeee* noises.

'We've got our release papers for Saturday,' Ning said. 'I put yours up by the window.'

Fay smiled as she reached for an envelope. Her expression changed dramatically when she'd read a couple of sentences.

'They're sending me to foster-parents in Elstree,' she yelled. 'Where's bloody *Elstree*?'

'Way north I think,' Ning said. 'Like, past Barnet, or something.'

'What gives them the right to send me to Elstree?

Surely they're supposed to release me back where I came from.'

Fay steamed down the hallway and entered Wendy's office without knocking.

'Elstree?' she screamed. 'I'm not from anywhere near Elstree. I thought you got released back into the care of whatever local authority you were arrested in.'

Wendy sat at her desk and looked resigned to another shouting match. 'You were arrested in Camden,' Wendy began calmly. 'But Camden has a network of foster-parents in other boroughs. And given that your aunt was murdered by a gang based in Camden, it was decided that you'd be better off living a few miles out of harm's way.'

Fay tutted. 'If Hagar had wanted me dead he'd have done it already. But I'm just a kid. He doesn't regard me as a threat.'

'Elstree is a perfectly nice place,' Wendy said. 'It's not like you've got friends or relatives in Camden.'

'I wasn't even consulted – as per usual,' Fay huffed.

'You might have had time to make changes if you hadn't got yourself locked up in seg,' Wendy said stiffly.

'Always *my* fault,' Fay said, before storming back to the cell.

'You can always come and visit me,' Ning said soothingly.

'Where are you?' Fay asked.

'The north of Islington,' Ning said. 'Some place called Nebraska House.'

*

Ryan still felt down after another morning of school, moving between lessons without really connecting with anyone. At lunchtime he queued up for sausage and chips at a takeaway near the school, then walked briskly towards the swing park.

The kids with links to Hagar's operation were a close-knit bunch of Year Nines and Tens. They lurked at the back of the park on a skateboard ramp, while Year Seven kids mucked about on the swings and the roundabouts.

Ryan got a text from James, All set?

He dabbed ketchup over the screen of his iPhone as he responded.

Ready when U R.

A couple of minutes later, six boys came into the park wearing the black blazers of the nearby Dartmouth Park school. None of the sextet had ever been near Dartmouth Park. They were all CHERUB agents, including Ryan's mates Max and Alfie and a kid called Jimmy who looked like he could break rocks with his head.

'St Thomas',' Jimmy shouted, as he approached the kids by the skateboard ramp. 'Why you got this park? It's nearer to our school than yours.'

A target of Ryan's named Ali took the bait. 'You got the massive reservoir park, right next to your school.'

Jimmy laughed. 'That's ours, but now we're taxing this park.'

Ryan picked up the last of his chips as eight of his target kids moved towards the six CHERUB agents.

'Why don't you start something?' a target called Andre shouted as he stepped out to the edge of the skating ramp. 'You bitches be lucky to leave this park on two legs.'

As Andre stepped forward, CHERUB agent Alfie DuBoisson met him with a fist in the face.

'Our park!' Alfie shouted.

The St Thomas' kids piled forward into the CHERUB agents. Blows flew in all directions, but the results were predictable as combat-trained CHERUB agents knocked three kids on their arses. One St Thomas' kid charged in with a lump of wood, but was swiftly disarmed by Max and had the wood shoved up the inside of his blazer.

As the melee erupted between fourteen- and fifteen-year-olds, most of the little kids scrambled out of the park gate. Ryan balled up his chip paper and charged towards the action.

'Think you're hard?' Ryan taunted, as he strode in with chest puffed and fists bunched.

The first rival Ryan faced was his friend Alfie. They'd fought in the dojo a few times and Ryan always got his arse kicked. But this time Ryan launched a pivoting roundhouse kick and Alfie acted out a backwards stumble, clutching his ribcage.

Jimmy had a Somali named Youssef in a headlock, until Ryan approached and karate-chopped him in the neck, forcing him to let go before giving him a two-fingered eye jab that didn't quite make contact.

As Jimmy stumbled back with his hands over his eyes,

another CHERUB agent charged at Ryan and ended up sprawled on his face from a trip.

'Any more of you wanna piece of me?' Ryan yelled.

The St Thomas' kids who'd been knocked down in the initial onslaught were still mostly crawling around on the ground, while four of the CHERUB agents were getting to their feet. At the centre of it all, stood Ryan.

'I got four of you,' Ryan yelled confidently. 'Where's your bravado now?'

Alfie was the first CHERUB agent back on his feet, but as Ryan stepped closer he turned and started running. Within a few seconds the other CHERUB agents had all turned and run away.

'Dartmouth Park,' Ryan taunted, as they ran off. 'Dartmouth Shite, more like.'

By this time, most of the St Thomas' kids were back on their feet. Abdi, who'd repeatedly blanked Ryan in science class, came up behind and gave him a friendly thump on the back.

'You see that eye gouge on the big kid?' Abdi shouted. 'He's gonna be feeling that one!'

'Where'd you learn your skills?' Andre asked.

Ryan smirked. 'I've been moved around a lot of schools and there's always someone waiting to take a pop at you.'

'Righteous,' another kid said, before offering to bump fists. 'Reckon we'd have handled it though. It's just they took us by surprise.'

'Surprise,' Abdi agreed.

'So where you from?' Andre asked.

Ryan made a circle with his pointing finger. 'All around. My parents died, so I live with my brother, James. He's got a job working as a mechanic, so hopefully we're gonna be here for a while.'

'Didn't I see you going in a house on the Pemberton estate?' Abdi asked.

Ryan nodded. 'That's right.'

'You should come over to The Hangout,' Abdi said. 'You must practically be able to see it from your house.'

'I've seen it,' Ryan said. 'I wasn't sure if it was cool, plus it's not like I know anyone round here.'

'Come tonight,' Abdi said. 'There's pool, table tennis, girls.'

'Not that they'll go near you, Abdi,' someone said.

Ryan tried to sound nonchalant, even though he was all excited on the inside. 'Guess I might check it out,' he said casually.

14. HANGOUT

Ryan got home from school just before five.

'And?' James asked.

Ryan smiled as he threw his school bag down in the hallway. 'Yeah, your plan worked,' he said. 'I had double maths after lunch and I sat with Abdi, Youssef and a guy called Warren. We were pissing around so much that we got a detention.'

'So, am I a genius, or am I a genius?' James asked.

'Clearly nothing beats a giant fake street brawl to win new friends,' Ryan said. 'Now I'm supposed to be meeting the guys at The Hangout in about an hour, so I'm gonna shower and change. Is there something I can blitz in the microwave?'

'That's the only kind of food I buy,' James said.

After his shower, Ryan felt anxious as he picked out clothes for the evening. He didn't want to look scruffy, but he might also get laughed at if he ponced himself up too much. In the end he went for a blue and white striped T-shirt, cargo shorts and a pair of Vans slip-ons.

From outside, The Hangout was a grafittied metal shed that could have been a youth club anywhere. The main doors were propped open because of the heat and Ryan stepped into a spacious hall with pool and table tennis tables, a line of vending machines and a lot of severely vandalised foam chairs.

There were about twenty-five kids in the space, and as Ryan walked in it seemed that every eye turned on him. He made about four steps over the sticky tiled floor before Youssef called.

'Ryan, get over here.'

Youssef was in the middle of a group of about ten lads, most of whom Ryan recognised from his target list. Nobody could be arsed to play ping-pong in the heat, but all the pool tables were busy, while another group of lads played poker. Despite the promise of girls, there were none to be seen, and most mysteriously of all, three sinister-looking heavies sat outside an office.

'You play pool?' Youssef asked, as he banged Ryan's fist. 'Guys, this is Ryan. He stepped in and saved our asses from those Dartmouth Park slags earlier on.'

Abdi objected to this description. 'He helped out, he didn't *save* us.'

Youssef shrugged. 'Whatever.'

A bulky Somali lad named Sadad spoke. 'Those arse swipes are lucky I wasn't there. I would have mashed them up.'

'I'd love to go up to Dartmouth Park and find those kids and take 'em down,' Abdi said. 'They only beat us because they took us by surprise.'

This wasn't what Ryan recalled, but he joined the nods around the group. As far as he was concerned, they could remember the fight any way they liked, as long as they were still his mates.

'So how do I get a game of pool?' Ryan asked.

Sadad answered. 'I'm up next, you can play the winner.'

As Sadad spoke a bearded guy in a waistcoat came out of the office and offered Ryan his hand.

'Hi,' he said, as Ryan shook. 'I'm Barry, from The Hangout. Welcome to the youth club.'

'Hey,' Ryan said, as a couple of lads imitated Barry's slightly pompous voice.

'You're a hundred per cent welcome here,' Barry said. 'But you do have to register and there's a two pound joining fee. If you could just come to my office.'

Ryan looked uncertainly at his new mates.

'Don't go,' Sadad said. 'Once you're back there he'll try to snog you.'

This caused an outbreak of wild laughter, but Barry seemed used to getting mocked. He led Ryan past the three scary-looking heavies and into a well-appointed office. It was equipped with a photocopier, two computers and two whirring air-conditioning units.

'Nice and cool here,' Ryan said.

Barry sat at his desk and found Ryan a small blue

form. 'Just fill in your name, address and telephone number. It's two pounds to join, but it doesn't matter if you don't have it with you right now.'

'I've got it,' Ryan said, as he rummaged inside his shorts.

'If you can just look up.'

Barry swivelled a webcam around and snapped Ryan's photo for his membership card.

'The laminating machine for your card takes a few minutes to warm up,' Barry explained, as he reached behind and handed Ryan a brochure.

The leaflet was printed in colour and entitled *The Hangout – There For You.*

'Make sure you give this a good read,' Barry said. 'The Hangout is a charity, funded entirely by donations. We work in six London boroughs providing youth clubs such as this one, day trips, sporting activities and support services.

'Now that you're a member, you can get involved in any of our activities, or make use of our confidential counselling and advice services. Keep hold of the leaflet and give it a read when you get home.'

'Thanks,' Ryan said.

Ryan spent a couple of minutes flicking through the pages while the laminating machine heated up to make his membership card. Once it was ready, Barry handed the still-warm card over and showed Ryan back out into the hall.

Sadad yelled, 'Hope you kept your mitts off him, Barry.'

Barry ignored it, but one of the three heavies stood up.

'Sadad, here!' he ordered. Then he pointed at Ryan. 'You, listen.'

Sadad looked nervous when he got close, and everyone in the room was looking.

'Show respect to Barry,' the thug told Sadad. 'Get a mop and bucket and clean the whole floor.' Then he looked at Ryan. 'Did you treat Mr Barry with respect?'

'I did,' Ryan said, nodding anxiously.

'OK, go back with your friends.'

Sadad walked briskly towards a cleaner's closet, not daring to show any dissent. Ryan rejoined his new friends. After giving it a few seconds and making sure that the toughs weren't looking at him, Ryan turned to Abdi and spoke in a whisper.

'Who are the three nutters?'

'They work for Hagar.'

Ryan acted innocent. 'Who the hell is Hagar?'

This comment caused widespread laughter.

'What's funny?' Ryan asked.

'How can you not know who Hagar is?' Youssef snorted.

'I moved here less than a week ago,' Ryan said. 'I don't know who anyone is.'

Abdi smiled. 'Hagar's the biggest drug dealer in this part of town.'

Ryan looked over. 'So which one's Hagar?'

This caused more laughter.

'Hagar's the top dog,' Abdi said, snorting with

laughter. 'He doesn't sit in a crummy youth club all day. Those are his lieutenants. They organise all the street dealers and dish out crumbs to us kids if we're lucky.'

'What kind of crumbs?' Ryan asked.

'If they like you, they give out jobs,' Abdi explained. 'Maybe twenty quid to take something from here to there, or go to Starbucks for coffees. Once they start really trusting you, you might get a package. That's when you sell drugs yourself.'

'Shit!' Ryan said excitedly. 'Can you make a lot of dough?'

Abdi nodded. 'There's guys our age making seven hundred a week, just for selling a few hours a day after school. But you've gotta be careful, 'cos if you mess up, Hagar's guys will batter you.'

'Maybe kill you even,' Youssef added, as the black ball rattled into a pocket on the nearest pool table.

The guy who'd lost handed Ryan a chewed-up cue, while the victor racked up the balls for another game.

'OK,' Ryan said, as he lined up to break. 'Let's play some pool.'

15. NEBRASKA

Fay and Ning left Idris STC shortly after noon on Friday. A prison service minibus drove south for an hour and a half before dropping Fay at a semi-detached house in the suburb of Elstree. Her new foster-parents were a couple in their late forties, who had two younger foster-kids and a house filled with china dolls and frilly curtains.

Ning reached Nebraska House just before five, but a mix-up in the paperwork meant it was nearer to 7 p.m. before she was allocated one of the care home's dingy single rooms. Dinner was evil and Ning sent Fay a picture message showing curry and rice with the word, EWW!

Fay texted back a few minutes later, I have a big double bed, the foster-mum makes Victoria sponge cake that's 2 die 4.

Once she'd settled in her room, Ning called her mission controller, James, to confirm that everything was OK.

'If you get a chance, pop into room sixteen and see if it still says *James Choke* on the wall,' James said.

'Who the hell is James Choke?'

'My pre-CHERUB name,' James explained. 'I was in Nebraska House for a while after my mum died.'

'The rooms look like they were painted quite recently,' Ning said. 'So how's Ryan doing?'

*

Friday night drew a crowd of more than fifty to The Hangout, and a few of them were even girls. It was officially a disco night, but although Barry had folded up the ping-pong tables to make space, nobody seemed interested in dancing.

Ryan sat at the back of the room with Abdi, who'd sneaked in an Evian bottle filled with vodka.

'Where's the rest of the gang?' Ryan asked.

Abdi pointed discreetly at the single heavy sitting outside the office. 'Friday and Saturday are busy,' he explained. 'Youssef makes deliveries for a dealer. Sadad's got a gig as a lookout that pays thirty pounds a night.'

Ryan smiled. 'You reckon I can make some money?'

Abdi nodded. 'Not right now, but they'll find you something once they get used to your face.'

'What if I just go up and ask?'

'If you're lucky they'll laugh, if you're unlucky they'll smack you down. Either way, being pushy's not gonna help your chances.'

'So how come you're not working?' Ryan asked.

Abdi looked shame-faced at the floor between his legs. 'A couple of months back I had a little gig selling cocaine and heroin from an alleyway beside my mum's hairdresser's shop. Two guys jumped me and stole two hundred quid's worth of gear. So now I've got to pay it back at ten pounds a week for thirty-six weeks.'

'That's three hundred and sixty.'

'Interest,' Abdi explained. 'The only reason I didn't get stomped is because my mum does hair for a lot of Hagar's boys' girlfriends.'

'But you can't help it if two guys jump you,' Ryan said.

'Rules are rules, Ryan. If you're man enough to take merchandise and sell it, you've gotta be man enough to look after it.'

'You wanna play pool?' Ryan asked.

'There's like twenty people waiting,' Abdi said, as he took a big slug from his boozed-up Evian bottle. 'Unless you wanna beat them all up like yesterday.'

Ryan pointed at a fit blonde girl sitting a few metres away. 'How do you rate my chances with her?'

'About two per cent,' Abdi said, as he offered Ryan a slug of his Evian. 'For courage.'

'Booze breath won't help,' Ryan said, as he stood up. 'Wish me luck.'

But before Ryan got anywhere near the girl he noticed a big Somali dude coming his way.

Abdi looked up eagerly. 'What can I do for you, boss?'

'Where is everyone?' the dude asked.

'Out and about,' Abdi said. 'I'm available.'

'You don't exist until you've paid your debts,' he said, before pointing at Ryan. 'Walk with me.'

A Flo Rida track started up as Ryan followed the thug across the room and out of the main door where it was quiet.

'You wanna earn a fast tenner?'

'Sure,' Ryan said.

'You know Dirtyburger?'

Ryan nodded. 'I've never eaten there, but I've been past it on the way to school.'

'OK, I've got some people on the Pardew estate that need feeding, you see?'

'Sure,' Ryan said.

'Get five burgers, five fries, five Cokes. Take them up to flat fifty-six. Make sure to ask Clive how it's going, then you come back and tell me what he says. Understood?'

'Understood,' Ryan said, as the man peeled twenty-pound notes out of a roll.

'Don't screw up. If you do, don't show your face around here no more.'

*

Fay went to bed early and set the alarm on her phone for 5 a.m. Her room was comfortable and decorated in neutral shades so that it would suit any short-term foster-kid, from a three-year-old girl to a sixteen-year-old boy.

After waking and taking a piss, Fay crept downstairs and looked in the cupboard by the front door. All she found were shoes and coats, so she walked through to the kitchen. She checked the cupboards for anything of value and rattled all the canisters to see if there was a hidden stash.

But the ground floor was a bust, so she walked back upstairs to the room belonging to her foster-parents. She opened the door quietly, then gave it half a minute to see if they stirred.

There was an encased radiator running along one wall and Fay saw her new foster-dad's wallet and keys lying on top of it. A floorboard made a noisy creak as Fay stepped forward. She monitored her foster-parents' breathing as she grabbed the wallet, keys and a travel card and tiptoed back towards the exit.

After backing into her room and making a relieved gasp, Fay was pleased to discover that she'd nabbed an Oyster season ticket that would let her travel around London. The credit cards in the wallet were of no use without the pin number, so she left them and took what she thought was a slightly disappointing haul of forty-five pounds.

Fay had prepared her escape the night before. She'd packed a lightweight rucksack with a couple of changes of underwear and some toiletries, and printed off a Google Map showing the fifteen-minute walk from the house to Elstree Station.

Fay slugged some orange juice and couldn't resist grabbing a slice of Victoria sponge, which she crammed into her mouth as she opened the back door and walked down twenty metres of garden. Using her foster-father's keys, she unlocked the shed and stuck her head inside, inhaling a mixture of cobwebs and creosote.

There was a tool rack against the back wall and she grabbed a shovel, plus screwdrivers and some other small tools that she thought might come in handy.

The first train south ran at 5:53 and Fay was keen to be as far from Elstree as possible before her foster-parents woke up. She called Ning on her mobile as she strode briskly towards the station, carrying her backpack and a garden shovel balanced on her shoulder.

'Yeah,' Ning said drowsily.

'You sound tired.'

'It's twenty-five to six,' Ning yawned. 'What were you expecting?'

'I looked on Google,' Fay said. 'The nearest underground to Nebraska House is Tufnell Park. You need to travel north to Totteridge and Whetstone. I'll meet you by the entrance at about seven-thirty.'

'What's at Totteridge?' Ning asked.

'You just be there,' Fay said firmly. 'We're gonna have a bit of fun.'

16. DIG

Totteridge was a moderately posh suburb, eight miles from the centre of London. Ning reached the underground station a few minutes before seven-thirty, bought a bottle of water from a newsagent and stared at rows of semi-detached houses for long enough to wonder if Fay was coming. She was about to send a where-the-hell-are-you text when Fay finally arrived.

'Nice shovel,' Ning said. 'Makes you pretty identifiable if anyone searches for you on CCTV.'

'True,' Fay said. 'I ditched Foster-Daddy's Oyster card at King's Cross because they can use them to track you. It's been a while since I've been up this way, but I think we need to get a 251 bus from a stop at the top of the hill.'

They waited twelve minutes for the single-deck bus. It took them on a twenty-minute ride, passing golf courses and mansions before reaching the edge of London's protected green belt.

'This is definitely the middle of nowhere,' Ning said, as they stepped off the bus on a road with no markings and hedgerows growing up past head height on either side. 'What is this place?'

'Not telling,' Fay said, smiling, as they crossed the road.

'For all I know you're planning to whack me with the shovel and kill me.'

Fay raised one eyebrow. 'Damn, you guessed.'

After a few hundred metres the pair reached a wooden gate crudely painted with *Greenacre Community Allotments – Please lock after entering.*

The dirt pathway inside was rutted with vehicle tracks. As they began walking, they passed a ramshackle shop which had two foul-smelling mounds of manure, on offer at £3 per bag. Beyond this, a network of paths lined with individual parcels of land stretched off in all directions.

Some allotments were beautifully kept, with painted sheds, neat rows of growing vegetables and greenhouses full of flowers. A few were tangled and overgrown, while the vast majority of plots fell somewhere between the two extremes. Even though it was early, there were already cars parked up and people picking fruit and hosing their plants.

'The British make me laugh,' Ning said, as she looked around. 'In China families do everything they can to leave the land and go live in the city. Here they work all week, then come and dig a piece of land like it's some kind of fun.'

'Don't knock it,' Fay said. 'My mum used to grow the best-tasting tomatoes. And the courgettes and strawberries were amazing.'

A couple of turns on the meandering tracks brought them to plot sixty-four. The eighteen-metre square was bisected by a crazy-paved path and had two large sheds at the far end.

'Looks neat,' Ning said, as she looked along rows of runner beans and raspberry bushes. 'Who's been looking after it?'

'You're not allowed more than one allotment, but a lot of people want two,' Fay explained. 'The woman on plot sixty-three said she was more than happy to look after it when my aunt got sent to prison.'

Fay lifted some anti-bird mesh and picked a couple of raspberries from a bush. She popped one in her mouth and offered the other to Ning.

'Nice,' Ning said as the taste exploded in her mouth. 'It reminds me of the village I lived in when I was little. Except we'd have ducks and chickens around as well.'

Fay led Ning along the strip of crazy paving, until she came to a curved reddish piece of stone that looked like it had once been part of a chimney pot. It was pretty solidly bedded into the earth and Fay had to dig with the fingers of both hands to prise it up.

Beneath the stone were half a dozen woodlice, and more importantly a round metal tin. Fay couldn't twist the rusty lid.

'Give us,' Ning said.

But Ning couldn't open the tin either, so Fay went down on one knee and prised the lid with a screwdriver. When it eventually popped open, the tin contained a bunch of keys wrapped in thick plastic to keep out moisture.

One of the keys opened a lock on the smaller of the two sheds. The exterior was tatty, but Fay led Ning into a cosy little space. Grubby windows in the roof and door let in light. There was a camp bed, a small camping stove fuelled by gas cylinders and a metal sink with a single tap that would provide cold water.

Fay opened a cupboard and found some tea bags. 'Fourteen months past the sell-by date! I guess I'd better go to Asda and stock up.'

'So you're planning to stay here?' Ning said.

Fay nodded. 'There's no heat or hot water, but at this time of year it should be fine.'

'What'll you do when it gets to autumn?'

Before Ning got an answer, Fay turned the tap over the sink. There was a violent chugging noise, followed by a splutter of brown water that made her jump backwards. After a few seconds, the pipe settled down and a drizzle of clear water ran out.

'By the autumn . . .' Fay said thoughtfully. 'By the autumn, I reckon I'll either be dead or I'll have killed Hagar and robbed enough drug dealers to afford better digs.'

'Always planning ahead,' Ning said chirpily. But on the inside she felt kind of sad because she'd started to like Fay and didn't like the idea that she might end up dead.

'So I'll have to go to the supermarket, get some groceries and some cloths and stuff to give this place a good clean. The allotment shop should have gas cylinders for the stove.'

'You came with a shovel,' Ning said. 'I assumed we were coming here to dig something up.'

Fay realised she'd forgotten and nodded excitedly. 'Yes! Next door.'

The second shed was larger, but had none of the frills. The windowless interior meant that the only light came through the open door, while the contents were a cluttered mixture of garden tools, pots, netting, and bags of fertiliser and compost.

'Shovels,' Ning said, laughing as she rattled some garden tools. 'So much for carrying one all the way from Elstree.'

Fay sounded narked. 'Well, I didn't know what tools I'd find here. I'd never have got the keys to the sheds without the screwdriver.'

'Joke,' Ning said airily. 'Don't blow your stack.'

Fay took a deep breath and held up her hands. 'I've got a temper, I know. But I'm putting a lot of faith in you, Ning.'

'How come?'

'You could go back home and grass me up,' Fay explained. 'Can I really trust you? I mean, how long have I known you? A week?'

'Barely,' Ning said. 'But you're the one who called me

at five a.m., asking if I wanted to come and have some fun.'

'Fair point,' Fay said. 'I need you to help me drag most of this stuff outside and lift up the floor.'

It took the girls ten minutes to drag tools and sacks out of the shed. Once the space was clear, Fay told Ning to stand up against the back wall of the shed.

'I'll lift the floor with the shovel, you grab hold and prise it up.'

Fay took three attempts before she got the shovel between the boards and lifted a big section of the shed's wooden floor. Ning struggled to lift it, so Fay threw the shovel down and after some grunting the pair managed to rest it against the side wall.

'Grab a shovel,' Fay said.

As Ning went outside for a shovel, Fay began digging. After the first couple of loads, her spade banged the top of a metal box. Ning moved in and the pair gradually unveiled an ex-army ammunition box a metre and a half long and half a metre wide. Fay dug a little hole at the narrow end to reach a handle and strained as she tugged the box out of the earth.

'Give us a hand.'

Ning grabbed the handle at the other end and the two girls lifted the box out of the earth.

'God that's heavy,' Ning said, as the box thudded down. 'What's inside?'

'I'm not sure exactly,' Fay said, as she grabbed the box's aluminium lid.

Ning was half scared, half impressed when she looked

inside. There was an arsenal of knives, but her eye was drawn to some small rolls of twenty-pound notes, tightly wrapped in clingfilm to keep out the damp.

'There's a few of these,' Ning said. 'Maybe a couple of thousand quid.'

'Enough to keep me ticking over for a few weeks,' Fay said, as she studied the contents at the other end and pulled out a set of body armour and a nylon pouch full of evil-looking knives.

'Ceramic blades, no rust,' Fay explained.

Removing the body armour had unveiled some cardboard boxes, each one vacuum sealed to keep out moisture. Fay used a craft knife to open a box, and Ning instinctively backed up when she saw the contents.

'Is that for real?' Ning asked.

Fay nodded as she lifted out a handgun. 'This is what I was hoping to find. Two Glock 17 police issue handguns and two hundred rounds of ammunition.' Then she pointed the plastic-wrapped gun at Ning and said, 'Bang, bang!'

17. BACON

Ryan woke up feeling pretty pleased with himself. He'd got in with the right crowd and had even been sent on an errand by one of the heavies from The Hangout. He found James in the kitchen, with a foot on the dining-table cutting his toenails.

'Now there's a sight,' Ryan said. 'And what happened to the nice cooked breakfasts I've been getting?'

James smiled. 'You get breakfast on a schoolday. On the weekend, it's self-service.'

As James said this, a big piece of toenail shot across the room in Ryan's direction.

'You'll have someone's eye out,' Ryan said, as he walked to the fridge and found a big pack of bacon.

'Bacon sandwich?' Ryan asked, as James clipped another nail.

'Count me in,' James said, as he put his foot down

and started pulling on a sock.

Ryan put a pan on the hob and poured in some cooking oil.

'So tell me more about your errand,' James said.

'Not a massive amount to tell,' Ryan said. 'The Somali guy gave me some cash—'

James interrupted. 'Name?'

'I didn't get a name, but Abdi or one of those kids will know. So anyway, he gives me fifty quid and sends me to buy burgers.'

Ryan paused while he laid out bacon rashers in the pan, then quickly washed his hands before walking to the cupboard and grabbing a white sandwich loaf.

'So what was going on when you got to this flat with the burgers?'

'Poker game,' Ryan said. 'I only got as far as the hallway, but I could tell from the noises they were making.'

'Makes sense,' James said. 'They're not gonna send an untested kid into the place where they count the money or something. But it's a really good sign.'

'How come?'

'They're interested in you,' James explained. 'For all we knew, Hagar's crew had fifty kids all eager to work for them and you wouldn't get a look-in for weeks. Did he take your mobile number?'

Ryan nodded. 'When I got back to The Hangout I asked for his number, but he just laughed.'

'What about the girls?' James asked.

Ryan looked mystified as he laid four slices of bread

on the countertop. 'What girls?'

James laughed. 'It was a disco, wasn't it? So I assume there were girls there.'

'Oh right,' Ryan said. 'There were a few fit girls, but I never got a chance to talk to any of them.'

'Keep your eyes peeled for an ex of someone who might know stuff,' James said. 'Are you still messed up over that Natalka chick you met in Kyrgyzstan?'

For a second Ryan wondered how James could know, but as a mission controller James would have read all the records of his past missions.

'It's a year since we had to go our separate ways,' Ryan said. 'I still think about her though.'

James nodded. 'I fell in love on a mission a couple of times.'

'Was that with Kerry Chang?' Ryan asked.

James laughed. 'Nah, I was usually cheating on Kerry.'

'Is Kerry still your girlfriend?'

James nodded. 'But she's at university in California so I don't get to see her much.'

'Bummer,' Ryan said.

As Ryan flipped the sizzling rashers he felt his iPhone vibrate in his pocket. He backed away from the noisy pan so that he could hear the deep voice in his ear.

'It's Ali,' the guy said.

'Ali who?'

'You went to Dirtyburger for me last night.'

'Oh, sorry!' Ryan said. 'You never gave me your name.'

As Ryan spoke he pointed at the pan and gestured for James to take over the cooking.

'Busy today, son?'

'No,' Ryan said. 'Just moved into the area. No idea what to do with myself.'

'Well, you wanna earn twenty-five quid for a few hours' graft?'

'Sure,' Ryan shrugged.

'I'll text you a location, Youssef will meet you there.'

*

Fay and Ning rode the bus back to Totteridge, then began the half-hour tube journey to Kentish Town. It was a beautiful day. Their carriage was empty apart from a woman with a buggy at the opposite end, but Fay's huge smile made Ning uneasy.

'Why so happy?' Ning asked. 'Aren't you worried?'

Fay shrugged. 'I've been dreaming about getting Hagar back since my aunt died.'

'But your mum and aunt were smart and Hagar got them.'

'The therapist at Idris said I was a *pathological thrill seeker*,' Fay said. 'A danger addict.'

'Where do we start?' Ning asked. 'I mean, presumably we don't just ask for directions to Hagar's house and then shoot him.'

Fay laughed. 'First off, it's unlikely Hagar even lives in a dump like Kentish Town. Second, I don't just want to kill Hagar. I want to get right in his face and make him mad first.'

After riding the escalator out of Kentish Town tube

station, Fay and Ning walked away from the shops and restaurants and headed for the Pemberton estate.

'That's The Hangout youth club,' Fay said. 'Hagar's people used to run a lot of small-time stuff out of there.'

'Like what?'

'Street-level dealers, mostly,' Fay said. 'They recruit local kids to do the jobs nobody else wants.'

'Are we going inside?'

'No point,' Fay said.

Instead, Fay led Ning to a shabby underground garage block, through a park that seemed seedy even on a bright summer's day, and finally to an industrial estate where a man lay sleeping on his back.

'He'll do,' Fay said.

The man was dirty, dressed in a denim jacket, football shorts and filthy trainers. His legs were so skinny that you could see every bone and tendon and he had scabs all over his body.

'Is he a drug addict?' Ning asked, looking shocked.

'Of course,' Fay said. 'You wanna know what's happening in the drug trade, go ask an addict.'

Fay crouched over the crumpled figure and pinched his cheek. 'Rupert.'

The man slowly opened one reddened eye and then began furiously scratching his arms, as if he had fleas.

'Piss off and leave me alone,' Rupert demanded. 'Bloody do-gooders.'

'I'm not a do-gooder,' Fay said firmly. 'Where are your friends, Bob and Tony?'

The man was intrigued by this show of knowledge and squinted from the sun as he sat up slightly. 'Bob was stabbed up and didn't make it. Tony's in prison.'

'That's a shame,' Fay said. 'You three were quite a team.'

'No offence, but who the hell are you?'

'You used to be friendly with my aunt Kirsten.'

'Kirsten was a nice lady! She used to fix me up good.'

Fay pulled a twenty-pound note and Rupert reached for it.

'No, no,' Fay said, snatching it out of reach.

'You're the wee girl Kirsten had with her sometimes? How is your auntie?'

'Dead,' Fay said bluntly.

'Ripping off dealers,' Rupert said. 'That'll get anyone killed.'

'I've got twenty pounds here,' Fay said. 'I'll take you to the greasy spoon up by the railway arches. I'll buy you something to eat and you can tell me all the best spots to buy heroin and cocaine. Is that a deal, Rupert?'

Rupert's smile showed off missing front teeth. 'Forget the food,' he said. 'Just give me thirty for my next two fixes and I'll tell you all you need to know about Hagar and Eli.'

'Eli?' Fay said. 'Who the hell is Eli?'

18. PHONE

'Youssef,' Ryan said. 'What's happening?'

Youssef was bulky and dark-skinned with a wispy beard. 'You're late,' he said coldly, as he got off a wooden bench and started towards the entrance of Kentish Town Station.

'Only five minutes,' Ryan said. 'I'm new in the neighbourhood, took a wrong turning.'

Youssef accepted this with a shrug. 'There's money to be made running stuff for Ali and that crew, but you gotta be punctual and fast.'

Ryan followed Youssef, blipping his Oyster card through the tube gates and down the escalator towards the platform.

'We're getting off at Tottenham Court Road,' Youssef explained, as he discreetly passed over a roll of money. 'That's three hundred pounds. When we get out we're gonna head towards Oxford Street. It's three miles long and has about thirty mobile phone shops. Our job is to go into every shop along the way, and pick up one of the cheapest phones in each shop.'

'Why not buy them all in one shop?' Ryan asked, as they stepped off the escalator and moved on to the southbound platform.

'Three minutes,' Youssef said, as he looked up at the train arrivals board. He didn't answer Ryan's question until they'd moved to a quiet area at the end of the platform.

'Mobile phones are convenient, but they're also a drug dealer's worst nightmare. Not only can the cops record every conversation, they can be used to triangulate your exact position. The only way to stay ahead of the cops is to never use a phone for more than three or four days.'

Ryan knew this already, but was keen to find out how deep Youssef's knowledge was. 'Why not just change the SIM card?'

Youssef shook his head. 'Every phone has a built-in number called an IMEI. Even if you swap the SIM card, the cops can still trace the phone or block it if it gets stolen.'

'So how often do the Hagars of this world change their numbers?'

'I've heard that Hagar doesn't carry a mobile,' Youssef said. 'If he wants something done, he'll put it in the ear of a lieutenant. The lieutenant probably has to change his mobile every two or three days.'

'Which is why we're gonna buy the cheapest ones we can get,' Ryan said.

'You're learning,' Youssef answered. 'And if you ever spot a dude stepping out of a sixty-grand car holding a twelve pound ninety-nine Nokia, I guarantee you he's crooked.'

*

It took some gentle persuasion to take Rupert to a greasy spoon café behind the Pemberton estate. He ordered a full English and a large tea, Ning asked for beans on toast, while Fay went for a bacon and fried egg sandwich.

'Tell me about Eli?' Fay asked.

Rupert shrugged. 'Don't know that much,' he said. 'But there's a rivalry going on. This part of town was all Hagar's undisputed territory. But the last few months this Eli has been mixing it.'

'So they're at war?' Fay asked.

'If they are it's a quiet war,' Rupert said. 'But at least healthy competition has upped the quality of the product. You get more kick from twenty quid's worth of gear than you would have done at the start of the year.'

They paused the conversation while the waitress put down three mugs of tea and the plates of greasy food. Rupert tucked in by skewering his sausage on a fork, but Ning was put off by a plate that didn't look too clean and the unwashed aroma of her dining companion.

'So where do you go to buy heroin these days?' Fay asked.

'Eli sells a decent product. You can usually pick it up

in the park over by the reservoir, or behind the Archway tower.'

'And Hagar?' Fay asked.

'He's got a dozen places, but I usually go up to the Pemberton estate.'

'Same for cocaine?' Ning asked, to Fay's surprise.

'Most places will sell you both,' Rupert said, as he erupted into a violent coughing fit.

Fay nodded as she greedily bit into her fried egg sandwich. 'Pemberton estate,' she told Ning. 'That's where we're headed next.'

*

It was a hot Saturday afternoon and the estate writhed with kids riding bikes, kicking balls and squirting one another with water pistols. Amidst the fun, Fay picked out an alleyway behind the refuse chute where a three-strong crew were peddling drugs.

'Three blokes,' Ning said. 'How would you rob them?'

Fay shook her head. 'It's never worth robbing a street crew. They're always on high alert for cops and even if you got close you'd be lucky to get two hundred in drugs and cash. You've got to go for big quantities to make robbing worth the risk.'

'So why *are* we looking at street dealers?'

'Rupert gave us an idea where to find dealers, now we need one of 'em to work for us.'

'An informant on the inside?' Ning asked.

Fay nodded. 'It's the hardest part of any operation, but my aunt taught me a few tricks.'

'Pretend you fancy them?' Ning asked.

'Only as a last resort,' Fay said, as she gave a little shudder.

After making a detailed tour of the estate, the two girls settled on a bench with a decent view over The Hangout. The youth club wasn't officially open but there was a group of teenaged boys hanging around near the entrance and every so often one of them went inside.

'What are we looking for?' Ning asked.

Fay shrugged. 'I'll know when I see it.'

'You reckon all these boys are working for Hagar?'

'Lookouts, runners and wannabes,' Fay said.

Ning was bored after half an hour on the bench, but Fay seemed fascinated. Ning was momentarily interested when she saw Ryan and Youssef roll up carrying heavily laden backpacks.

'Could be drugs,' Ning said.

Fay laughed. 'What, in broad daylight in the centre of the estate? You've got a *lot* to learn.'

'So who are they?'

'Well, if they come out with those backpacks empty, we'll know they've delivered something.'

'Like what?'

'Anything drug dealers need,' Fay explained. 'Milk powder for cutting drugs, plastic bags, mobile phones.'

Sure enough, Ryan and Youssef emerged a few minutes later minus their backpacks and looking pleased with themselves. Ryan briefly stood around with the mini-crew outside The Hangout, before taking the two hundred-metre stroll back home.

A few minutes after Ryan left, another kid appeared. He was nothing special to look at but Fay's eyes were wide open.

'Check out Mr Frizzy Hair,' she said.

Ning was mystified. 'What about him?'

'The body language,' Fay said. 'All the other kids want to bump fists with him. And he's a little better dressed, like he's someone with some money in his pocket.'

CHERUB had trained Ning to pick up signs like this and she felt stupid for missing them. 'He could just have wealthy parents,' she said.

'If he did it's unlikely he'd be hanging around here.'

'So what do we do?'

'We'll follow him,' Fay said. 'I want to know where he lives.'

19. WARREN

Fay and Ning followed their target across the Pemberton estate and on a short bus ride to a shabby housing block close to Hampstead Heath. Shortly before 7 p.m. he left his house on a bike and they had no way to follow him.

When it got dark just before ten, Fay moved in close and looked through the ground-floor apartment's front windows.

'Looks like it's just his mum at home,' Fay said. 'No sign of a father or siblings as far as I can see.'

'I'm tired,' Ning moaned. 'Someone's gonna spot us if we keep hanging around.'

Fay sounded irritated. 'Just *go* if you want to.'

'You can't stay here all night,' Ning said. 'You've got to sleep some time.'

It was a quarter to midnight when their target

returned and wheeled his bike into a hallway. He turned on a light in a first-floor bedroom, and threw the window wide open to catch a breeze.

'I reckon he's in for the night now,' Fay said, as she glanced at her watch.

'The last train to Totteridge will have gone,' Ning said. 'But I reckon I can smuggle you into my room at Nebraska House.'

Ning earned a mild rebuke from the night supervisor for staying out after curfew and smuggled Fay into her room via a door at the back of the kitchens. The slender bed wasn't big enough to share, so Fay wound up on the floor with bundled clothes for a pillow. Both girls slept well and nobody raised an eyebrow as Fay showered and ate breakfast with the other residents of Nebraska House.

'What's today's plan?' Ning asked.

'Back to our target's apartment,' Fay said.

'For how long?' Ning asked wearily.

'However long it takes,' Fay answered. 'This is my battle, if you're not interested I'll handle it on my own.'

As a CHERUB agent Ning knew she had to stick with Fay, but as a human being she didn't relish the prospect of another hot, boring day following people around. After sneaking off and making a quick call to update James, Ning followed Fay back to their target's apartment.

It was half past ten when the target's mother headed out, dressed in a bright yellow suit and a matching hat like she was going to church.

'We're in luck,' Fay said. 'Let's roll.'

'Is there a plan?' Ning asked.

Fay threw over a scarf. 'Tie this over your face and follow my lead.'

The two girls tied scarves over the bottom half of their faces as they mounted the apartments' front steps. Fay pressed the doorbell and slid the Glock handgun out the back of her jeans.

They waited long enough for Ning to say, 'Maybe he went out again.'

But after a full minute and a second press on the doorbell a blurred figure could be seen behind the frosted glass in the front door. The teenager opened up: fifteen years old, with scruffy Nike tracksuit bottoms and a muscular chest glazed with sweat.

His first reaction to the two masked girls was vague amusement. 'Can I help you?'

Fay barged the door with her shoulder then stuck the gun right in the youth's face.

'Back up, hands high,' Fay ordered.

The youth did as he was told, backing down a hallway decorated with peeling floral wallpaper.

'Who else is in the house?'

'Nobody.'

Fay looked at Ning. 'Check it out.'

Ning wasn't armed and didn't relish the prospect of checking out all the rooms. She checked the kitchen and living-room first, before racing upstairs to do the bedrooms and bathroom. Meantime, Fay had the youth backing up the stairs to his room.

'What's your name?' she barked.

'Warren,' the kid said.

Fay and Ning met up in Warren's tiny bedroom.

'Christ it stinks in here,' Fay said, as she stepped over a floor mounded in tangled clothes and underwear.

Ning recognised the backpack Warren had gone out with the night before. She unzipped it and found about thirty plastic bags filled with cocaine.

'How much do you sell these for?' Ning asked. 'Twenty?'

Warren nodded.

'Sit on your bed, hands on head,' Fay ordered.

Ning tipped the contents of the backpack out over the floor. 'What's gonna happen to you if we steal this?'

Warren kept a wary eye on Fay's gun.

'They'll kick my ass and I'll have to work to pay it back.'

Fay nodded. 'And when word gets around that you got robbed by two girls?'

Warren just shook his head. 'So you wanna take my stash, take it, bitches.'

'Don't call me a bitch,' Fay said angrily, as she closed in on Warren with the gun. 'Six hundred quid's worth is chicken shit! We don't want—'

Before Fay could finish, Warren lunged and grabbed the end of the gun. Fay stumbled forward as she tried to keep hold. Ning's first reaction was to dive for cover in case a wild shot went off during the struggle, but once she was sure the gun wasn't pointing her way she lunged for the bed and launched a flying kick at Warren's head.

The powerful blow sent Warren into a daze and enabled Fay to stagger back with the gun. Ning made sure Warren got the message by punching him hard on the back, while Fay cracked the pistol across his brow with enough force to make a cut.

'That's what happens if you mess with us,' Fay shouted, as Warren slumped sideways on the bed, making a low groan. 'Now sit up straight before I pull you up by your hair.'

'Hands on head,' Ning added.

Warren coughed as he straightened up. Fay picked one of the little packets of cocaine off the carpet and flung it contemptuously at his midriff.

'I don't care about your chicken-feed six hundred-pound stash. I need information,' Fay began. 'If you're dealing for Hagar's crew, you must have a lot of info.'

'I'm not a snitch,' Warren said.

Fay laughed. 'Imagine your mommy coming home from church and finding your brains splattered all over that lovely IKEA wardrobe. If you tell me what I need to know, that doesn't have to happen. I won't even steal your drugs.'

Warren looked down into his lap. 'What is it you want to know?'

'This whole thing with Hagar and Eli.'

'What about it?' Warren asked.

'How did it start?'

'I don't know every detail,' Warren said. 'But there

used to be an informal agreement. Eli would sell weed, Hagar dealt in coke and heroin. Then, six months back, Hagar started selling marijuana and Eli got pissed off and started up with cocaine.'

'So is there a war?' Fay asked.

'Eli and Hagar hate one another's guts. There's been a few beatings-up and some scuffles over territory, but mostly they've been tiptoeing around each other.'

'Evenly matched?' Fay suggested.

Warren nodded. 'There's been untold rumours that Hagar is about to make some big move against Eli's crew but I've not seen any sign.'

'Do you report to Hagar?' Fay asked.

Warren started to laugh. 'I've only ever seen Hagar like twice. I get my supplies from a guy named Steve.'

'Steve,' Fay said thoughtfully. 'Is he close to Hagar?'

'Close as anyone, I'd guess.'

Fay smiled. 'How much do you make selling drugs?'

Warren shrugged. 'I'm pretty small-time. A hundred, maybe two on a really good week.'

Fay nodded. 'How would you like to earn an extra hundred a week?'

'For what?'

'Tell me everything you hear about Hagar and Eli and anything you hear about drugs.'

Warren liked the idea of the money, but still seemed reluctant. 'Are you working for Eli's crew?'

'We're working for ourselves,' Fay said, sounding more friendly as she lowered the gun.

Fay grabbed a pencil and wrote a mobile phone

number on one of Warren's school books.

'Call me any time,' Fay said. 'I'll make it worth your while.'

20. CUT

Ryan had earned twenty quid for his Saturday afternoon phone-buying spree. More importantly he'd been noticed by Craig Willow, a goon who Youssef reckoned was Hagar's chief enforcer.

For the next three nights Ryan mooched around The Hangout, but nobody came over to give him any kind of work. He was almost desperate enough to make a direct approach to one of Hagar's people when Craig arrived and came right towards him.

'Shoo,' Craig said, as he waved off Abdi and Youssef. 'Ryan innit?'

Ryan nodded.

'I'm told you're tasty in a dust-up.'

Ryan shrugged like it was nothing and said, 'I don't take shit from anyone.'

'That's a good motto,' Craig said, as Ryan noticed the

big Spurs cockerel tattooed on his forearm. 'You up for a run into enemy territory?'

'How much?' Ryan asked.

'Twenty-five quid.'

Ryan made a wary nod. 'What am I doing?'

'There's tension between our boys and Eli's crew over on the Elthorne estate, so I need an unfamiliar face to bring in the resupply.'

'Drugs?'

Craig smiled. 'What else? Go and wait outside house seventy-two. Someone will give you a package. You take it straight up to Elthorne, block seven apartment F3.'

There was a warm summer sunset as Ryan headed out of The Hangout. He waited twenty minutes before a guy he'd not seen before passed over a backpack with a slightly doom-laden, 'Good luck.'

The pack was full, but not particularly heavy. As Ryan started to walk he guessed that there had to be at least a couple of hundred packets of drugs, and with a gram of cocaine costing at least £25, that meant he was packing five grand's worth of merchandise.

The Elthorne estate was in Highgate, twenty minutes' walk north. The sky was a dark purple colour as Ryan approached a graffitied map showing the layout of the dilapidated housing blocks. The first part of Ryan's route was down a lawned expanse between blocks, then he had to turn into an alleyway with houses backing on to both sides.

A cat shot out from behind a mound of boxes, giving Ryan a fright before he made a final turn, ignoring the lift and starting up concrete stairs to the third floor. As he rounded the first-floor landing he passed two solid-looking guys, one of whom was smoking a cigarette. When he reached the second floor, he heard the two men moving quickly up the staircase behind him.

Ryan sped up, but as he tried getting up to the third floor he found a body blocking his path.

'Excuse me, mate,' Ryan said.

The man didn't move. He was a monster, with sunken black eyes and arms like railway sleepers. The other two were coming up from behind, which left Ryan's only option as a run along the balcony in front of the second-floor apartments.

He ran seventy metres, passing reinforced front doors and windows fitted with bars. At the end he found a blue door with a fire exit sign. Ryan pushed the metal bar to unlock the door, but was horrified to discover that it was jammed.

With the three men less than twenty metres away, Ryan leaned out over the balcony. He was too high up to jump, but he reckoned he could stand on the railing and reach out to pull himself up to the next floor.

His legs swung precariously as he pulled himself up and rolled over a railing on to the third-floor balcony. He reckoned that his opponents would only take half a minute to double back and reach the third floor, so Ryan looked around desperately for apartment F3.

The heavily reinforced front door was only a few metres away. The apartment's front window was boarded up and there was a CCTV camera pointing along the balcony.

'Hello!' Ryan shouted, as he pressed the doorbell and banged on the door. Then more desperately, 'Can you open the door?'

But there was no sign of life inside the apartment. The man with enormous arms was coming around the balcony, and the other two had somehow got through the fire door Ryan hadn't been able to move and were closing in from the other side.

'Give us the bag,' Giant Arms said.

'Come and get it,' Ryan said, feeling fairly confident that he was speedy enough to dodge the fat man's blows. But a clicking noise came from behind and Ryan jolted when he saw a handgun out the corner of his eye.

'Give us the bag, kid.'

The sight of the gun pushed Ryan into shock and he backed up to the apartment. One guy put a hand on the backpack and Ryan didn't resist as he ran the strap down his arm. As soon as his opponent had the pack, the big dude swooped with a fist in the guts.

As Ryan doubled over, another guy punched him twice, and with the gun pointing at him he didn't dare fight back. Next came a blow to the mouth, and a kick in the back of the legs that left Ryan sprawled across the ground in a daze.

As Ryan covered himself, fearing more blows, a hand went down the pocket of his shorts and extracted his mobile phone. Finally Ryan felt a kick to the head that knocked him cold.

*

Fay had sneaked back to her foster-home in Elstree to pick up more of her stuff, but she'd yet to attend her school there and spent most of her time in the Kentish Town area, finding out as much as she could about Hagar's operations.

'You wanna sneak into Nebraska House tonight?' Ning asked, as she sat alongside Fay on a park bench, watching the dramatic sunset.

Fay nodded. 'Nobody's noticed me so far, and that airbed you found is quite comfy.'

But as Ning stood up, Fay felt her mobile vibrate in her pocket. The voice on the other end was familiar, but took her a few seconds to place.

'Warren?' Fay said.

'You know what you said about information?' Warren said. 'What's my cut?'

'I can give you fifty quid for any decent info.'

Warren laughed. 'I'm not gonna sell my crew out for fifty quid. I want a cut, a percentage.'

Fay paused for a minute. 'A cut of what?'

Warren spoke softly, like he was afraid of being overheard. 'Hagar's got a house off Tufnell Park Road. It's like a secret backup. Even if Hagar's entire supply gets stolen, he can use what's in the house to stay in business.'

Fay looked intrigued. 'How come you know about this place?'

'My cousin's a carpenter, who does odd jobs for Hagar. He spent three days working in the house, putting in CCTV. I only know because it's near my nan's place and he kept coming round blagging sandwiches and cups of tea while he was on the job.'

'So there's a lot of security?' Fay asked.

'I guess there's some. But there's no guards. Just Hagar's brother, Clay.'

Fay perked up when she sensed the opportunity to get at someone close to Hagar. 'So where is it?' she asked.

Warren laughed. 'I want a third of whatever money you make.'

Fay tutted. 'What risks are you taking? Finder's fee is never more than ten per cent.'

'Twenty-five,' Warren said.

'Twenty.'

Warren paused for a second. 'All right, I'll text you the address.'

Once Warren hung up, Fay explained the deal to Ning.

'What if Warren didn't like us invading his crib and this is his plan to get back at us?'

'I suppose that's possible,' Fay said.

'And surely anything valuable will be kept in a safe?'

'Probably,' Fay agreed. 'Jobs like this always take planning, but it's nothing I can't handle.'

21. LIPS

'Are you all right, son?'

Ryan opened one eye and saw a blurry female figure standing over him. His mouth was full of blood and his abs exploded with pain when he tried to get off the concrete. His instinct was to call James, but he found an empty pocket where his phone should have been.

The middle-aged woman offered Ryan an arm. He took it, and used it along with the balcony railing to haul himself up. His mouth was uncomfortably full of blood and he had no option but to spit it out. He felt around with his tongue, fearing he'd lost a tooth, but he actually just had a nasty cut on his bottom lip.

'I've called the police,' the woman said.

Ryan wasn't keen on having to explain what had happened to the cops. 'I've got to get going,' he said.

But Ryan's knee buckled as soon as he tried to walk and when the woman's husband appeared holding a plastic garden chair, he settled into it gratefully.

Ryan was worried that losing the drugs would be the end of his association with Hagar's crew and wondered what he'd say to the cops. But as he sat on the lightweight chair his biggest concern was the amount of blood pouring into his mouth.

Two policemen arrived a few minutes later.

'Two guys jumped me, stole my pack, my phone and ran off.'

'Can you describe 'em?'

Ryan invented two fairly nondescript muggers.

'There's CCTV in the lobby,' one cop said. 'We'll try and get the tape.'

Ryan doubted that the cops would put too much effort into tracking down a case of a kid getting mugged. They asked where he lived, but Ryan couldn't speak without blood running out the corner of his mouth and the cops decided to take him to hospital.

The larger of the two officers let Ryan put an arm around his back as they walked towards the lift.

*

James was in the kitchen in the flat when Ning rapped on the frosted-glass front door.

'Come in, come in,' James said warmly.

Ning took a seat at the kitchen table and sighed. 'Working with Fay is intense. She's focused on Hagar twenty-four/seven.'

'Tea?' James asked. 'Or a cold drink?'

'Can of Coke, or something like that would be great,' Ning said.

'So what's she been finding out?' James asked.

'Tons of stuff about Hagar's people. Where they're working from, what they're selling, who's important.'

'Is she discreet?'

Ning shook her head. 'Fay's clever, but she's been going around asking lots of questions about Hagar's operations. Sooner or later someone who matters will notice.'

James nodded as he placed two cans of Diet Coke on the table and sat opposite Ning. 'You'd think she'd be *ultra*-cautious after her mother and aunt were both murdered.'

'She's got that thrill seeker mentality,' Ning said, as she pulled the tab on her can.

James looked thoughtful. 'So I've got a vengeful thrill seeker, walking around with a loaded Glock in her pocket. We're gonna have to play this carefully.'

'How do you mean?' Ning asked.

'Let's just say that my new career as a mission controller will be short-lived if you and Fay get involved in a bloody shoot-out.'

'I'll try my best to avoid that scenario,' Ning said, smiling but also aware that it wasn't a totally unrealistic prospect. 'I need to bring something to the party to keep close to Fay.'

'Like what?' James asked.

'Fay has been doing a lot of stuff on her own, while I'm at school. She's also getting information out of Warren. The only thing I'm offering Fay right now is a bunk on the floor of my room at Nebraska House.'

James shook his head. 'I don't think that's true. I thought you were friends.'

'We get on fine, but Fay's focused like a laser beam. If you want me to stay close to her and all the information she's gathering on Hagar's crew, I need to bring something to the table.'

'What have you got in mind?' James asked.

'Fay thinks she's got a better chance of getting at Hagar if she forms an alliance with Eli's crew. Trouble is, she's spoken to a few street dealers and can't get anywhere when it comes to finding out who's who.'

James nodded. 'So if I can get you a name and location for one of Eli's lieutenants, you'll seem a much more worthwhile friend to Fay.'

'Exactly,' Ning said.

'I'll speak to the local drugs squad,' James said. 'How will you say you got the information?'

'Tell her I found out from a kid at school, or something.'

James picked up his Coke to drink, but downed it when he felt his phone vibrating inside his pocket. He didn't recognise the number.

'It's me,' Ryan said, with a slurred voice. 'I'm in accident and emergency.'

*

Ryan lay shirtless on a hospital bed, with his head tipped back to stop the bleeding.

'I'm really sorry,' he said, when he saw James.

'What have you got to be sorry for?'

'I screwed up the mission,' Ryan said. 'I'll never get

back in Craig's good books.'

'You can't be certain,' James said.

'They'll probably kick my arse if I show my face at The Hangout.'

'They must have known the risks.'

As James said this a youthful doctor stepped into the cubicle.

'Will he live, doc?' James asked cheerfully.

'He'll live, but he's taken a battering. Two or three days in bed resting those swollen ribs.'

'Nothing broken?'

The doctor shook her head, then craned forward and tapped Ryan's cheek. 'Is it numb yet?'

'Yeah,' Ryan agreed.

The doctor placed a sterile pack on the table beside the bed. After telling Ryan to sit up straight she ripped the pack open and took out a needle, pre-threaded with sterile cord.

'Unfortunately your lip is going to need five or six stitches.'

Ryan flinched and felt queasy as the doctor moved the needle towards him.

'The more you fidget, the longer it'll take,' the doctor warned.

And while his face was numb, Ryan still felt like he was going to puke as the needle speared his bloody lip.

22. GATES

Two days later

Fitting in at a new school is one of the trickiest jobs for a CHERUB agent. Ning hadn't formed a close bond with anyone and felt lonely as she joined the flow of kids streaming out of the school gates.

'Ning!'

Ning recognised Fay's voice coming from across the street.

'Nice day at the office?' Fay teased.

'Why make me start a new school three weeks before summer holidays?' Ning moaned.

'Bunk it,' Fay said. 'I do.'

'I just might,' Ning said. 'Although I'd get grounded if they found out at Nebraska House.'

'So, ask me what I've been up to.'

'What?' Ning asked.

'I tracked down that Shawn guy who works for Eli. The one you told me about.'

'What for?'

'I needed to know if Eli was up for buying some cheap product.'

'And?'

'He's keen.'

'And where's this cheap product coming from?' Ning asked.

'I've been watching Hagar's backup safe-house. Warren was right, it's ripe for taking down.'

'How can you be sure?'

'There's one guy living there,' Fay explained. 'Every so often his girlfriend comes over. Once or twice a week, he comes in or out with a big bag. And since there's never anyone else there, he must have access to the safe, or wherever it is the drugs are being stored.'

'So what's the plan?' Ning asked.

'Nothing sophisticated,' Fay said. 'Masks and balaclavas, wait until about eleven p.m., then we knock on the front door and point a gun in the dude's face.'

'What about security?'

'We know there's CCTV, but I peeked through the window when the house was empty and there's no sign of any gates.'

'And when are we doing this?'

Fay cracked a smile. 'No reason to wait. If you're up to it we'll go in as soon as it gets dark.'

*

Ryan had an egg on his forehead, stitched lower lip and a purple splotch under his right eye. He'd not gone back to school since the mugging, so he sat at the dining-table in cargo shorts and a Jack Wills polo.

'You sure you're OK with this?' James asked, as he stood at the kitchen worktop setting up a radio which would give him a link to a minuscule transmitter that had been tweezered into Ryan's ear.

Ryan sounded a touch irritated. 'I'll be right.'

'I'm just playing it by the book,' James said. 'You took a beating. All CHERUB agents have the right to drop out of missions at any time.'

'Blah, blah,' Ryan said, as he cracked a smile.

'OK,' James said, as he flipped a switch on the little radio transceiver on the countertop. 'Testing audio, one, two, three.'

Ryan heard James' voice repeated inside his ear, then double-tapped his earlobe to activate the com unit and heard his own phrase repeated through the receiver unit.

'I'll be on the bench outside. If it gets hairy say *bulldog* and I'll pile in and rescue you,' James said.

Ryan's chair grated as he stood up. Bright sunlight made him squint as he cut across the dirt patch between his apartment and The Hangout. As Ryan sidestepped dog turds and broken glass, James followed him out, sat on a wooden bench overlooking the bunker-like youth club and opened a copy of *Motorcycle News*.

There were a dozen kids milling about inside The Hangout. Nobody noticed Ryan because there was some kind of ruckus going on around the pool table and a Mediterranean-looking kid was getting headlocked by an overweight thug almost twice his size.

'Let him go,' Youssef shouted, joining a chorus singing a similar theme. 'You lost the game, fair and square.'

The victim's face kept getting redder as Youssef approached Ryan.

Youssef smiled, but sounded alarmed. 'You've got some balls showing your face here,' he said, as he glanced furtively around.

'You got my text about what happened?' Ryan asked.

Youssef looked shifty. 'No offence, but it's not good to associate with you right now. I'm out on a limb because I like you, but you'd better get out of here before one of Hagar's crew eyes you.'

Over at the pool table, the bully had finally released the headlock and his victim slumped against the pool table, gasping for breath.

'He moved the black,' the bully squawked angrily. Disapproving glances came at him from all sides as he grabbed his school bag and blazer off the floor.

Meantime, Youssef's expression had turned deadly serious. 'Craig's here, Ryan. He breaks limbs with a baseball bat.'

Ryan had waited to make his move until he knew Craig was in the building, but he acted surprised.

'My house is two hundred metres away,' Ryan said. 'They know where I'm at if they want to get me. I know I'm not gonna be in anyone's good books, but they might at least respect me if I have the class to face up and apologise.'

Youssef didn't agree. 'Give it another week and talk to one of the younger lads. Going in when Craig's here is *not* sensible.'

Ryan tried to sound all confident. 'I'm not a pussy. I'm gonna stick my head in the lion's mouth. Wish me luck?'

'I've known these people longer than you,' Youssef said.

But Ryan was determined. There were two offices out back. One belonged to Barry the centre manager. The other was primarily used by members of Hagar's crew. Ryan caught the outlines of two bulky men behind frosted glass as he rapped on the office door.

The voices stopped. Craig stuck his head out into the hallway and put his pointing finger in Ryan's face.

'Wait,' he ordered, pointing at a plastic chair before going back inside and closing the door.

The conversation between Craig and a spindly Asian guy kept going long enough for Ryan's gut to turn somersaults. The guy sprinted off on some errand, leaving the office door open.

'Let's hear it then,' Craig said, inviting Ryan in.

The office was small. The little desk was covered in tangerine peel. There was a fan running and a window open, but Craig's aftershave dominated.

'Got some balls showing up here,' Craig said.

'You deserve an explanation.'

'Why wait three days?'

'I only got out of hospital yesterday evening.'

'You could have called.'

'I don't have your number.'

Craig snorted. 'The likes of you don't get my number. But you could have called one of your pals. Abdi, Youssef or whoever.'

'They nabbed my phone,' Ryan explained. 'It had all my numbers on it.'

'So, what's your cock-and-bull story?'

Ryan shook his head as Craig took an ominous step closer. 'I'm not lying, I swear. Someone must have tipped them off. They were in the stairwell, like they knew I was coming or something.'

'It's funny,' Craig said, before a dramatic pause.

'What?' Ryan asked.

'I've been sending lads up to that place on deliveries for ten years. Some lads have made the trek a hundred times and not one of 'em has lost gear.'

'I don't know what to say,' Ryan blurted. 'They were waiting on the stairs, and there was nobody inside apartment F3.'

'I run a tight ship,' Craig said, as he thumped his chest and moved so that he was almost touching Ryan. 'If they were waiting for you, it must have been you blabbing your mouth off to someone.'

'No way,' Ryan said. 'I never spoke to anyone. Face to face, or on my phone.'

'So have you got my money? I reckon about three-six should cover it.'

'How could I get that?' Ryan asked.

'You live with your big brother?'

Ryan nodded warily.

'He's been seen on a motorbike,' Craig said. 'If he sold that he could pay us back.'

'This has got *nothing* to do with my brother.'

Craig cracked a slow smile. 'In my book, it's got everything to do with anyone who doesn't want to see you get your legs smashed.'

'Look,' Ryan said, putting on his most pleading expression. 'I'm smart. I'm good in a fight and I swear I didn't rip you off. You must have jobs I can do to earn my way back. Anything you like. I can carry stuff around, run errands. I'll scrub toilets if that's what you want.'

Craig looked thoughtful before he spoke. 'Can you clean cars?'

Ryan smiled. 'Sure . . . I mean, I've never actually washed a car, but I'm a fast learner.'

'There's an industrial estate near King's Cross Station. You can't miss the yellow sign for the Kalifornia car-wash. I want you there on the weekend and every day after school. If you work hard, I might eventually find it in my heart to forgive you.'

'How long?' Ryan asked, but went further when he saw the baffled look on Craig's face. 'I mean, how many hours before I pay off my debt.'

Craig turned his lips into a sneer. 'You'll work there until I say so.'

23. SAFE

Fay hadn't forgotten any of the stuff her mother and aunt taught her. She made Ning bunch long hair under a baseball cap and wear a boob-squishing T-shirt and baggy hoodie. Cheap slip-on shoes a couple of sizes too big completed a look that would pass the pair off as young males to anyone who didn't look too hard.

'Only speak if you have to, and try to deepen your voice,' Fay said. 'If Hagar hears he got robbed by two women, I'll probably be the first person he thinks of.'

Being July it was 10 p.m. before it got dark enough to leave Nebraska House. It was after Ning's curfew, so the two girls nabbed a toddler's ride-on fire truck from the outdoor play area and used it as a step-up before vaulting the back fence.

'It's like wearing clown shoes,' Ning said, as she

walked briskly. 'I'd have put extra socks on if it wasn't so warm.'

Both girls were sweating when they arrived. The moon was brighter than they'd have liked as Ning took a first glance at the shabby end-of-terrace house. The only hint that there might be something valuable inside were the bars over the front basement window.

'First-floor windows open,' Fay said. 'Flickering light.'

'TV?' Ning asked.

Fay nodded. 'If his girlfriend's not around, he seems to go up to the bedroom early. I've had to be careful on lookout 'cos he sits by the window when he smokes.'

'So how do we get inside?' Ning asked.

'Let me worry about that,' Fay said. 'How are your nerves?'

Breaking into a house with one guy inside was mild compared to many situations Ning had been in, both before and since joining CHERUB. But Fay didn't know about that stuff so Ning made herself appear suitably wary.

'I guess you know what you're doing.'

'For sure,' Fay said, placing a reassuring hand on Ning's shoulder before setting off towards the house.

The gate creaked, so Fay stepped over a low wall with Ning a couple of steps behind. Fay started down some uneven steps. Both girls pulled army-green balaclavas over their heads, as Fay took a lock gun from her pocket and approached the basement door.

A lock gun makes opening a lock easier than using a manual pick, but it still requires significant skill. Ning was impressed by how swiftly Fay managed to open a complex deadlock. Then she switched to a larger pick and effortlessly turned the main lock.

The door hadn't moved in a while and it rained cobwebs and dust as Fay shoulder-barged it. After opening twenty centimetres, Fay felt a jolt as a thick chain pulled tight.

'Damn,' Fay said.

Ning thought Fay was lucky that the door had moved at all, because there might easily have been bolts on the inside.

'Open my pack,' Fay said.

Ning unbuckled the bag strapped to Fay's back and pulled out a set of small bolt cutters. As Ning was stronger, she took charge of snapping the chain and led the way into a muggy basement with mildewed carpet and blistered plaster.

Nobody had lived down here for years, but the moonlight gave them a glimpse into a living-room populated with high-backed chairs and family photos from the 70s and 80s. The ground floor had a more modern vibe, but the occupant was a slob. There were mounds of dirty men's clothes, a bin stuffed with takeaway boxes and a sink spewing dirty plates.

'Mucky pup,' Fay whispered.

All the doors were open because of the heat and Ning could hear the TV in the upstairs bedroom as Fay pulled out the Glock holstered to her belt and began creeping towards the flickering colours coming from the TV upstairs.

The last step made a loud creak as Fay lifted her foot, but there was no sign of movement in the bedroom. Gun poised, she craned her neck into the bedroom and was shocked to see nobody inside. She moved quickly to check under the bed, ripped open two wardrobes and looked out the window, instantly concluding that it was too high for Clay to have jumped.

'Shit,' Fay said, as Ning stood out on the landing, glancing behind at a couple of closed doors, then up at a loft hatch directly above her head.

Fay jumped when she heard a chirping noise, but it was a text message coming through on an HTC smartphone lying on the bed. The screen said *Imelda*.

'Must have rushed out if he left his phone,' Ning said, as Fay stepped out on to the landing.

Clay might not have had his phone, but Ning was scared because there was a chance he'd gone to grab a weapon and she'd be a dead duck if he shot through one of the closed doors. She backed up to the wall and reached nervously towards a door handle. It was another bedroom, with a dozen pairs of immaculate Nikes lined up along the back wall.

Fay went for the other door, but it moved before she got there. A muscular arm snatched Fay's wrist and yanked her forward into a cramped bathroom. She tried aiming the gun, but the jerking motion knocked her off balance and her back slammed painfully against a towel rail inside the bathroom as her gun flailed out of control.

Ning remembered CHERUB teaching her to create

as much space between herself and a loaded weapon as possible. But she was fond of Fay and acted on instinct, charging into the cramped bathroom, as Clay twisted the weapon out of Fay's hand.

The handgun landed on a lemon bath mat, as Clay and Fay wrestled near the edge of the bathtub, getting tangled in a clingy shower curtain. Clay drove up with his legs, knocking Fay back towards the sink, then strained to grab the gun. But Ning got there first, hooking the pistol with her oversized shoe, sending it spinning between her legs and stopping when it reached the hallway carpet.

Fay lunged at Clay, but he pushed her off and shoved her through the tangled curtain and into the bottom of the bathtub. Clay stood up to charge at Ning, but she swiped him around the head with the butt of the pistol.

The blow sent Clay to his knees in front of the sink, blood welling around a cut as Fay sat up in the bathtub. Ning took a half-step forward and stuck the gun in Clay's face as he thought about making another move.

'You're too young to die,' Ning said firmly. 'Put your hands on your head.'

Clay's face stayed angry, but Ning eyeballed him until his palms rested flat against his shaved head.

Ning spoke to Fay, trying to sound manly by deepening her voice but not too sure if it just sounded idiotic. 'Is there a phone around? Has he called anyone?'

The two girls both glanced around, looking for a handset. They didn't find one, but Ning did spot a can of pepper spray standing between the bleach and the toilet brush.

'This what you came in here for?' Ning asked, as she inspected the packaging and flipped off the lid. Clay winced when she aimed the nozzle at his face, but she just laughed and handed it across to Fay, who seemed dazed as she stepped out of the bathtub, clutching ribs that had banged painfully against a handrail.

'Thought Hagar might have managed a gun for his little brother,' Fay scoffed.

'There's nothing here for you girls,' Clay said.

Ning sighed inwardly: so much for passing themselves off as young men.

Fay had regained her composure, and held the pepper spray menacingly as she stood directly behind Clay.

'I've been watching this place for a while,' Fay said. 'Plenty of comings and goings. And now you're gonna show us to the safe.'

'Ain't no safe here,' Clay said.

'I think there is,' Fay said, touching on sarcasm. 'Unless all those visitors were coming here for tea and cakes.'

'You see any safe?' Clay asked.

Ning and Fay were certain there was a safe in the house, because Warren said that his cousin had helped to install it. Unfortunately, Warren didn't know where the safe was, and Fay hadn't been able to work anything out while surveying the building from outside.

'You're gonna tell us where that safe is,' Fay said firmly. 'Then you're gonna open it for us.'

Clay sucked air through his teeth and shook his head. 'No safe here. You're tripping.'

Although Ning had acquitted herself brilliantly during the tussle, Fay still regarded her as a subordinate and insisted on taking back the pistol. She kept the gun on Clay's back as they escorted him downstairs.

Ning began a hunt while Clay sat on the sofa with Fay standing guard.

The fact that Warren's cousin was a carpenter was a major clue. Ning started by looking behind a couple of pictures on the living-room wall, then moved into the kitchen and checked inside all the cabinets.

She was about to head down to the basement when she noticed a narrow gap running along the wall close to a radiator in the hallway. She rapped on the wall and got a hollow sound, and when she dug a penknife blade into the gap, the radiator wobbled.

'Bingo,' Ning shouted, as she grabbed the radiator, which appeared not to be connected to the central heating system.

Behind the heavy panel was a half-metre-deep cavity and a row of green LEDs on the front of a safe built into the floor.

'It's a keypad,' Ning shouted, as she stepped back into the living-room. 'We're looking for a number, not a key.'

'Well?' Fay said, as she eyeballed Clay.

'It's on a timed lock,' Clay said. 'Even if I wanted to open it, I can't do it without getting the master authorisation code from my brother.'

As the words left Clay's mouth, Ning was already typing the name and model number she'd seen on the safe into the browser on her smartphone.

'He's lying,' Ning said, as she swiped down the page. 'Tecumax 416R safe with a four- to six-digit code. There's no mention of any timing facility.'

Fay nodded in agreement. 'I've seen people come and go at all times, day and night. There's no timed lock on that thing.'

Even with a gun aimed at his temple, Clay still acted cocky. 'My brother's gonna get you for this,' he blurted. 'He'll pimp you out to every guy who wants you, and when you're all beat up and nasty, he'll slit your throats.'

Fay had done enough raids with her mother and aunt to know that a lot of guys don't believe that a woman really has the guts to hurt them, even if they have a gun pointing at their head. She'd learned that the best way to shock a man out of this mindset was to do something unexpectedly brutal.

Keeping one eye and the Glock on Clay, Fay reached into her backpack and pulled out a disposable surgeon's scalpel. She used her teeth to rip off the sterile packaging and flicked off a plastic safety guard with her thumb. Then she swiped the blade, making a huge gash across Clay's cheek.

As Clay moaned in pain, Fay began a speech she'd learned from her aunt.

'The human body contains nine litres of blood. The wound I just gave you should clot and heal before you bleed out. But if you don't tell me the safe combination within one minute I'm going to cut you again. And again one minute after that, if you don't tell me the combination. By the time I've given you three cuts, your chances of dying from blood loss are greater than fifty per cent.'

'I'm gonna have a scar, you crazy bitch,' Clay said, clutching his face but apparently still not prepared to believe what Fay was telling him.

'It would be a shame to completely ruin this nice carpet,' Fay said, as she moved the reddened blade up to Clay's other cheek. 'And please stop calling us bitches. It's sexist and just as offensive as if I called you a monkey.'

'You're crazy,' Clay shouted.

Fay moved in with the scalpel again. 'The combination,' she demanded.

'Two four one three zero,' Clay blurted.

Fay looked up at Ning. 'Go tap it in.'

Ning walked into the hallway, crouched through the gap to the floor-mounted safe and tapped in five digits. The LEDs flashed as a motor drew back the bolts and the door sprang open by a couple of centimetres.

'We're in,' Ning shouted.

A light came on inside as Ning lifted the heavyweight door. It revealed nine vacuum-packed one-kilo bricks of cocaine, and three knotted carrier bags filled with hundreds of mini bags, containing one gram of cocaine each. There were also several large tubs filled with mysterious white powders, which Ning guessed were used by Hagar's people to bulk up the cocaine when it was sold on the streets.

'Ten to twelve kilos,' Ning said excitedly, as she came back into the living-room.

Clay was on the couch with blurry eyes and his shirt collar soaked in blood.

'Pack all the gear up into our rucksacks,' Fay said. 'Then come back here. I'll need you to make sure he doesn't try any funny business while I tie him up.'

24. KALIFORNIA

Two days later

Kalifornia Kar Kleen was situated on the forecourt of an abandoned petrol station behind King's Cross railway station. Eight quid got your car washed by a crew of surly East Europeans in soggy blue overalls. Twenty-five got your car cleaned inside and out, while fifty got you a full valet with detailing. Kar Kleen didn't accept cards or cheques, which made it a perfect business for its owner, Hagar, to launder cash made in the drug trade.

Ryan was average height for fifteen, but he was smaller than the adults he'd been sent to work with, so he'd landed the awkward job of cleaning car interiors. Vacuuming wasn't too bad, but customers who dropped fifty quid for a valet expected perfection, so he had to crawl around inside cars with cleaning sprays, cloths and brushes hanging off a tool belt.

Ryan had done a full day at school, and was now into his third hour at the car-wash. He'd begun to hate Minis, because there were millions of them around and there was no comfortable way for a normal-sized human to clean out the back of a small two-doored car.

The Mini Ryan was in right now was particularly bad because the owner had a couple of brats and the back seats were crusted with Ribena stains, crayon and puke. He worked some cleaning mousse into a nasty blotch on the seat, then wiped down the seatbacks and headrests before returning to attack the stain with a plastic scraper and a nail-brush.

Ryan's neck and shoulder ached as he scrubbed, but the stain just blurred around the edges. He reckoned he'd get another bollocking from Milosh the supervisor, a man whose unwillingness to believe that a stain couldn't be removed was matched only by his unwillingness to climb inside a car and have a go himself.

After giving up on the seat stain, Ryan delved into dirt and crumbs under the front seat. He was pulling out a Thomas the Tank Engine sock and a mildewed digestive when a rap on the back window made him jolt.

Ryan gently bumped his head on the padded door trim as he rolled on to his back. Craig was eyeballing him, making an aggressive *get out* gesture.

The bottles hooked to Ryan's belt sploshed as Craig led him across the soapy courtyard and into a large office. It had once been the garage shop. The cashier's desk was still in place and magazines and newspapers yellowed on a rack by the door.

'The boss here reckons you're OK,' Craig said, grudgingly. 'You passed your trial.'

Ryan was surprised enough to manage an involuntary smile, because all he'd heard from Milosh was abuse.

'You'll work off your debt at ten pounds an hour, starting tomorrow,' Craig said. 'You'd better work hard. I want you here every day after school and eight till seven on Saturday. If you call in sick you'd better be dying. If you cause me any kind of grief, I'll make sure you regret it. Understood?'

Ryan's feelings were split. On one hand, he'd found a path back into Craig's good books. On the other, the prospect of slogging it out after school and all day Saturday didn't exactly leave him brimming with glee.

'When do I do my homework and stuff?' Ryan asked.

'Not my problem,' Craig answered tersely. 'I don't give a shit about *you*. I just want the money you owe me.'

'OK,' Ryan said.

Ryan's OK came out grumpier than he'd expected and made Craig turn nasty.

'Any more of that attitude and I'll slap the piss out of you. Now get back to it.'

As Ryan headed out of the office, a Mercedes E-class was pulling up on the forecourt. It looked new, but it was understated, apart from black privacy glass which gave the vehicle an air of menace. As a tall, mixed-race man emerged from the driver's seat, Milosh rushed across and did a kind of semi-panicked Japanese bow.

'I'll get it washed straight away, sir,' Milosh fawned. 'Won't hold you up at all.'

Ryan had seen the driver in dozens of security photos while preparing for the mission, but he'd been knocked off kilter by Craig's anger so it took a couple of seconds for him to register that Hagar had walked past and was heading into the office to see Craig.

'You, you,' Milosh was shouting, as he pointed at a couple of guys and ordered them to start jet-washing Hagar's car.

Ryan was curious to get a look inside Hagar's wheels. 'You want a hand, boss?' he asked.

Milosh buckled a cleaning belt, as he gave Ryan a look of horror. 'Finish the Mini,' he said. 'Mr Hagar's car has to be done by an expert.'

*

Fay caught her first glance at Eli's lieutenant, Shawn, across the food court of Wood Green Shopping City. He had a goatee, a yellow Lakers basketball vest and shiny green tracksuit bottoms over legs so long it looked like he was up on stilts. He sat at the plastic table and used a voice way posher than the gangsta look might have led you to expect.

'Pleasure to meet two such fine-assed creatures.'

Fay and Ning had Cokes, fries from Burger King, and rucksacks stuffed with Hagar's cocaine standing between their legs. Fay wasn't sure she could trust Shawn. She'd arranged to meet somewhere public, but the mall was about to close so it felt pretty desolate. Shawn had also brought muscle, in the form of two guys standing against a shuttered Donut Magic stall.

'You Shawn?' Fay asked, sounding uncharacteristically nervous.

'Who else?' Shawn asked back. He seemed unnaturally chilled and Ning suspected that he'd been smoking weed.

'I didn't know you were bringing company,' Fay said, pulling back her coat to show the holstered Glock, before making a nod towards the guys across the food court. 'I don't want any funny business.'

Shawn smiled like the gun didn't mean a thing, and rocked his chair on to its back legs.

'Don't sweat,' he said slowly. 'Here's how this goes down. I take a couple of tasters from your bricks and hand them to my pharmacist over there. He goes to the WC with his chemistry set, tests the gear and makes sure you're not ripping us off. As soon as he gives me the nod, I've got the cash and we'll be ready to rock and roll.'

Fay nodded, then pointed at Ning. 'If your boy gets to look at the coke, my girl gets to check the cash.'

'Fair play,' Shawn said, as he produced a T-shaped probe from his tracksuit.

The tool was designed for farmers and geologists to take soil samples, but in the cocaine trade it was used to dig into packets of drugs to ensure that purity was more than skin deep.

Fay kicked her backpack under the table towards Shawn, who glanced around to make sure nobody was looking before furtively taking random samples from three out of the nine bricks of cocaine. He tapped each sample into a plastic tub, then went down Ning's pack and took samples from a couple more bricks before taking a few of the one-gram bags.

Fay sounded tense. 'I already told you, the bricks are eighty-five per cent pure. The one-gram bags between twenty and twenty-five.'

Shawn shrugged. 'I'm not calling you a liar, but I don't know you ladies and my butt's on the line if I spend money on the wrong shit.'

The tattooed pharmacist walked between tables, took the sample bottles off Shawn, then locked himself in a disabled toilet behind the escalators. Shawn kicked a bag across to Ning. She opened up and saw five-thousand-pound bundles, made up of fifty- or twenty-pound notes and held together with elastic bands. As far as she could tell it was all genuine.

Shawn broke the tense silence that followed. 'Pretty gutsy stinging Hagar's stash house. I hear he's going all out looking for you two.'

Fay shrugged. 'That was just the beginning. I'll be getting my hands on more of his merchandise if you're interested.'

'Always,' Shawn laughed. 'But if it was me in your sweaty Nikes, I'd take what you earned from this score and clear out. Hagar's got a lot of bodies and you've only got to slip up once.'

Fay smiled. 'I'll be careful.'

Shawn didn't respond because he'd just received a

text from his chemist. 'Eighty-four point six for the bricks, thirty-three on the gram bags,' he said.

'Told you,' Fay said.

'I'll give you six thousand per kilo for the bricks. Three for the gram bags.'

Fay growled. 'We agreed. Seven and four, seventy-five grand in total. Take it or leave it.'

Shawn laughed. 'You've got a heap of merchandise and one of the biggest gangsters in north London hunting you down. Do you really wanna risk shopping this gear around to get a better deal?'

Fay didn't like being knocked down, but tried to stay cool. 'I've got connections in places where nobody has even heard the name Hagar,' she said icily. 'Manchester, Glasgow, Belfast. Eighty-five per cent pure at seven grand a kilo, they'll be biting my arm off.'

'If that's how you roll,' Shawn said, giving his goon a thumbs down gesture and pushing back his chair like he was about to leave.

Ning looked anxious, but Fay smiled. 'You're full of shit,' she told Shawn.

Shawn raised one eyebrow. 'How so?'

Fay smiled, as Shawn leaned back across the table.

'First off, seven grand a kilo for coke this good is stupidly cheap,' Fay began. 'Eli will make his entire outlay back just from selling the one-gram bags on the street. You're just trying to push the price down because Eli will give you a taste of any money you manage to shave off his bill.'

Fay took a big breath before continuing. 'I've spoken

to a lot of people on the street and I happen to know that Eli and Hagar hate each other's guts. I'd bet my last twenty quid that the first thing Eli does when he gets hold of this merchandise is get someone to take a photograph and send it to Hagar, just to wind him up.'

Shawn shook his head slowly. 'No flies on you, are there?' he said, as he cracked a wicked smile and pointed at the bag with the money inside. 'Take the cash, you've got your deal.'

Ning nodded to indicate that she was happy with the amount of money in the bag.

'I'll be back in touch when I have more gear,' Fay said.

Shawn snorted as he grabbed the two cocaine-filled backpacks and stood up. 'You girls be careful,' he warned. 'You both seem smart, but that don't make you invincible.'

25. PASSION

The next morning, Warren answered his front door dressed in Diesel jeans, Lacoste polo and slightly too much aftershave.

'Well, don't you smell nice?' Ning teased, as she stood in the doorway with rain soaking through the top of her hoodie.

'You look like you've seen a ghost,' Fay added. 'Are you gonna leave us standing out here in the rain or what?'

Warren stepped away from the door, and glanced around guiltily before closing it behind the girls.

'Your mum home?' Fay asked, as Warren led them to the kitchen.

'She does office cleaning on Saturday. Won't be home till lunchtime.'

Fay and Ning dumped wet umbrellas on the lino, as

171

Warren nervously opened the fridge.

'You want a drink?' Warren asked. 'Coke, juice? Or I can make a brew.'

'We're good,' Fay said. 'Sit down at the table. What's with all the pacing about?'

Warren stood by a little dining-table, fingers clenching a chair back as the girls sat down.

'Why am I nervous?' he said, sounding like he'd just been asked the world's stupidest question. 'Because you two should not be coming here. Eli sent Hagar a message saying, "Thanks for the drugs," and Hagar blew his stack. Word's over the street like a rash. All kinds of nasty stories about what Hagar will do if he catches you, and anyone who tipped you off.'

Fay remained calm. 'You're not stupid. You must have known Hagar wouldn't be happy when you tipped us off.'

Warren shook his head. 'I didn't think you'd be dumb enough to sell the gear straight to Hagar's biggest rival.'

'I know what I'm doing,' Fay said.

'He's worked out your name and everything,' Warren spat. 'Your aunt and your mum used to rob him. You're out for revenge, but that's not what I signed up for.'

'Yeah, you signed up for this,' Fay said, as she took a bundle of money from the inside pocket of her sodden jacket and pushed it across the tabletop.

'Fat lot of use it does me if Hagar slits my throat,' Warren said.

Fay reached towards the money. 'We got fifty grand

for the cocaine,' she lied. 'Your share comes to ten, but if you don't want it . . .'

Warren reluctantly grabbed the money, and actually looked impressed as he fanned the stack of notes.

'Be careful how you spend it,' Ning said. 'People will ask questions if you start throwing money around.'

'I'll save it for university, *if* I live that long,' Warren said.

'So what about the other place where you said your cousin worked?' Fay asked. 'The grow house?'

Warren shook his head. 'Screw you. Hagar's on the warpath and I'm keeping my profile so low that ants will be looking down at me.'

'Why chicken out now?' Fay asked. 'If we pull another job, what's Hagar gonna do that he's not gonna do already?'

'Why did the two of you rock up here?' Warren blurted. 'You could have called. We could have met up somewhere in town where nobody would see you.'

Ning also felt that Fay was being reckless, but she was playing the role of naive sidekick so she hadn't been able to speak up.

'Next time, I'll call,' Fay said, acting like it was all a big joke. 'Tell me about the grow house and I'll make you a full partner. Even three-way split.'

Warren finally felt calm enough to sit at the table. Fay glared across, but Warren looked at the stack of money like he was expecting it to give him an answer.

'I need another job, Warren,' Fay said. 'Tell me now.'

'No way.'

'Hagar can't cut your balls off twice.'

Warren thumped the table. 'Stop going on about my balls. This isn't a game, you know?'

Fay changed tack. 'If you turn yellow on me, word might find its way back to one of Hagar's people, about the carpenter with the big mouth and his little cousin.'

Warren stood up. 'Now you're blackmailing me?' he shouted.

Fay stood up too, and sounded upset. 'Hagar killed my mum and my aunt. You seem like a really nice guy, but I'm gonna do whatever it takes to get revenge.'

'Why not just kill him?' Warren asked. 'You've got guns.'

Fay shook her head. 'I don't just want to shoot Hagar. When he dies, I want him to know that he didn't get away with killing Auntie Kirsten and my mum.'

A tear streaked down Fay's cheek. Ning couldn't tell if Fay was putting on an act, but if she was she was making a good job of it.

Warren stepped around the table and placed a hand awkwardly on Fay's back. 'I know he's really hurt you and you must really hate him. But surely this isn't what your mum and aunt would have wanted you to do?'

Fay sobbed, and gritted her teeth. 'I can't live a normal life until Hagar's paid for what he's done.'

Warren swept a hand through his hair and sighed. 'I'll tell you what I know, but it's vague. Nothing like the info I had on the safe-house.'

'Thank you,' Fay said. She dabbed one eye with a

tissue, before her tone regained its normal authority. 'So are you gay, or what?'

Warren sounded offended. 'I'm not gay. What makes you even say that?'

Fay smiled. 'You're always nicely dressed and you wear cologne. You could take me on a date some time if you like.'

Ning cringed as she saw the torment on Warren's face. He thought Fay was hot and didn't have a girlfriend, but Fay was borderline mental and definitely dangerous.

'One evening next week?' Warren said, uncertainly.

'You're taking me out tonight,' Fay said, before breaking into a laugh. 'You get the *cutest* expression when you're scared.'

*

Ryan had learned to love wet weather, because people don't pay to have cars washed when the shine will get ruined. He'd started at half eight and worked through a couple of valet jobs for a nearby Volkswagen dealer. After that he'd been sent to McDonald's to buy breakfasts, but by ten he'd been idle for a full hour.

The forecast said rain all day, so Milosh had sent some of the guys home. The five that remained sat under the warped petrol station canopy reading newspapers and trading stories.

'Need a shit,' Ryan said, as he pocketed his mobile and stood up.

'Have one for me while you're up there,' one of the guys joked.

The toilet was a stinking beast in a cabin behind the former shop. But Ryan had seen a couple of blokes leaving the office and driving off about ten minutes earlier, and that was his true destination.

Since Ryan started work at Kar Kleen he'd regularly seen Hagar, Craig and some of Hagar's other senior people meeting up in the office. James had decided it would be good if Ryan could get inside and plant a couple of miniature video cameras.

When the car-wash closed at night, Milosh or the duty manager would put a big chain and padlock on the office door, but in the day it was only secured with a straightforward door lock. Rather than risk carrying a lock gun, Ryan had already checked the make and model of the lock and a skeleton key had been sent down from campus.

The CHERUB security department knew their stuff, but Ryan was still relieved when the key turned and the lock opened. The office had large windows along two sides, so he kept low as he walked inside.

He unzipped his Kar Kleen-branded overall and pulled three coin-sized rubber disks out of his pocket. Two were the same size and contained video cameras. He'd already worked out the best spots to place them, and he quickly rested one on top of a curved security mirror and the other on a disused fire extinguisher. The cameras were designed to automatically point their lenses towards any sound, and if anyone found them, they just looked like bits that had fallen off of something else.

The third device was even smaller: a limited-frequency microphone designed to pick up the sound of computer keyboards. This recent addition to CHERUB's espionage gear was used with a piece of software capable of detecting the minuscule variations in the sonic signature of each key on a keyboard. Predictive software then determined which key corresponded to which letter of the alphabet, and meant that you could log every keystroke from several computers just by placing this microphone in a room.

Once he'd stuck the microphone under the corner of a desk, roughly halfway between the room's two laptops, Ryan backed out into the drizzle and found Craig strolling towards him.

'What the hell are you doing?' Craig shouted.

Like all good CHERUB agents, Ryan had an excuse ready. 'I was looking for you,' he explained calmly. 'I wanted to know how many more hours I had to work to pay off my debt.'

'How'd you get in the office?'

Ryan acted innocent. 'I thought you were in there. It wasn't locked or anything.'

Craig looked at the open door and seemed to accept Ryan's explanation. 'Who was in here last?'

'The blond guy,' Ryan said, not letting on that he knew the bloke's name from surveillance photos. 'And the chubby one who always wears a pullover.'

'Right,' Craig said. 'They'll be getting a rocket up their arses for leaving the office unlocked.'

'Yeah,' Ryan said weakly. 'So I was kind of wondering

about my hours. Milosh said he's not keeping track, and you're only here now and then. So I was thinking I should make a log or something.'

Craig didn't seem to care. 'Fine, you do that. Just don't let me catch you cheating.'

'I wouldn't risk it,' Ryan said.

Ryan went for a piss in the toilet, but his stomach flipped when he stepped down from the cabin and found Craig on his case again. He gave Ryan a *don't move* gesture, while rabbiting into the cheapo Nokia mobile at his ear.

'Well . . .' Craig said. 'No . . . no, no. You tell him to stay and I'll get it picked up.'

Ryan wondered if he'd left any evidence in the office, but the devices he'd planted looked completely innocent, so he couldn't see how.

Craig started losing it with whoever was on the other end of the phone. 'I told Luke where and when,' he yelled. 'It's not brain surgery, is it? And I don't give a monkey's if he's sick. If Luke's sick, he makes a call and someone will sort it out. But knowing that lazy shite, he's been on the piss all night and can't get his head off the pillow.'

After a few more sentences and some serious swearing, Craig ended the call and glared at Ryan. 'I need a job done. You know Kentish Town?'

'Only vaguely, but I've got maps on my phone.'

Craig nodded. 'I need you to get up to Kentish Town Road and pick up a package from a man standing outside Iceland. Then I'll need you to take it somewhere across town.'

Ryan was intrigued, but made himself sound wary. 'I haven't worked off my debt, so I'd rather not risk getting robbed again.'

Craig's expression hardened. 'I'm not asking, I'm telling,' he barked. 'I haven't got the details for the delivery address, but I'll get someone to text it to you.'

As Craig said this, he pulled a wad of twenty-pound notes out of his jeans and gave three of them to Ryan.

'That's for a taxi if you need one.'

'Right,' Ryan said, as he unzipped his overall and started pulling off his trainers.

'What are you fannying around at?' Craig asked angrily.

'I'm assuming you don't want me carrying gear around London with the name of this place embroidered across my back.'

Craig gave Ryan a respectful nod and a hint of a smile. 'Good thinking,' he said. 'Brains seem to be in short supply in this organisation these days. There might just be hope for you, kiddo . . .'

26. HUNT

Warren reluctantly spilled the beans to Fay and Ning.

'Back in the day, before Craig gave me my package and I started making real money, I did a Saturday job in my cousin's carpentry shop. One week I got there and it was mayhem. My cuz and two guys who work for him were making these trellis things and wooden racks. Plus there's an electrician there, wiring banks of lights on chipboard for hanging from a ceiling.'

'Sounds like a grow house to me,' Fay said. 'What's the address?'

Warren smiled awkwardly. 'That's where it gets tricky. Like, me and my cousin all knew what the stuff was for, but Hagar's people weren't gonna blow the location. This geezer kept coming along in a van to pick stuff up as soon as it was finished. I don't know where he went, but there's a couple of decent clues.'

Warren paused for dramatic effect, which made Fay look pissed off.

'First up, the van was unusual. It was a white Transit, with two navy stripes coming up one side, across the roof and down the other. And it must have originally belonged to some company because you could see a name sprayed over.'

Fay shook her head. 'So it's a white van. Hagar's crew are bound to have sold it on or dumped it by now.'

'Most likely,' Warren agreed. 'But if you stop interrupting, I'll get to the juicy bit. The van was going back and forth, picking up stuff and delivering it to the grow house. But a few times that van made the round trip in ten minutes.'

'Five minutes there, five back,' Fay said thoughtfully. 'At thirty miles per hour, that's still a two and a half-mile radius from your cousin's workshop.'

Ning shook her head. 'It's not. Where in London can you drive at a constant thirty miles per hour for more than a minute or so? By the time you count for junctions, traffic lights, you're not gonna get much more than a mile in five minutes.'

'I guess,' Fay said.

'Most important, that van was fully loaded,' Warren added. 'It took at least ten minutes to load up with wood each time. It was probably faster unloading at the other end, but even if they drove flat out and had a team of guys unloading, they can only have driven two minutes maximum.'

Ning pulled out her phone and opened the calculator

app. 'So,' she said, as her fingers tapped the screen. 'Two minutes' driving, and let's say the average speed was fifteen miles per hour. That's a radius of half a mile from your cousin's workshop.'

Fay looked at Warren. 'Get Google Maps on your laptop.'

Warren seemed to have got over his angst about the girls being in his house as he led the pair from the kitchen to his bedroom.

'Oooh, very nice,' Fay said, as Ning did a 360, taking in a neat room, with a big LCD on the wall and framed photos of giant wooden rollercoasters.

'Strange choice of pictures,' Ning said.

Warren sounded a touch embarrassed. 'I'm a bit of a coaster geek. Like, going on websites where people talk about the biggest and fastest rollercoasters and stuff and I belonged to this club. I hardly do any of that stuff now though.'

Fay wasn't listening and had opened the lid on Warren's laptop. 'Where's your cousin's workshop at?'

Once they found the workshop on Google Maps, Fay printed a page out and Warren got a compass from his school pack, worked out the scale and drew a half-mile circle around it.

'Still a lot of streets,' Fay said, dejectedly. 'Searching them all would take days, and it's not like a grow house is gonna have a sign out front saying, *Spliff grown here.*'

Ning sounded more enthusiastic. 'We know it's a big building,' she said, as she turned to Warren. 'How much space do you reckon all of that trellis would take up?'

'More than would fit in a normal-sized house,' Warren said. 'And there were forty-eight banks of lights.'

Ning nodded. 'We should be looking for a commercial building. Disused factory, warehouse, or something like that.'

'I'll scan the Google sat view and see what comes up,' Fay said.

'They were picking up and dropping that trellis and banks of lamps in broad daylight,' Warren noted. 'So I reckon they must have been able to park the van on a secluded driveway, or reverse into a garage.'

Fay switched to satellite view and zoomed in on a street in the top-left corner of Warren's circle. The view was full of the roofs of terraced houses. She dragged the map downwards until she came to a T-junction.

'I'll mark off the streets on the printout,' Ning said, picking up the printed map, before grabbing a pen off Warren's desk and stripping the cap with her teeth.

Over the next couple of hours, Warren, Fay and Ning huddled over the laptop screen. When they found a large building, they'd switch from satellite to street view. They inspected churches, schools, shops and police stations, but amongst these unlikely locations for a marijuana grow house, they found sixteen places that seemed large enough and had a secluded driveway.

Saturday night was peak time in the drug trade, so Warren had to go out and sell his package. Fay and Ning drew a wonky line down the map and decided to head out on the street and check eight possible grow house locations each.

*

Ryan's first job took him out east to Canary Wharf, delivering fifty grams of cocaine to a hot Russian in a thirty-fourth-floor penthouse. He assumed he was done, but over the following five hours the bargain basement Alcatel that Craig had given him rang at least twice per hour, with unknown voices on the other end telling him where to go next.

He picked up multiple packages from a woman in Chinatown and took them to the offices of a nightclub security firm just off Leicester Square. He dropped more cocaine in Soho and a huge block of weed to a van in an underground car park. When there was too much cash to pocket, he began stuffing it in his backpack.

Just after five, Ryan got told to await further instructions. He sat on a street bench scoffing a pepperoni pizza slice when a message came through saying it was all good and to bring the wodges of cash to a minicab office behind Finsbury Park bus station.

As he headed towards the one-storey cab shack behind the bus station, Ryan caught sight of a fat bloke standing hands on hips at a car-wash place across the street. He was tired and his first thought was that his brain was playing tricks, but the harder Ryan looked the more certain he was that he was looking at one of the three men who'd robbed his money and slapped him around earlier that week.

Suddenly excited, Ryan changed track, heading away

from the minicab office and joining a bus queue. Hidden amidst passengers, Ryan watched the man over by the car-wash. He seemed to be bossing around staff, who wore blue overalls like the ones he wore at King's Cross.

Ryan wasn't sure how to handle the situation, so he pulled his phone and called James.

'Hi,' James' voice said. 'My cell must be out of signal area and I can't take your call. To connect to the mission control building on campus, press five.'

Ryan was about to press five when the fat dude waved goodbye to no one in particular and started heading uphill, away from the station. Ryan pocketed his phone and set off after him.

The guy wore a too-tight polo shirt and cargo shorts that afforded you a glimpse of a pimply arse crack. A break in traffic allowed Ryan to jog across the main road, as his target turned into a side street and pulled a car key from his shorts.

Ryan lost sight when the man turned the corner, so he sped up. When he got a look down the side street, his target stood in the road, unlocking a Peugeot people carrier. Snug clothing meant there was no way that the guy could be carrying a weapon, and in the absence of any advice from James, Ryan figured he could earn serious brownie points with Craig if he nailed the man who'd robbed his gear.

The guy had most of his bulk inside the car when Ryan broke into a run and slammed the driver's door on his trailing leg. Ryan swiftly rounded the door, yanked it open and kneed the man in the face.

'Rob me now, golden balls,' Ryan said, as he landed two quick punches. One cracked the guy's nose and the knee had already bloodied his bottom lip.

The man was dazed as Ryan hauled his bulk out of the car. He hit the pavement hard and Ryan whipped the wallet bulging out the back of his shorts. Back on the main road, an old woman with a shopping trolley looked on, while a fit-looking bloke in plaster-splattered jeans and steel toecaps yelled.

'Oi.'

Ryan didn't fancy his chances and broke into a run as soon as he'd made sure there was ID in the wallet. The plasterer was in decent shape and had closed the gap to a couple of metres when Ryan scrambled left into a tree-lined residential terrace.

Ryan's fitness level paid off as he powered up a steep hill. He opened a twenty-metre gap and as Ryan reached the crest of the hill, the plasterer staggered to a halt a few hundred metres back, leaning against a lamppost to catch his breath.

Finsbury Park wasn't Ryan's neighbourhood. After a 360 glance, he randomly chose a footpath between two low-rise housing blocks and ended up back on the main road, about a kilometre from where he'd started. He slowed to a stroll, crossed the street and walked into a Tesco.

Ryan opened the wallet he'd stolen and studied the ID. Then he took out the little Alcatel, looked at the calls received and dialled the number of the guy who told him to go to the minicab office.

'Hey, it's Ryan,' he told the phone, still a touch breathless.

A deep voice came back at him. 'Who?'

'You told me to drop the money at the cab office, but something happened.'

The man sounded suspicious. 'Something like what?'

'I got jumped a few nights back. I saw one of the guys who jumped me standing by the car-wash across the street from the cab office. I managed to knock him out and nab his ID.'

The guy sounded shocked. 'You're the one that just knocked Fat Tony out? What the hell did you do that for?'

Ryan was confused. 'I don't know who Fat Tony is, but he was part of the trio who robbed me the other night.'

'Fat Tony runs our car-wash. He works for Hagar, same as everyone else. You'd better get your arse back here and explain yourself.'

'I . . .' Ryan stuttered. 'Hang on a minute, I'll call you back.'

As he pocketed the phone, Ryan couldn't work out what was going on and his mind was whirling. If Fat Tony was one of Hagar's people, he must have been working for the other side. Ryan had over twenty grand of Hagar's money in his backpack, but there was no way he was going to walk back to the cab office. It would be his word against Fat Tony's, and what were the chances they'd believe a kid they'd never met before?

After pocketing the Alcatel, Ryan pulled his regular CHERUB-issue iPhone out of his pocket and called James.

'You should have called me before you took Fat Tony out,' James said, once he'd grasped Ryan's rapid-fire explanation.

'The guy was getting into his car. You had no signal and I had to make a decision.'

'Fair enough,' James said. 'Keep walking uphill towards Crouch End, I'll come and pick you up on the bike.'

'Thanks,' Ryan said.

'See you in ten,' James replied. 'Fifteen tops.'

'Can you make head or tail of this?'

James thought for a couple of seconds. 'Yeah,' he said. 'As it goes, I think I've got a pretty good idea what's going on.'

27. PLANTS

Of the eight Xs marked on Ning's map, there was one she liked most. It was a rectangular shed, easily big enough for all the trellis and forty-eight banks of lights. There was a well-hidden car park with dandelions growing out of cracks in the concrete, a peeling sign that said Marston Bowling Club and the best of the empty parking bays reserved for the club president.

Besides Fay's trawl of Google Maps, Ning had done extra research, using local newspaper archives and the Camden Council planning website: the bowling club had sold up and built a new indoor green on cheaper land to the north, but a developer's plans for luxury apartments had been refused planning approval.

Even more interestingly, Ning had found a Land Registry record online, which showed that around the time Warren's cousin was building all the trellis for a grow house, ownership of the former bowling club had been transferred from the property developer to an untraceable shell company based in Jersey.

It was impossible to tell if Hagar owned the shell company, but it was exactly the kind of set-up a drug dealer would use if he was trying to protect assets from detection by police and tax authorities.

Ning followed her hunch and went to the bowling club first. It felt good working alone, pursuing her mission to bring down a drug empire without the constant handicap of having to act as Fay's sidekick.

She approached warily, shielding her face with the brim of a baseball cap. If this was Hagar's grow house, there would certainly be security cameras, and after taking down the stash house his entire crew would be on the lookout for someone matching Ning's description.

With her face aimed at the gravel, Ning entered the car park, holding a beer bottle and wavering about so that she seemed drunk.

The first signs weren't promising. The car park was empty, there was no noise from inside, no obvious security cameras, and the building's windowless aluminium siding gave no clue about what, if anything, was happening inside.

The building's entrance was down an alleyway, through wrought-iron gates, with chipped gold lettering that read, *Marston Bowling Club est. 1852.* There was no light coming through the glass entry doors, but Ning observed that the gates weren't padlocked, and the security grilles and electronic lock on the main doors appeared to be recent additions.

Ning was pretty sure of her hunch now, but thought she might need more to convince Fay. Still acting drunk, Ning walked past the gates and cut down another alleyway which ran between the indoor bowling green and a breeze block wall that separated the club from the street.

Some of the weeds here came up to Ning's knee, and there was litter and broken glass underfoot. Intriguingly, the building had ventilation grilles cut into the metal and every one had been covered over with a piece of hardboard. Shiny metal screw heads indicated that the boards were recent additions, presumably to keep up humidity inside and stop light escaping that might be visible from the street.

The further Ning walked, the more she also became aware of a hum of electrical equipment inside. She was now certain about her hunch, but though she hadn't seen any CCTV cameras, Ning still reckoned there was a good chance she was being watched.

To complete the impression that she'd just wandered in drunk, Ning lobbed her empty beer bottle, pulled her denim shorts down to her ankles and squatted. It was creepy thinking that some random guy was probably sitting inside watching her pee, but it was the only thing she could think of that gave her a legitimate excuse to have wandered off the street and down the alleyway.

As her urine continued trickling towards a gutter, Ning staggered across the parking lot, and back on to a street of well-kept semis. As soon as she was out of sight of the club, she pulled out her phone to call Fay. But Ning didn't want Fay to think she was too smart, so she decided to go back to Nebraska House for a couple of hours, take a shower, give James an update and call Fay up later.

*

James' bike rolled up outside a laundrette, with Ryan riding shotgun.

'Looks dead in there,' James said. 'Best not go back to the flat until this is sorted. Craig won't like you hanging on to twenty grand of his money and he's bound to have asked one of the lads from The Hangout to watch our front door.'

Ryan stepped off the bike, and pulled out the Alcatel as James led the way into the empty laundrette. He was a little shaken from James' aggressive riding, but his attention was drawn by four missed calls on the phone.

'They're certainly keen to get hold of me,' Ryan said.

The rain had finally stopped and they sat on a wooden bench, well out of the low sun. Ryan rested his crash helmet at his side.

'I think Craig was messing with you,' James explained.

Ryan looked curious. 'How'd you mean?'

'How many kids want to work for Hagar's crew?'

'Loads,' Ryan said. 'Guys like Warren who get a package are making hundreds of pounds every week. Some of the guys talk about *when they get their package* like winning the lottery or something.'

James nodded. 'Hagar's organisation needs a way to sort the kids who'll work hard and stay loyal from the ones who are just attracted to the bling. How can you do that?'

Ryan nodded. 'Some kind of test?'

James nodded. 'So they send you off in the middle of the night to some bullshit safe-house, with a bag that looks like it's full of cocaine, but it was probably just powdered milk or something. When you get there, Craig fixes it so that three of his guys are there to mug you. And the reaction to how you deal with the mugging shows your true character. Some kids – most I expect – will feel out of their depth and panic. A few – the good ones – will say sorry and spend some time scrubbing cars or whatever. And the ones who come out of that process, putting in some graft and showing determination to be part of the crew, are the ones Craig is really interested in recruiting.'

'Makes sense,' Ryan agreed. 'And me bumping into that guy at the car-wash was pure coincidence?'

'More of a balls-up on Craig's part than a coincidence,' James said. 'Sending you to deliver the money in the place where one of the goons who jumped you works.'

'So it's another car-wash that belongs to Hagar?'

James nodded. 'I'll bet you that car-wash, and probably half the car-washes in north London, are fronts for Hagar to launder drug money. Maybe they wash fifty cars a day, but if you look at the books, you'll see cash going through for a hundred or more. Minicab offices are another classic way of laundering money, 'cos everyone pays in cash and half the drivers are illegal immigrants.'

'But me beating up Fat Tony, surely they'll be pissed off?'

'Fat Tony won't be happy that you caught him off guard. But in Craig's eyes, my guess is that it'll just be another sign that you're someone worth recruiting. The only thing is, Craig's gonna get worried while you're holding twenty grand of Hagar's money and not answering your calls.'

'I still don't fancy walking into that cab office,' Ryan said.

'I'm with you on that,' James said. 'What you need to do is call them. Make it clear that you don't want to rip them off, but you'll meet Craig personally and give him the money.'

Ryan sounded wary. 'He's a moody bastard. Craig stomped Youssef's brother because he got chocolate on his favourite chair at The Hangout.'

'Craig's Hagar's number two,' James said thoughtfully. 'For that job you need a good head on your shoulders, and a reputation as someone not to be messed with. I wouldn't expect Hagar to pin a rosette on you or anything, but as long as you're not too gobby he should be OK.'

'What if you're wrong?' Ryan asked. 'I mean, I can handle myself, but he's a hard bastard and he's likely to have backup.'

'I grabbed your com unit before I left the house. Wherever Craig wants to meet, I'll be right outside and

I'll come in with all guns blazing if things get hairy. OK?'

'I reckon I can live with that,' Ryan said, as he pulled out the Alcatel. 'The longer I'm off grid, the angrier Craig will get, so I'll call right away.'

28. EXCHANGE

Ryan felt his heart thumping as a black Audi limo pulled up alongside a puddled kerb. Craig had insisted on picking him up in a car. Ryan had a tracking device tucked down his briefs so James could follow on his bike while keeping out of sight, but being on the move meant it would be much longer before James could intervene if things turned hairy.

The Audi's back door opened electronically, revealing a big leather armrest, with Craig on the far side.

'Get in,' Craig said.

Ryan stepped in, placing his backpack on the armrest as he checked out the muscle in the driving seat. He was a proper thug, with a chain tattooed around his neck. Ryan knew him from surveillance pictures he'd looked at before the mission and was fairly sure he was named Paul.

'Drive,' Craig said, as he glanced over his shoulder out the back window.

Tyres squealed as Ryan got pressed back into his seat. His nostrils were overwhelmed by a mix of damp leather and Craig's cigarette smoke.

'So,' Craig said, giving Ryan his best granite expression. 'You're showing some chops saying you'll only hand the money direct to me. What have you got to say for yourself?'

Ryan clipped his seatbelt into the holder and tried to keep the tension out of his voice. 'The way I see it, either Fat Tony is ripping you off, or you sent me up to that estate the other night with a bag full of milk powder and an ambush ready and waiting.'

The driver turned and smiled, but then caught himself. He only resumed laughing when Craig cracked a smile.

'Which is most likely?' Craig asked.

'The test,' Ryan said. 'Every kid wants a taste of your action and you need a way to know who can really step up and do the job.'

Craig looked suspicious as he grabbed the backpack.

'Money's all there,' Ryan said.

'No doubt,' Craig said, as he put the bag on the carpet between his legs. 'You must be pretty bright.'

The compliment made Ryan feel more confident. 'I'm clever and I work hard.'

'You keep your mouth shut about the test,' Craig said.

Ryan nodded. 'So you're not gonna make me go back

to the car-wash?'

Craig left Ryan's question hanging. The car took a corner as Craig reached across, grabbed a lump of Ryan's cheek and squeezed almost hard enough to be painful.

'I'm a big fan of common sense,' Craig said, sounding more aggressive as he pulled Ryan across the armrest by his cheek. 'Guts and loyalty count for a lot. But over the years, I've had more aggro from blokes who think they're smart than anyone else. Know why?'

'Why?' Ryan asked, words distorted by the hold on his cheek.

'Credit where it's due, clever blokes can be useful,' Craig began, as he let Ryan go. 'But they usually think they know best, and they struggle with their place in the pecking order. Sooner or later the brainy ones always try to rip you off.'

'I just want to earn dosh, for nice stuff. And maybe put a bit of money aside for uni,' Ryan said.

Craig laughed. 'That's what you say now.'

'I'm no genius,' Ryan said. 'It was pure coincidence that you sent me to a cab office with Fat Tony's car-wash on the same lot.'

'Bit of a balls-up,' Craig admitted. 'But most people still wouldn't have figured that it was a test.'

'So I'm too smart to carry on working for you?'

'Don't put words in my mouth, son,' Craig warned. 'But know this: I've been in this game nigh on twenty years. I've seen every scheme and scam and I've seen off guys a lot tougher and smarter than you.'

Ryan pushed his point. 'So, the car-wash?'

'You're off the hook,' Craig said. 'But Fat Tony had jobs lined up tomorrow, and since you were tasty enough to take him down, I think you'll make a fitting replacement.'

'Doing what?' Ryan asked.

'Putting in line what needs to be put in line,' Craig said. 'I'll drop you off at the tube station at the end of the road. Stick that phone in a public bin, it was already a couple of days old when you got it. I'll have them push another one through your door this evening, and you can expect a call from my good friend Clark in the morning.'

*

Fay had a bunch of surveillance equipment in the allotment shed, but years stored in damp conditions had got to the circuits and no amount of fiddling would bring it to life. When the shops opened on Sunday morning, Fay and Ning bussed it to a retail park and picked up a wireless CCTV kit and a couple of pairs of cheap binoculars.

Ning hadn't been impressed by Fay's method of openly asking questions about Hagar's organisation, or the cavalier way she'd handled the stash house takedown, so she made an intervention before they got anywhere near the bowling club.

'I didn't see any cameras,' Ning said, as the pair sat at a stop waiting for the bus back into town. 'But they'd arouse suspicion if they made cameras obvious. I looked some stuff up about surveillance online. Apparently when the cops start a surveillance they do it really patiently. Like, they'll spend a day or so just watching a gate. Then send someone in a bit closer. Then maybe back off for a few days.'

Fay gave a dismissive shake of her head. 'Kirsten and my mum never bothered with all that.'

'And look where they ended up,' Ning said bluntly.

Fay reared up. 'Don't you diss my family.'

Ning stood her ground. 'I'm not dissing your family. I just keep thinking about the stash house. What if there'd been a bolt instead of a chain on the lower door? We'd have blown it completely. And even though we got in, we took so long and made so much noise that Clay knew we were coming. He might have shot us both if he'd had a gun.'

'The raid went well,' Fay said. 'We made our money. If you want to play this game, there's no such thing as a risk-free job.'

'I'm just not sure we're doing enough to minimise risks,' Ning said.

'What do you know?' Fay snapped.

'All I'm saying is, what's the mega rush?' Ning asked. 'We made more money than we can spend on the last job. So why not make this one a slow burn? Wait until Hagar's crew drop their guard a little.'

'He killed my mum,' Fay said. 'If you're chicken, go back to Nebraska House and watch TV. I don't *need* you.'

'Warren was right, Fay. Your lust for revenge is clouding your judgement. Get yourself killed if you want to, but that's not what I signed up for.'

Fay didn't say a word. This was a challenging moment for Ning. She needed to be close to Fay to learn about Hagar's organisation and progress the mission. But it was too risky to carry on this way, so Ning decided to call Fay's bluff.

'There,' Ning said, as she put down a carrier bag with the new pairs of binoculars in and stood up. 'Take the equipment. I'm out.'

'Don't be such a drama queen,' Fay said. 'I can't believe you.'

Ning pointed up the street. 'I'm hungry,' she said. 'That sushi place we walked past looked good. I'm gonna go up there and grab some lunch. Then maybe I'll go watch a movie in town, or go back to Nebraska and chill in my room. If you want, I'll go back to the bowling club once it's dark and we can start our surveillance by watching who comes and goes from the end of the street. But going back in broad daylight and staring through binoculars, before we know how many people are inside, or where the CCTV cameras are, is stupid and I don't want any part of it.'

'So you're an expert all of a sudden?' Fay said.

'You don't need to be an expert to see that you're pushing too fast.'

With that, Ning started walking up the road. She was desperate to look back and see Fay's reaction, and massively relieved when Fay finally stood up and shouted, 'OK!'

Ning turned and placed her hands on her hips. 'OK, what?'

'Maybe I don't know it all,' Fay admitted. 'And I highly doubt Kirsten or my mum would want me to get killed.'

Ning turned back as Fay walked towards her.

'Lunch and a movie?' Ning asked.

Fay nodded, then the two girls put down their shopping and hugged it out.

'You said you looked up some stuff about surveillance,' Fay said.

Ning nodded. 'I bookmarked a few pages. We can check them out when we get back to my room at Nebraska House.'

'No harm in taking a look at them,' Fay said. 'And I've not been to the flicks in ages.'

29. KENT

Clark was a nickname, earned by black hair and plastic glasses reminiscent of Superman's alter ego, Clark Kent. He was touching thirty, with an awkward face caused by a pummelled nose and fat lower lip.

'All right?' Clark said, in an accent that came from somewhere north.

Bright sun made Ryan squint as he slid off a low wall and accepted Clark's firm handshake.

'Craig tells me you can handle yourself.'

Ryan acted modest. 'I guess.'

'You'll need a stab vest,' Clark said. 'I've got a few round my flat.'

Clark lived on the opposite side of the estate to Ryan. His furniture was old but every spare inch of wall was fitted with hooks. These held weapons, from child-sized knuckledusters to Kalashnikov assault rifles.

'Are these real?' Ryan asked, as he swept his finger along a dusty shotgun barrel.

'Hundred per cent,' Clark said, as he opened a chest of drawers and started rummaging.

There was enough illegal gear on display to get you a life sentence, but Clark didn't seem to care. After a minute he pulled a stab-proof vest from the drawer and flung it at Ryan.

'Should fit,' Clark said, as he rapped his knuckles on something hard beneath his sweatshirt. 'I never leave home without mine.'

The stab vest was easily visible underneath Ryan's T-shirt, so he took a balled-up hoodie out of his backpack.

'Gonna cook in this weather,' Ryan said, as he zipped up.

'Better than risking a knife in the guts,' Clark said, as he walked to his kitchen and came back with two bottles of Evian. 'Cold one,' he said. 'You'll need it.'

As Ryan dropped the bottle into his backpack, Clark surprised him with a lunge. He tried getting an arm around Ryan's waist, but Ryan spun and backed off. He tripped over a lamp cable and clattered into a wall lined with baseball bats.

'Nearly!' Clark gasped, smiling as he took another swipe.

This time, Clark anticipated Ryan's speed and hooked his ankle. Ryan's bum hit the carpet and he shuffled back towards a sofa as Clark closed in. The nature of Clark's attack and the fact he was smiling made Ryan sure he was just mucking around, trying to test his mettle.

When Clark got within arm's length and leaned forward to grab, Ryan darted head first between Clark's legs, locked arms around the big man's calves and thrust upwards, lifting Clark's feet off the ground.

Clark crashed forward. No harm was done because he landed on the couch, then rolled on to his back, howling with laughter.

'Slippery bugger,' Clark said, as he waved his palms to make it clear that hostilities had ended. 'Not bad at all.'

Ryan couldn't decide what to think. Clark seemed friendly, but it also felt weird wrestling a guy he'd met less than half an hour earlier.

'Take this,' Clark said, as he unhooked one of the batons on the wall. The metal stick started off twenty centimetres long, but when Clark twisted the base a prong shot out, tripling its length. Ryan swooshed it through the air a couple of times before whacking a camouflage cushion.

'You're my eyes and ears,' Clark said. 'I'll handle the clients. You keep lookout.'

They travelled in a Prius minicab, presumably another of Hagar's money-laundering companies. After weeks of stress, Ryan was pleased that he was finally getting closer to Hagar and might soon have something useful to report back to his mission controller.

Clark and the driver bantered in a way that made Ryan sure they worked together often. A twenty-minute drive took them north to a private dental practice in Edgware.

The waiting area was smart. Clinical white walls, a big screen showing daytime TV and a busy waiting room lined with smart leather armchairs and posters offering to *Whiten your smile from as little as £149.*

Clark leaned on the reception desk and turned on what little charm he had. 'My son has an eleven-thirty appointment to see Mr Lladro.'

'Take a seat, we'll call you through.'

Clark sat in the armchair furthest from the reception desk and spoke to Ryan, barely above a whisper.

'Mr Lladro set this place up about four years back. His credit score was dog shite, so no bank would touch him. One of Hagar's companies put up most of the money, but now the little runt's behind with his payments.'

Ryan looked around at three receptionists, a dental nurse and another coming through the door.

'It looks like they're coining it to me,' Ryan said.

Clark nodded. 'A dentist is gonna make money for as long as people have teeth. But Lladro's wife died eighteen months back and he's been on a bender ever since. Cards, cocaine, call girls. He owes half the loan sharks in London and he's become a very tricky man to pin down.'

Ryan nodded. 'So you made an appointment.'

The nurse came through on the dot of half eleven. Her white Crocs squeaked on polished tiles as she led them to a frosted glass cubicle filled with a big skylight and all the latest dental hardware. Clark's expression turned sour as soon as he came through the door.

'Where's Lladro?' he asked grimly.

The slender young dentist spoke politely, as he pulled on a blue nitrile glove. 'I'm Mr Greenwin. Mr Lladro is indisposed, so I'll be taking care of his patients today.'

'Indisposed where?' Clark asked.

'I believe it's a personal matter.'

Clark smiled. 'So you know where he is?'

'I can't divulge personal information about practice staff. I'll be taking care of Mr Lladro's patients today and I can assure you—'

Before Greenwin finished, Clark turned to Ryan and spoke hurriedly. 'Block the door.'

Clark snatched a sharp-ended dental probe from a cabinet beside the dental chair. With a single deft movement, he shoved Greenwin against the frosted glass with the point held at his throat. The nurse gasped and made a dash for the door, but Ryan blocked her as Clark made a threat.

'One more step, missy, and this goes straight through his face.'

While the nurse stood rigid, half a step from Ryan and the door, Clark began grilling Greenwin.

'How well do you know Lladro?'

'Not particularly well,' Greenwin said. 'He's been my boss here for four years, but we don't socialise.'

'Where is he?'

'I honestly don't know.'

'You didn't say you didn't know before. You said he was indisposed.'

Greenwin made a nervous squint and shook his head. 'I don't know his movements when he's away from the practice.'

'When's he back here?'

'He hasn't seen a patient in over two weeks.'

'If you had to guess where he was?'

'He plays a lot of golf.'

As the nervous exchange went on between Greenwin and Clark, Ryan warily eyeballed the nurse. He was certain he could handle her if she tried to get out, but there was only a glass screen separating them from other cubicles so people would hear if hostilities broke out.

'Which golf club?'

'Highgate, I think.'

'He doesn't answer his mobile any more,' Clark said. 'Has he got a new number?'

Greenwin shrugged. 'Probably, I don't know.'

'But you're covering all his patients. You must have to speak to him from time to time.'

'Mr Lladro's behaviour has been very erratic since his wife died early last year.'

Clark snorted. 'Your boss owes money to my boss, and to some other serious villains. My job is to make sure we get paid before the money runs out. One of the girls on reception must know his new mobile number. Shall I go and smack it out of one of them?'

Ryan watched the nurse's hand disappear into her trouser pocket.

'Hey,' he warned, but she kept moving and delicately removed an iPhone.

'I've worked with Mr Lladro for a long time,' the nurse said, speaking deliberately to try and diffuse the tension in the room. 'I'll give you his new mobile number if you promise to leave immediately. I know he's moved into an hotel, but I don't know where it is. But he usually plays a round of golf on Monday morning and you should catch him in the clubhouse for a late lunch.'

Clark sounded pleased as he took the pointed tool away from Greenwin's throat. 'Now that wasn't hard, was it?'

'It's not Mr Lladro's fault,' the nurse said, her voice rising a few octaves. 'He's been through hell since his wife died.'

'He's a big boy,' Clark said. 'Now I'm going to leave. In case either of you thinks of calling the police, or decides to tip Lladro off, remember this: my boss has a secured loan over this practice, so barring a miracle you'll be working for him soon. Your home addresses and next of kin details will be on file here, and I'm sure you wouldn't want me turning up at your house with a couple of angry pals . . .'

To emphasise his point, Clark flicked over a framed picture of Greenwin's kids. The dentist looked furious, but kept a lid on it as Clark and Ryan backed out.

The receptionist was expecting them to pay for a check-up, and yelled, 'Excuse me,' as the pair headed out the door and got into the grungy Prius mini-cab.

'Right,' Clark said, as he looked at his watch. 'It'll be a while before golden bollocks finishes his round of golf, so who's on for a big fry-up?'

30. PLANT

Ning had discreetly placed one of the wireless CCTV cameras in a hedge so that it showed the entrance to the former bowls club parking lot, then set up camp with Fay in a little swing park a few hundred metres away. Any lingering doubts about having found the grow house got quashed when the Transit van with two blue stripes rolled up outside.

A park keeper came just before midnight, turfing them out and locking the gate. But the fence was only shoulder high, so the girls had no trouble climbing back in once he was gone.

A pattern emerged through Sunday night and Monday morning. Every eight hours, two guards would enter the former bowls club and two would leave shortly afterwards. Sometime between nine and ten in the morning an additional crew of three men would arrive, one on foot, one in the striped van and one in a battered Honda hatchback.

Occasionally, members of this trio would emerge, either through the main entrance or a set of emergency exit doors. Drums of liquid fertiliser went in full and came out empty, bags of waste got loaded in the van. Their shift seemed to last until mid-afternoon, and the van owner always came out first with two or three bulging rubbish sacks. The guy who arrived on foot got a lift from the guy with the Honda. The only other visitors were a postwoman and moped riders delivering from a nearby pizza place and curry house.

It was 1 p.m. when Fay arrived at the swing park, and Ning was surprised to see Warren holding her hand. They joined Ning on a bench at the edge of a soft play area.

'And?' Fay asked bluntly, as Warren put his hand around her back and gave her a peck on the cheek.

'Looks like the same pattern,' Ning admitted. 'The gardening crew and two guards are inside the building right now. I waited until about five minutes after the food delivery, then I walked around the back and hid a second camera.'

Warren didn't get it. 'What's the significance of the food delivery?'

'They're less likely to be concentrating on the screens when they're eating hot food,' Fay explained.

Ning demonstrated her handiwork by holding up the little LED monitor that came with the CCTV kit. It showed the second camera perfectly centred on the rear fire doors.

'Next time they open up, we ought to get a look inside.'

Fay nodded as she pulled away from Warren. 'Good work.'

'You two seem to be getting along pretty well all of a sudden,' Ning noted, as she wondered if Fay really liked Warren, or if the kissy-kissy stuff was just a way of keeping their best source of information on side.

'He's lovely,' Fay said jokily, as she slid her hand across Warren's lap.

'What about the security cameras?' Warren asked.

Ning looked at Fay. 'Is lover boy a full partner now?' she said, a touch irritably.

Fay's yes came in the form of a guilty smile. 'Where would we be now without him?'

'Must have been some date on Saturday night,' Ning said acidly, before changing the subject. 'Hagar's security guards must have CCTV, but I can't see any cameras.'

'So how much longer do you think we should keep up this surveillance?' Fay asked.

'I reckon another day, unless something surprising happens,' Ning said. 'The park keeper's already giving me funny looks when he turns up and sees I'm still here.'

'The best way is to wait until the three guys open up the back doors and then jump 'em,' Fay said.

Ning shook her head. 'If the two security guys are doing their job they'll be on high alert every time that door opens. And unless the set-up is a total shambles, they'll probably have guns within reach and come out shooting before we can even take down the gardeners.'

'You have a good brain for this sort of thing,' Fay complimented. 'So we're better off at night, when it's just the two guards in the building?'

'We need to find a way of getting in without them knowing,' Warren said. 'There must be a blind spot, if we can only find the CCTV cameras.'

'I suppose there might not be cameras,' Fay said.

Ning shook her head. 'The cheapo wireless cameras we bought yesterday are pretty titchy. Someone with Hagar's money can probably get cameras so small that you'll only find them if you climb up the side of the building.'

'So we're screwed,' Warren said.

Fay and Ning both shook their heads. Fay spoke first, saying almost exactly what Ning was thinking.

'If we can't get inside without the two guards seeing us, we need to find a way of getting the guards to come out and meet us.'

*

Clark picked out Lladro's Jaguar saloon in front of the golf club. After a circuit of the car park, they parked the Prius on the street opposite the club entrance. This gave them a vantage point over everyone coming in and out of the clubhouse.

Ryan played games on his phone, until he got worried about the battery dying, Clark farted noisily and thought it hilarious to tell the others to *sniff that*, while the driver perched his newspaper on the steering wheel and occasionally read a crossword clue aloud.

Three hours had gone by when Clark looked up and raised a smile. 'There's the little bastard!'

Lladro was a portly bald man. At only five feet tall, he barely seemed bigger than his bag of golf clubs.

He spoke in a clipped shrill voice with a superior manner as Ryan and Clark approached. 'What are you two gentlemen after?'

Clark's silence gave the fat little dentist a dose of nerves. He turned to run, but Ryan quickly circled behind as Clark grabbed the collar of his polo shirt.

'What do I want?' Clark asked thoughtfully, as he shoved Lladro against the back of his Jaguar. 'How about three hundred and eighty-three thousand pounds?'

'Now listen . . .' the dentist began, trying to sound authoritative as Clark forced a hand down his trouser pocket. 'I've already spoken to your people. The cheque is written and on the desk at my home.'

'That's an old record, I've heard it,' Clark said.

Clark slugged Lladro in the gut, then took a half-step back and threw a Jaguar key fob at Ryan. 'Open her up.'

Ryan stared at the little plastic pebble and took a stab at the green button with an unlocked padlock icon. The indicators blinked and there was a whirring sound from the door locks.

'The boot, dumbass,' Clark shouted.

Lladro made a high-pitched howl as Clark thumped

him again. Ryan pressed the only other button on the key fob and the boot popped up, hitting Lladro gently in the face.

'Time for a ride, baldy,' Clark said.

Ryan watched in shock as Clark hoisted Lladro up by his trouser belt. The dentist's stubby little legs kicked comically in mid-air as Clark raised him high, then shoved him into the boot of his own car.

'Keys,' Clark ordered, as he slammed the boot down. 'Put his clubs in, they're probably worth money.'

Lladro kicked and thumped as Clark settled into the driving seat, and Ryan loaded the golf bag on to the rear seats. As soon as Ryan had dropped into the front passenger space, Clark reversed aggressively out of the parking space, missing a Range Rover in the row behind by centimetres.

Clark spun the wheel with the palm of his hand and triggered the anti-lock brakes as he accelerated hard. A sharp left took him out of the golf club, and Ryan saw the Prius minicab tailing in the rear-view mirror. Ryan considered the possibility that Clark was going to kill Lladro. If it came to that he'd have to try and save the dentist, but that would completely blow his role in the mission.

'You look like you've seen a ghost,' Clark told Ryan, golf clubs clattering across the rear seat as he took a corner too fast.

'It just happened really fast,' Ryan explained. 'And I'm wringing wet under this stab vest.'

Clark took a hand off the steering wheel and gave

Ryan a friendly jab on the upper arm. 'Don't worry,' he said warmly. 'We just nailed the tricky part. Now we get to have some fun.'

31. LOANS

The Jag had baked in the afternoon sun and Lladro fought for air as Clark popped the boot open.

'Hey, slaphead, how's it going?'

'Let me talk with your superiors,' Lladro said, trying to hide fear.

'They don't wanna talk to you,' Clark said, smiling as he grabbed Lladro's belt.

'I demand—'

Lladro's sentence ended abruptly, with Clark's fist smashing into his mouth.

'You don't demand,' Clark shouted. 'You listen.'

Lladro found himself being yanked out of the boot, by shirt collar and belt. He hit the ground hard. He was dizzy from the heat in the trunk and his vision blurred from the punch, but he could see enough to work out that he was in an underground parking lot, with the headlamps of the Prius aimed in his eyes.

'Here's what my superiors have to say,' Clark said, before booting Lladro in the stomach. After a couple more brutal kicks, he set his heel on Lladro's belly and turned back to Ryan. 'You gonna take a couple of shots at our tubby little butterball?'

Ryan felt bad, but figured Clark was going to do whatever he was going to do. He didn't want Clark to see his reticence, but Ryan's timid steps gave him away.

'What are you scared of?' Clark demanded.

Ryan swung his trainer. Lladro had balled up, so he kicked him in the back, but not massively hard. Clark didn't look satisfied, so Ryan reluctantly launched a second, harder kick.

'That's more like it!' Clark said approvingly, as Lladro groaned. 'Here's another few for you, doc.'

Clark launched more kicks, by the end of which Lladro was slumped on his back, dribbling blood and close to unconscious.

'Get the petrol can,' Clark shouted.

Ryan looked confused.

'From the Prius.'

The driver popped the Prius' hatchback and Ryan looked inside at assorted weapons and a kids' plastic cricket set. He found a rusted metal can and tried to think how he might help Lladro escape. The dentist was in no state to run off, so Ryan would have to knock out Clark, then somehow take out the driver sitting in the car ten metres away.

Clark snatched the can out of Ryan's hand and rust

grated as he unscrewed the cap. Lladro screamed as Clark sloshed petrol into his eyes.

'Fat little piggy like you,' Clark teased, as he pulled a lighter out of his pocket. 'You'll make good crackling when you burn.'

'You think I care?' Lladro shouted defiantly. 'I can be with my wife.'

'Aww, baby,' Clark mocked. 'How much have you blown on whores since the old bag copped it?'

Ryan grasped the extendible baton in his trouser pocket, and took a step up so that he was close enough to whack Clark over the back of the head. Ryan was sure he could flatten Clark with one blow and get to the driver before he had too much time to think. Unless the driver had a gun in his glove box, in which case he'd just have to hope that his stab vest gave some protection from bullets too . . .

Clark erupted in a booming laugh as he squatted in front of Lladro and pocketed the lighter. 'Death's just letting you off easy, tubs!' he said. 'We're taxing the Jag and the golf clubs. Hagar's giving you two weeks. Either pay the three hundred and eighty grand you owe him, or go to a lawyer and get papers written up to hand over full ownership of the dental practice.'

Ryan felt relieved as Clark backed off. Lladro managed to sit up slightly, hands trembling and eyes stinging. Despite the pounding he'd taken, he still managed a patronising manner.

'If I could just speak to Hagar personally. I'm sure he'll be more accommodating when he understands the facts.'

Clark looked at Ryan, giving him a kind of *can you believe this* expression, then contemptuously kicked the near-empty petrol can at his victim.

'One more thing, Lladro,' Clark said, as he stood with one arm on the driver's side door of the Jaguar. 'Just in case suicide or running away seems tempting. A little bird tells me that your daughter is studying History and Politics at Portsmouth. Trafalgar Halls, room 309. If you disappear, she'll jump right to the top of my visitors list.'

Ryan was shaken by what had happened, but also relieved that Lladro had only been beaten and threatened. The ever present Prius cruised behind the Jaguar as Clark drove up a ramp and out of the underground car park.

'Have you ever killed anyone?' Ryan asked bluntly.

Clark broke into a big smile and shook his head. 'Hagar wouldn't approve.'

'Why not?' Ryan asked.

'You ever seen a dead man paying a bill?'

*

Clark liked his fried food and Ryan followed him on a sunny ten-minute walk to a café. He threw Ryan a compliment as he tore a corner out of a bacon sandwich.

'You're a good lad,' he said. 'I spoke to Craig about you last night. How do you feel about going solo on a job?'

Ryan swallowed a mouthful of chips before replying. 'What kind of job?'

'You should be familiar with the technique,' Clark said, smiling. 'There's a lad about your age, we're giving him a bag of drugs – well, icing sugar – to look after for a couple of days, and a place to deliver it.'

Ryan smiled and nodded. 'And my job's to make sure he loses it?'

'Got it,' Clark said. 'There's sixty quid if you handle it right. The kid goes to your school so you shouldn't have much trouble finding him. I haven't got the details on me, but I'll text them through when I get back to my digs.'

*

A Honda moped puttered up a steep hill, crash-helmeted driver looking for house number sixteen, and a box on the back branded with the logo of *Top Pizza – No1 For Delivery*. Number eighteen lived behind a neat box hedge, but the house next door had scaffold up the front and boards from a construction company.

As the moped came to a wobbly halt, the rider's trainer caught mud dragged off the building site. Getting sent on spoof deliveries was part of the job, but the rider decided to call and double-check the address before riding back to base.

As the teenaged rider unzipped his padded jacket and pulled out a phone, two girls dashed out of an alleyway between houses, one of them waving her arms.

'You our pizza guy?' Fay asked. 'Ham and pineapple. Barbecue chicken wings?'

The driver felt relieved. His boss always acted like it was somehow the rider's fault when you came back to

Top Pizza and had to ditch an order in the yard out back. Every delivery was also a chance to earn a tip.

'I thought it was a wind-up,' the rider explained, as he flipped up his helmet visor and stepped off the bike to grab the pizzas from the insulated box over the rear wheel.

'We're having a sleepover in the field out back,' Fay explained. 'How much do we owe?'

The rider pulled two cardboard boxes out of the pouch and looked at the till receipt taped on top.

'Twelve twenty-eight,' he said cheerlessly.

He watched Fay digging a hand down her jeans, as Ning circled behind and reached out, like she was going to take the boxes.

'Busy night?' Fay asked.

The driver shrugged. 'Monday's always pretty dead.'

As the last word left his mouth, the driver felt his legs collapse beneath him. Ning had taken him down with a sweeping kick behind the knees. As Fay closed in and saved the tumbling pizza boxes, Ning expertly flipped the rider on to his chest. She straddled him, then yanked his arm up tight behind his back.

'Fight me and I'll break it,' Ning said firmly.

The road was muddy and Ning's knees squelched as Fay joined her on the ground and started undoing the rider's chinstrap. As his helmet got yanked off and rolled towards the kerb, Ning pulled his other arm up behind his back and bound his wrists with a thick garden cable tie.

Once the rider's hands were bound, Ning was free to

place one hand on his chin and lift his head out of the dirt.

'Open your mouth.'

The rider ignored the instruction so Ning pinched his nostrils shut. When he had to breathe, Fay moved in, forcing a rubber bouncy ball into his mouth. Then the girls worked together, pulling a nylon luggage strap over his mouth and buckling it tightly behind his head to hold the gag.

'You're doing great, pal,' Ning said, getting a guilty thrill out of the successfully executed takedown as she stood up and locked another plastic tie around the rider's ankles.

Now that mouth and limbs were all out of action, each girl grabbed the rider under a sweaty armpit. He moaned into his gag as they dragged him into the alleyway between houses.

'Don't panic,' Ning told the rider. 'We'll let someone know where you are when we're done with the bike.'

Back in the street, Ning scooped up the helmet and pulled it on.

'Are you sure you know how to ride this thing?' Fay asked.

Ning nodded. 'Everyone has them in China. I've ridden them a million times.'

Fay put the pizzas back in the insulated box, then straddled the bike, pulled on a spare helmet they'd brought with them and shuffled up behind Ning.

'Hold tight,' Ning said, as she pressed the electric starter on the handlebar.

The anxious fingers dug into Ning's abdomen made her suspect that Fay wasn't confident in her riding skills. But after a wary start, Ning stopped wavering and built up speed as she rumbled off into darkness.

32. HARVEST

It was ten minutes to midnight as the moped stopped in the street outside the bowling club. Fay hopped off the back and flipped up her visor before taking a quick peek into the car park.

'Van's there,' Fay said. 'You got your patter clear in your head?'

Ning nodded. 'Show a little faith. I did OK with the bike, didn't I?'

Fay said good luck as Ning got off the scooter, grabbed a barely warm pizza out of the back and balanced it on one arm as she walked towards the wrought-iron gates. With the crash helmet on, Ning hoped that the guards inside wouldn't make any connection with the girl who'd squatted and peed on the other side of the building a few days earlier.

The doors had blackout blinds fitted, but enough

light leaked around the edges to read the intercom buttons on the door lock. Ning pressed the big button at the bottom, setting off a hearty buzz inside.

After twenty seconds, a gruff male voice came back through the intercom. 'What you want?'

'Pizza,' Ning said brightly.

The voice came back, sounding puzzled. 'Nobody here ordered pizza.'

Ning assumed they were watching her on camera, so she pretended to read the white address slip taped to the pizza box.

'Marston Bowling Club,' Ning said. 'This is the right place, isn't it?'

'You're at the right place, but we didn't order no pizza.'

'Is there anyone else inside who might have ordered pizza?'

Now the man sounded annoyed. 'There's *nobody* here ordered pizza. How many times I gotta tell you?'

'Right,' Ning said weakly. 'Must be a mix-up. I'll call my dispatcher.'

Ning stood at the doorway, flipped up her helmet visor and made a pretend phone call. She had no idea if they could hear from inside, but she went through the motions and made a fake call.

'Hello . . . This order, they say they don't want it . . . OK . . . OK . . . He sounded like he doesn't want to be disturbed . . . OK. See you tomorrow. Bye.'

Ning acted nervous as she pressed the intercom again. 'Hello?'

The voice sounded even more irritated. 'For the love of god . . .'

'Yeah,' Ning said weakly. 'I'm really sorry. We close at midnight. My boss says sorry for disturbing you. He got you mixed up with another regular customer. You're good customers and all, and since the pizza will just go to waste, he says it's on the house if you want it.'

'Hang on,' the man said. Then he turned away from the intercom and spoke to someone else. 'You want pizza . . . ? OK. Hello?'

'I'm still here,' Ning said.

'What kinda pizza is it?'

Ning tried to think what pizza most people liked best. After a second she had an idea that might raise her chances. 'It's a half and half. Ham and pineapple, and pepperoni melt.'

The man at the end of the intercom repeated this, and Ning caught a background voice saying, 'I could go for some pepperoni.'

Then the man turned back to the intercom. 'My friend can't say no to food. His big butt is on its way.'

Then in the background the other guy said, 'Kiss my arse.'

Ning felt really nervous now. The two guards couldn't have been more than ten paces from the door because she saw shadows moving on the blind almost immediately. After a couple more seconds the latch turned inside the door, followed by a click as the man pushed a button to release the electronic bolt.

'Evening,' the guy said, as the door came open. He

was nearly six feet tall, and stocky rather than fat. The air coming from inside was humid and Ning caught a whiff of marijuana plants.

'Free pizza's the best kind,' the man said, giving Ning a smile.

She held out the pizza box, but the man didn't take it straight away. Instead he rummaged in the front pocket of his jeans until he found a two-pound coin.

'Couple of pounds for your trouble,' he said.

As he reached forward, Ning swung the pizza boxes to her left. This meant the guard inside didn't see as she pulled a short-handled 75,000-volt cattle prod out of her jeans. The dangerous end made sharp cracking sounds as it hit the man's thigh. Ning squealed in fake shock as he fell forward, knocking the pizzas out of her hand as he hit the ground, roaring in pain.

Ning's rapid movement with the cattle prod meant that even the guy on the ground didn't get what had happened.

'Oh my god!'

The other guard's voice came urgently through the intercom. 'What was that?'

Ning made her voice all shrill. 'He's shaking. I think he's having a heart attack, or something.'

Then she went for her mobile. 'I'm calling an ambulance.'

The guard inside didn't like the idea of an ambulance on his doorstep. 'Hold off, I'm coming out.'

'I just felt this massive spasm,' the guy on the ground said, clutching a dead leg as the other guard reached the doorway.

This man was a proper giant. He went down on one knee, grabbed his colleague's wrist and started feeling for a pulse. While he was focused on this, Ning sneaked out the cattle prod again and zapped the back of his neck, then his calf as he sprawled forward.

The guard who was already on the floor now understood what had happened, but he couldn't react because his giant colleague had just landed on top of him. Still in a crash helmet, Fay started a sprint across the car park. By the time the gasping men had rolled away from each other, they had two girls aiming handguns at their chests from point-blank range.

'Inside,' Fay ordered.

The first man tried to stand up, but Ning yelled at him. 'Down,' she ordered. 'Crawl.'

Ning got an intense blast of humidity and the pungent marijuana smell as she followed the crawling men down a short corridor. A room off to one side had the door ajar, and was dominated by a long desk lined with monitors showing CCTV images from both inside and outside of the building.

A thick black curtain had been hung across the end of the corridor, and Ning was almost blinded as she stepped into a growing area lit with huge banks of lights. The flooring comprised spongy green carpet which had once been used for bowling. Lines of cannabis plants grew in long plastic troughs.

The former bowling green had been divided with plywood partitions. Fay opened a door into another area and immediately realised that each room contained plants in a different stage of cultivation.

'Where are you going?' Ning asked. 'We've got to tie these guys up.'

Fay kept her pistol on the two guards as Ning swiftly trussed their arms and legs, then used a pair of leather straps to tie each of them to a concrete post.

'Keep the noise down or I'll gag you as well,' Ning warned.

As the tying up got finished, Warren arrived from the swing park. His gaze was drawn to what had once been the club's lounge. Five PCs stood on a traditional mahogany bar, behind which lay a network of computer-controlled pumps and dozens of clear plastic tubes.

Warren sounded awed as he spoke through his balaclava. 'This shit looks state of the art.'

'Hydroponic cultivation,' Fay explained. 'Water and fertiliser are in direct contact with the roots, so plants grow much faster than in soil. It looks like each room has a crop in a different stage of cultivation, from seed germination, to plants in different growth phases and finally drying the end product. The computers control the amount of light, water and fertiliser that gets sent to each zone. And by having crops at different stages of maturity, Hagar has a steady supply of fresh cannabis.'

Warren nodded. 'Eli's lost a lot of regular custom, because Hagar's shit is better quality. And now we know why.'

Fay went down her backpack. She pulled out two

rolls of extra-strong bin liners and hurled the first one at Ning.

'Look for product,' Fay said, as Warren caught the second roll of bags. 'Drying leaves, mature plants and seed, in that order of importance.'

'What's wrong with smaller plants?' Warren asked.

'They're worthless. They're not potent enough to smoke until they come into flower and they'll die before anyone gets a chance to replant them.'

'What are you doing?' Ning asked, as Fay grabbed a bar stool.

Fay smiled. 'All these pumps and computers must have cost Hagar a fortune. If I smash it all up, the younger plants will die and he'll have to start growing again from scratch.'

The humid air and lush green plants had a serene air. Ning didn't feel like she was in the middle of a robbery as she moved through a couple of growing areas filled with young plants. The networks of tubes and troughs gave a soothing vibe of trickling water, disturbed occasionally by the whirr of an electric pump.

The third room Ning entered was full of larger plants and all the lights were out. She didn't have a torch, so she used her mobile screen for illumination. Ning realised she'd reached the back of the building, so she cut left through a rubber-sealed door that made a strange sucking sound as she opened it.

The light and heat in this room were less intense. Instead of high humidity, the air seemed to suck all moisture out of Ning's lungs and the plant aroma was so strong that it stuck to her mouth and throat.

Instead of plant beds, there were deep wooden cabinets fitted with mesh-bottomed drawers. Each drawer was layered with a couple of centimetres of marijuana leaves, ranging from just picked green, to much drier leaves that crumbled when you touched them.

Ning was no expert, but she decided it would be best not to mix up leaves in different stages of the drying process. It seemed the gardeners used bin bags too, because Ning was able to stretch the mouth of a black bag over a wire frame screwed to the wall. She then began pulling out the lightweight drawers and tipping the contents inside.

Within a few minutes she had a pile of empty drawers up to her shoulder and a black bag filled with some of the driest leaves. She squeezed out as much air as possible, knotted the bag, then reached inside her crash helmet and double-tapped her ear to open up her com system.

Ning had used the com on all of her missions, but she still found it creepy having a mission controller's voice seeming to come from inside her own head.

'You OK?' James asked.

'All going smoothly,' Ning whispered. 'Just thought you'd want an update.'

'Excellent,' James said. 'I'm two minutes away if you need me.'

Ning was about to say goodbye when the rubber seal on the door made a ripping sound. She glanced back and was relieved to see that it was only Fay.

'You found the drying room,' Fay said happily. 'Warren's got two rooms full of flowering plants to harvest. The only downer is, there's no sign of any finished product.'

'This is gonna take a while,' Ning said, as she waved her hand towards cabinets with well over a hundred drying drawers.

'Chill,' Fay said, as she looked at her watch. 'There's no shift change till morning.'

*

Four hours after they'd arrived, Ning grabbed a set of van keys from a hook in the CCTV room, then reversed the striped Transit van up to the bowling club's rear fire doors. As Fay and Warren ran around inside the building, dragging bin bags stuffed with dried cannabis leaves and mature plants up to the doorway, Ning opened the van's back doors and dragged a big bag of garden tools and half a dozen empty fertiliser drums out of the rear compartment to make space.

Ning picked up a couple of bags of dried leaves and was surprised to feel water splashing her legs as she lobbed them deep into the van.

'How'd they get wet?' Ning asked.

'I slit loads of tubes, smashed up the computers and left all the pumps running,' Fay explained. 'It's getting soggy in places.'

'Just make sure you don't stack wet bags on top of dry leaves,' Ning said.

The trio took a couple of minutes to load up the van

and, it being high summer, first light was breaking over the surrounding houses as they pulled out of the club car park. Ning drove a mile before pulling up in front of a row of shops. She and Fay took their crash helmets off for the first time in close to five hours.

Warren pulled off his balaclava and laughed as he saw the girls' sweaty, tangled hair.

'It's not a good look,' Warren teased, as he moved in and kissed Fay's reddened cheek. 'But the raid was bloody awesome!'

Ning was irritated by Warren and Fay's relationship, and became all-out hostile when the pecking turned to a full-on snog.

'Pack it in,' Ning moaned, as she put the van back in gear. 'In case you haven't noticed, we're still on Hagar's turf and the cops will pull us over if they see three teenagers driving a van at four in the morning.'

'Mum's right,' Fay said, as she palmed Warren away.

The tatty van wasn't a civilised ride and Ning crunched gears as she pulled off.

'I'd better call Shawn and let him know we've got some stuff for his boss,' Fay said.

But Shawn must have switched phones because the number Fay had was dead. She ended up calling one of Eli's street dealers, who gave out an up-to-date number after a lot of arm twisting.

Ning could only hear Fay's half of the conversation from the driving seat, but Eli's lieutenant clearly wasn't enthusiastic about a 4 a.m. call.

'Yes I do know what time it is,' Fay said cheerfully.

'But I've got news. Good news! Right now I'm riding in a van, stuffed with Hagar's entire cannabis crop. I'm looking for a quick sale and I've trashed Hagar's grow house at no extra charge.'

Fay paused while Shawn said something. Her face sank and her next sentence sounded wary.

'OK, I guess . . . You've got my number. I'll wait for your call.'

'Problem?' Ning asked, as Fay pocketed her phone.

Fay shrugged. 'I expected him to be more enthusiastic. He's gonna call me back after he's spoken to Eli.'

'Who's gonna be enthusiastic at four in the morning?' Warren pointed out.

'So where am I driving?' Ning asked.

'It's too risky leaving the van in town,' Fay said. 'Warren wants to be dropped off, then we can drive the van up to the allotments.'

33. CALLS

Two days after the raid on the grow house, Ning woke up on an airbed in the allotment shed. She sat up, eyeing a bluebottle crawling up the inside of a dirty window and the striped van parked next to a compost mound at the bottom of their plot.

Ning's knee clicked as she stood up. She thought about making a hot drink on Fay's little gas stove, but went for a little bottle of Tropicana orange, which floated in an enamel bowl to stay cool. She needed the toilet, which meant trudging over several hundred metres of dirt and gravel to a smelly shed, where you could hear your waste drop into a big composting tank below.

After pulling on leggings, wellies and a striped T-shirt, Ning made the toilet trek and bumped into a stern-looking Fay on the way back.

'Morning,' Ning said.

'My phone's hit-and-miss on the allotments, so I walked up to the street to get a better signal,' Fay said grumpily. 'There's still no text or anything from Shawn and his phone's dead when I try to call.'

'Probably switched it again,' Ning said.

'It's been *two* whole days,' Fay said. 'What's he playing at?'

'Stay cool,' Ning said. 'You're selling, he's buying. He probably doesn't want to seem too keen. I bet he'll make out like he's already got tons of cannabis and try to screw us on the price.'

'And I saw that lady from plot twelve, the one who gave us the nice strawberries. She made some comment about how I always seem to be around. I think she knows I'm living on site.'

Ning nodded. 'You can't keep staying here full time. I'll sneak you in at Nebraska House. I need to go back for a proper shower and clean clothes anyway.'

'I don't like leaving the van,' Fay said.

'You need to take your mind off stuff,' Ning said. 'We can go see a movie or something.'

Fay's face turned sour. 'I'm waiting on Shawn. How can I sit in a bloody cinema with my phone switched off?' she growled, as she pointed at the van.

'All I'm saying is, worrying won't get you anywhere.'

'You stating the bloody obvious every five minutes doesn't help much either,' Fay snapped.

Ning shook her head. 'Does it matter if Eli's crew buys the drugs? Hagar must still be mad that his grow house has been located and trashed.'

'What about the money?' Fay asked.

Ning shrugged. 'We've got more than we can spend from the stash house rip-off.'

'My whole plan is to make Hagar so mad that he does something rash. And nothing is going to make Hagar madder than knowing that I'm ripping him off and selling the gear on the cheap to his deadliest rival.'

'What makes you think Hagar will do something rash?' Ning asked. 'He's ultra-cautious. Warren's never seen him, and he reckons that apart from Craig his lieutenants barely see him either.'

'I know Hagar,' Fay said firmly. 'My mum and my auntie robbed him a dozen times. You don't get into Hagar's position in the drug business without being smart. But red mist is his weakness. When things go his way he's cautious and methodical. But if something gets under his skin, he loses it. And that's when I'm going to pop up and blast his nasty little head off.'

Fay seemed like her old self as she glared at Ning, but a chime from her phone put her straight back into an anxious frame of mind.

'Is it Shawn?' Ning asked.

Fay tutted and shook her head. 'Warren's texting from school. He's asking if I want to meet up with him at lunchtime.'

*

The Year Sevens and Eights sat on the floor at the front of the school hall, while older kids filed into rows of metal chairs. It was the end of summer term. The mood was heady with the thought of six weeks' holiday, while Year Thirteens had gone for all-out anarchy, throwing flour and eggs, stripping off shirts and staging school-tie-burning ceremonies.

'Quiet,' a deputy head roared. 'Year Nine, I'm talking to you.'

But Year Nine collectively told the deputy head where to stick the idea of being quiet and a girl ran off yelping as someone stuck an orange ice pop down her back.

Ryan had made a few friends at school, but he ignored them as he entered the hall, cutting back amidst rows of chairs into an enclave populated by Year Eleven and Twelve kids.

A group of Year Thirteen girls started singing a rude song about one of their PE teachers, before collapsing in shrieks of giggles. A teacher waded in and plucked a titchy Year Eight boy who was whistling with two fingers in his mouth.

'We hate Tottenham and we hate Tottenham,' some Arsenal boys chanted.

Amidst all of this randomness, Ryan sat in an empty chair directly behind a stocky kid named Ash Regus. Ash was a typical Hagar recruit: a brighter-than-average kid, who wanted to make some money selling drugs at parties to ease his way through university.

Ash was beefy, with cropped hair and angry pimples all over his neck. There was a black Eastpack on the polished wood between Ash's legs, and Ryan had just received a text message confirming that he'd collected a package from Craig during his lunch break.

'I'm happy to wait all day,' the head said, though most of his fellow teachers looked like they wanted a sunlounger and a cocktail ASAP.

A science teacher made a token effort to stop kids from leaving, but these lads weren't coming back for Year Twelve so the school had no power over them, and a couple of guilty-looking girls followed.

'Knooooob head!' the last lad shouted, having a little tussle with the science teacher as he left the school hall.

Things calmed down slightly as someone dimmed the lights. A big group of Year Thirteens came in, looking a lot like they'd been boozing. They got shushed by a teacher, so they all started shushing each other noisily and grated seats as the headmaster began his drone.

'. . . so we reach the end of another school year. Some of us have experienced their first year of secondary school, and are just settling into their lives here. Our Year Thirteens are at the other end of this journey and we wish all of them well as they begin adult lives and . . .'

As the headmaster droned in a voice that could have made a story about Jesus riding a unicycle naked down the school corridors seem boring, Ryan kept focused on the Eastpack. Ash clearly regarded the contents as important, with one strap gripped in a tight fist and the other hooked around his ankle.

Just as Ryan decided that his chances of sneaking the package out of Ash's bag were nil, one of the Year Twelves sitting behind kicked his chair. He glanced back furiously.

241

'Go sit with the other Year Tens, saddo,' a lanky kid said.

'Or what?' Ryan asked.

He got his answer with another kick in the back.

'Move,' the kid demanded.

The noise made Ash and just about everyone else in the surrounding seats look around. Ryan was annoyed because the last thing he wanted was for Ash to clock him. Ryan tried to ride it out, but he got kicked again.

'Move.'

Ryan was furious that his plan to spy discreetly on Ash had been ruined. As soon as he stood up, even more kids looked around and at least one teacher was giving him a *what the hell are you standing up for* stare.

As Ryan made a step towards a group of kids in his own year, another boy kicked an empty chair into his path, making him trip.

'Mind where you're stepping,' the lanky kid who'd kicked him three times said, as all his mates sneered.

Having so many people looking and laughing made something snap. Ryan spun around furiously, yanked a seat out of the way and launched himself at his tormenter.

Ryan got one arm around the lanky kid's neck as a roar of excitement ripped through the assembly and he landed several powerful body shots and a smack in the mouth. When the Year Twelves realised their friend was losing, they started dragging Ryan off.

He broke free, at the cost of a torn shirt sleeve, swung at one of the kids who'd moved behind and struck him clean in the temple, knocking him cold. He ducked a punch as two PE teachers came piling between the chairs to stop the fight. But before they got there, another ruck had broken out between Year Tens siding with Ryan and Year Twelves who weren't.

As Ryan backed up into Ash's chair, surveying the damage he'd caused – including three damaged and one unconscious Year Twelve – about twenty other boys were facing off, with a big group of Year Tens squaring up to physically bigger but less numerous Year Twelves.

'Everybody sit down!' the headmaster yelled.

Ryan looked back and saw that all the Year Sevens and Eights were starting to stand up and turn around to see what was going on behind them. One of the teachers got a hand on Ryan's shoulder but he was too riled up to submit.

'Hands off me, prick.'

The teacher didn't take kindly to this and the scuffle between Year Tens and Twelves kept getting bigger as the teacher started giving Ryan a *how dare you* type speech.

A few kids had started shouting, 'Bundle!' and overexcited Year Nines trying to get a look at the action forcefully shoved a couple of weedy kids into the rows of plastic seats.

'This is not acceptable,' the headmaster yelled.

The scuffles didn't seem to be breaking up, even though more than a dozen teachers were now trying to pull kids apart. Mostly it was just shoving and jeering, but there were a few punches being thrown and at least one bag had sailed across the hall hitting a girl in the back.

At this point a drunk Year Thirteen girl in a shocking-pink wig set off the fire alarm by the main doors. Kids began pouring out. Ryan managed to break free of the PE teacher who'd been giving him a lecture, while the headmaster desperately told people to stay in their seats. Then, after a brief consultation with one of his deputies, the head changed tack and told everyone to follow the fire rules and meet at the assembly points on the Astroturf pitches.

Ryan tried to keep Ash in sight, but he'd bolted when the fire alarm sounded. He saw Ash's head bobbing out of the fire doors, but by the time Ryan got out into sunlight himself Ash had disappeared in a melee, with most of the lower-school kids heading obediently for the Astroturf, and the older ones going straight for the school gates.

'Young man,' the PE teacher said, grabbing Ryan's shoulder as he desperately tried to spot Ash. 'I haven't finished talking with you.'

Ryan was pissed about getting taunted and losing Ash. He came within a quarter second of chinning the burly teacher, but thought better of it. He might need to come back to this school if the mission dragged on for six more weeks, and while fighting a teacher would probably make him a legend amongst the friends he'd made on this mission, it was much less likely to impress the senior staff back on CHERUB campus.

'Wait outside the headmaster's office, now!' the PE teacher yelled.

Ryan reluctantly let the teacher take his arm and begin marching him towards the head's office. Kids walking past on either size stoked Ryan's anger by making hissing noises and chanting stuff like *you're in trouble* or *you're getting excluded.*

And while all that was going on, Ash and his fake package of drugs had completely vanished.

34. REJECTION

Ning got hassled by a social worker when she got back to Nebraska House, because she'd been AWOL for two days. Getting grounded would have been a pain, but luckily she was just docked a week's pocket money and banned from a seaside trip that she had no plans to go on anyway.

Smuggling Fay into Nebraska House was easier than explaining her presence in the shower room to a nosy ten-year-old. Both girls felt better for a shower, clean clothes and a shared box of Maltesers. They watched trash on E4 and for the first time in two days, Fay relaxed enough to stop checking her phone for messages every two minutes.

Good cheer lasted until 4 p.m., when Shawn finally returned Fay's call. The two girls shuffled up close on the bed so that Ning could hear both ends of the conversation.

'Sorry it took so long to get back,' Shawn said. 'I've been having a lot of conversations with the boss about this. We've got plenty of supply right now.'

Fay and Ning both suspected that this was a ploy to bring down the price.

'I'm not asking for fortunes,' Fay said. 'There must be a price you're willing to pay.'

'Afraid not,' Shawn said firmly. 'We just paid you girls a lot of money for cocaine and cash flow ain't great since Hagar moved in on our business. You're smart girls. If I were you, I'd ditch this gear, or ship it to your pals up north, if they're for real. Keep your noses clean, and live it up with the cash you made already.'

Fay's voice became tense. 'Shawn, this is top-notch, hydroponic, high-THC weed. The quality of this stuff is the reason Hagar took all your best customers. This is your chance for a role reversal. Your crew could be selling the best gear in town, while Hagar's got nothing but a grow house full of rotting plants.'

Shawn laughed uneasily. 'What do you think's gonna happen when we start putting this stuff on the street? One sniff will tell Hagar that it's his own shit we're selling. He's already pissed off about the stash house. If we start selling his weed to his own customers, it's gonna be all-out war.'

Fay snorted. 'I didn't realise Eli was scared. Hagar's a wolf. If you don't stand and fight, he'll keep biting chunks out of your business until you've got nothing left.'

Shawn made a more relaxed sigh, and Fay was starting to feel like he was talking down to her. 'Hagar and Eli are businessmen. They'll tweak each other's noses, but all-out war costs lives, money and brings the law down on your backs. Hagar and Eli have been known to parlay. I've sat in as a bodyguard and you know what they talk about? Not street hustles and gangster wars. They talk about villas in Ibiza, diamond watches and whether my boss's new Porsche is faster than Hagar's new Ferrari.'

'But Hagar's taken a big chunk out of Eli's business.'

Shawn tutted with contempt. 'Fay, you're a kid. You think you're smart because you listen to some street talk. But your sources know dick about how shit works at the top level. You've got as much chance of making Eli go to war with Hagar as I have of making Canada go to war with the United States.'

Fay wanted to lash out, but she *was* just a fifteen-year-old girl and Shawn was sowing doubts in her head.

'Is there anyone you can put me in touch with who might buy the gear?' Fay asked weakly.

'I'd help if I could,' Shawn said. 'But Eli's mind is set. He wants *nothing* more to do with you girls. I like how you girls roll, but Eli was even talking about setting up a buy, then tipping off Hagar's crew so that they got to you first.'

'Jesus,' Fay said, moving the phone away from her face because she hated what she was hearing.

'Listen to what I'm saying and stay out of trouble,' Shawn said, before hanging up abruptly.

'Shit,' Fay hissed.

She pulled her arm back to lob the phone, but Ning snatched her wrist.

Fay spent the next few minutes staring silently into her lap, while Ning tried to find soothing words. Ning's mission brief was to keep Fay involved with Hagar so that she could gather intelligence. But Fay could be reckless to the point where she endangered both of their lives, and Ning had a lot of empathy with a girl who'd lost her entire family, just like she had.

'Maybe Shawn's right,' Ning said softly.

After a pause, Fay began shaking her head. 'Shawn probably understands Eli, but he doesn't know Hagar.'

'You've never actually met either of them,' Ning pointed out.

'No,' Fay said, nodding. 'But there's just too many stories out there. When Hagar's rattled he gets crazy. And that's when I'll get my chance to nail him.'

'Maybe we could find someone else who'll buy the gear in the van,' Ning suggested. 'You can keep my share and you'll easily have enough to live on for a few years.'

Fay's expression had changed from meek to determined. 'I'm not giving up on this just because Eli's got no balls.'

'There's not much we can do without his muscle,' Ning said.

Fay nodded in agreement. 'But we don't actually need Eli to start a war with Hagar, do we? We just need Hagar to *think* Eli's starting a war with him.'

Ning smiled. 'And how the hell do we do that?'

James walked through the main entrance of Ryan's school and caught a whiff that reminded him of every other school he'd ever been to. The place was deserted. Reception was unmanned, but he eventually found a cleaner running a floor polisher.

'I had a call,' James explained. 'I've got to see the head about my little brother.'

The cleaner gave directions and James ended up in a waiting area outside the head's office. Ryan sat on a foam-backed armchair, along with a couple of other kids who'd played major roles in disrupting the assembly that never happened. One of the kids had an anxious mum waiting alongside him.

'What happened?' James asked.

Ryan couldn't mention the mission with two other kids earwigging. 'I thumped this kid who kept kicking my chair and it kinda started a mini-riot.'

'Impressive,' James said, smiling but then regretting it.

James was now CHERUB staff, but he was only twenty-two and he often found himself sympathising with CHERUB kids and feeling an impostor in the role of a responsible adult. He was quite surprised that Ryan had lost his temper, but it was exactly the kind of thing James would have got in trouble for when he was an agent.

'Is anyone in the office?' he asked, pointing to the door with *Headteacher* written on it.

The mum sitting with her son spoke quietly. 'The

headmaster's in there. But he said he had to make some phone calls before he could deal with us.'

'Did he?' James said knowingly. Senior teachers don't actually have many powers to punish kids, but they always like to make them sit around, nervously awaiting their fate.

The mum gasped as James knocked on the head's door and stepped in without waiting for a reply. The head was on his laptop, looking at second-hand car listings.

'I'll call you in when I'm ready,' the head said.

James cast a deliberate glance at Autotrader.com and tutted. 'I'm a self-employed mechanic. Time is money.'

'You must be Ryan's brother,' the head said, with a slight air of disapproval. 'And his legal guardian?'

James nodded. Ryan got called in. Nervous Mum looked angry because she'd been waiting over half an hour. The head gave a long spiel about what had happened. Ryan said he was provoked, but accepted that he should have told a teacher or moved away, rather than losing his temper and starting a brawl. So far, the police hadn't been involved, but they might be if one of the parents made a complaint. The head wanted Ryan to have a fresh start after the holidays, so his only punishment was to write a 1,000-word essay on Gandhi and other historical figures who'd achieved their goals through non-violent protest.

'Sorry we barged in,' James told the mum, as they headed out.

'Sorry,' Ryan said, as James led him out of the school,

straddling splattered yolks and flour lobbed by Year Thirteens earlier in the day. 'Is this gonna go on my mission report?'

James was conflicted. He sympathised with Ryan and wanted him to feel upbeat about the mission. On the other hand, this was one of James' first jobs as a mission controller and he wanted to do things by the book.

'I guess it depends,' James said, letting the sentence hang until Ryan responded.

'On what?'

'Well, I'm finding laundry a chore. And emptying the dishwasher, vacuuming. I might be prepared to be lenient if those things got taken care of.'

Ryan smiled and nodded. 'I'm on school holidays now, anyway.'

'Maybe the odd foot massage,' James added, but it was such an obvious joke that Ryan didn't bother to respond.

'Thanks,' Ryan said.

'What about Ash's package?' James asked. 'When's he due to deliver it?'

'Monday morning.'

'What's your plan?'

Ryan shrugged. 'I don't have one yet. But they've given me his home address, and it's a safe bet that Ash will keep it in his house until he goes out to deliver it.'

35. GEARS

The girls watched *Warm Bodies* on Ning's MacBook and switched out the light just after eleven. An hour later, Fay lay on a floor softened with cushions and beanbags. It wasn't particularly comfortable, but at least she couldn't hear rats scuttling about like on the allotment.

Ning had a foot dangling over the side of her bed, and made a gentle whistle with each breath. Fay kept one eye on Ning as she sat up and began feeling for her things in near darkness. She slid on a T-shirt and jeans, but could only find one balled-up sock so she gave up and pulled her All Stars over bare feet.

After checking that her wallet and keys were in her pockets, Fay unplugged her phone from its charger and began creeping out. It was warm, so the door was ajar, but the hinge still squealed and Fay was relieved when she glanced back and heard Ning's familiar whistle.

At this time in the morning, Nebraska House's main door was locked and could only be opened by a button in the staff room. Fay crossed a hallway, entered a room that she knew was unoccupied and unlatched the window.

They were on the ground floor, but this side of the building was raised up, so Fay jumped off the window ledge and dropped a metre and a half on to woodchips. There were CCTV cameras, but Fay knew nobody watched them full time. She made a dash, before stepping on to a low wall and swinging her legs over a mesh fence.

Fay mixed doubt, excitement and the odd yawn as she walked briskly towards Kentish Town underground. She arrived twelve minutes later, finding metal grilles over the station entrance and a sign inside saying that the last train had now departed.

Feeling slightly dumb, Fay headed to a bus stop to work out which night bus would take her to Totteridge. The map at the stop only showed the local area, so she resorted to her phone and worked out a two-bus combo that would take her north to the allotment.

*

Ryan had spent his Friday night belly down on the flat roof of a day-care centre. The spot gave him a view over the ground-floor apartment where Ash lived with his mum and brother. Ash had been visited by a hot Year Eleven girl, and Ryan felt jealous as the pair spent an hour behind closed curtains.

The girl left just after 9 p.m. Twenty minutes later an

elderly BMW coupé came by and blasted its horn. Ash and his ten-year-old brother got in the back carrying overnight bags, and Ryan figured that the man had to be their dad.

Once the boys had left, Ryan looked into the living-room. Their mum sat in a big armchair, surfing with an iPad and watching TV, with the window wide open and curtains billowing on a night breeze. Ryan willed her to go out or go to bed, but three hours ticked by, during which the scratchy roof felt dimpled his skin and he twice had to crawl behind an air conditioner and take a piss.

It was half midnight when Ash's mum closed the window and switched off the TV. Ryan couldn't see the windows out back, but he gave it forty minutes, by which time he felt fairly certain she'd be asleep.

Ryan would have preferred an empty house, but all things considered Ash and his brother spending the night with their dad wasn't a bad result. He stifled a yawn as he crossed the street. There were two drunk couples walking arm in arm, so Ryan diverted around the block and headed back to Ash's flat when the street looked empty.

His aim had been to get in through the front door, but Ryan was disappointed to find a good-quality mortise lock, and grilles that would stop him getting in if he broke the glass. A frosted bathroom window had been left open, but he'd have had to be a lot skinnier to crawl in through there.

This left the large living-room window as his best

option. Ryan put on a pair of gardening gloves and gave the white plastic frame a shove, but a sturdy catch stopped it moving. He tapped delicately on the pane and the tinny sound left Ryan reasonably confident that the glass wasn't toughened.

After a furtive glance up and down the street, Ryan took a roll of sticky-backed film from his backpack. It was a fiddle getting the backing off in the dark. The adhesive was really strong and he would have had a fight if he'd needed to reposition it. Once the square was in place, Ryan grabbed a strange-looking device which comprised a suction cup about the diameter of a coffee mug, attached by tube to a miniature version of a bicycle pump.

Placing the sucker against the glass, he worked the pump. The sucker was actually split into two parts, with suction on one side and pressure on the other. When the difference between pressure and suction grew high enough, the glass would crack in a straight line between the two halves.

There was a satisfying click as the pane cracked. Ryan turned a valve to release some of the suction, then he pushed the suction disk upwards, drawing a neat line of cracked glass behind it. He made a rectangle just inside the edge of the plastic film, then moved the suction cup to its centre.

The film was too strong to simply pull away, so Ryan sliced around the cracked glass with a craft knife, while keeping his left hand on the suction cup. When he'd cut three sides of the plastic, the glass swung outwards like an uneven door, with the strong plastic acting as a hinge and stopping it from hitting the ground.

'Not too shabby,' Ryan muttered to himself.

The sucker was an expensive piece of kit, so Ryan returned it to his backpack before reaching through the glass and releasing the catch. After he'd pushed up the window, his Nike got in a tangle with the curtains before he landed on the living-room floor with his leading leg slotted awkwardly between a mirror-topped table and an overstuffed magazine rack.

Ryan moved towards the living-room door, then leaned into a hallway. The door and hallway were wider than you'd expect and Ryan figured that the place had originally been built for someone with a disability.

The flat's layout was confusing, but there were reassuring snores coming through an open bedroom door. There were three other doors off the hallway, but Ryan's nose guided him through another door into a space whose smell reminded him of some of the grungier kids' rooms on CHERUB campus.

There were bunk beds, and judging by the superhero posters behind the top bunk and *FHM* pin-ups below, Ash slept on the lower bunk. Ryan took a torch out of his pocket. The first thing it lit was a line of Lego sets built along one wall. Ryan recognised Ash's school blazer, and his PE kit balled and stinking in a carrier bag.

Ash had celebrated the end of term by lobbing a bunch of tatty pens and school books in the bin, but there was no sign of his backpack. Ryan knelt down and started shining the torch about. There was nothing on the desk or chairs, so he knelt down and started looking under the furniture.

Ash's school bag was under the bed, amidst shoes and sweet wrappers. But it felt light when Ryan pulled it out and the only things inside were two textbooks and a geometry set. Ryan knocked a few shoes out of the way and smiled when he saw what he was looking for.

Ash had pushed the clingfilm-wrapped package deep under his bed. Ryan crawled in until his shoulder got wedged between carpet and bed frame, but even at full stretch he could only get his fingertips to the edge of the package.

Ryan backed out and grabbed a couple of rulers off the desktop. He used the rulers like chopsticks, getting behind the package and flicking it forwards. He almost had it in his grasp when he heard a gentle sound on the carpet, and noticed a shift in the light.

'MUM,' a girl shouted urgently.

Clutching the package with one hand, Ryan pushed himself out from under the bed as he saw the spokes of a wheelchair coming towards him.

'There's a burglar in the boys' room,' the girl shouted.

Ryan was furious with himself. How could he have watched the flat all evening and not seen that Ash had a wheelchair-bound sister?

As he tried to get out from under the covers, the front wheels of the wheelchair hit Ryan's legs, pinning them to a bedside cabinet. As he bucked and twisted, the girl raised a metal crutch up above her head and sank the rubber tip into Ryan's stomach.

He moaned in pain, as he managed to twist around enough to get a proper look at the girl. She was only about twelve, but while her legs ended at the knee, her upper body was well muscled from playing sport.

Ryan braced his legs against the bedside cabinet as he took another whack from the crutch. He was trying to push the wheelchair back, but the brake was on and he only got free by hooking his foot inside the cabinet and violently kicking it over.

As Ash's mum came into the room, Ryan had got all of his limbs free, but was still cornered by the wheelchair.

'Sophia, be careful, he could have a knife,' Ash's mum warned.

But Ryan was on the wrong end of the crutch twice more before her mother wheeled a reluctant Sophia out of the way.

'Go call the cops, sweetie. I'll take charge of him.'

Ash's mum grabbed the crutch off her daughter and held it up high over Ryan as he sat up.

'You move a muscle and I'll knock you for six,' she warned.

Out in the hallway, Sophia was talking to the 999 operator. Her mother was a bulky lady, and Ryan hoped that would make her slow as he sprang up and scrambled on to Ash's bunk. As he'd hoped, the swinging crutch hit the bed rather than him.

As a clonk rang through the metal bed frame, Ryan crawled up to the end of the bed. He threw a couple of pillows back at the woman and clutched the package to his chest with one hand as he slid off the end of the bed and stumbled out into the hallway.

Ryan went for the front door, but grabbing the handle didn't help because it had been deadlocked. Sophia dropped the cordless phone in her lap and wheeled fearlessly towards Ryan. The chair's front wheel skinned Ryan's ankle, but the twelve-year-old made a much less formidable opponent without the crutch and Ryan managed to squeeze past and charge for the living-room.

Ryan ducked as Ash's mum swung the crutch, but it caught the back of his leg, knocking him off balance and sending him stumbling towards a couch. The big woman swung again, but Ryan rolled across the couch as the crutch hit the sofa cushions with a *whump* that could have knocked him cold.

'The cops are two minutes away,' Sophia shouted from the hall.

Ryan's leg buckled as he stumbled forward and somehow launched himself through the open window, going out the way he'd come in. Much to his own surprise, Ryan realised that he still had the package as he stumbled across a little patio and stepped over a low wall and on to the street.

At the same time, Sophia had got the front door open and began wheeling herself speedily towards the front gate. Ryan was hobbling, and Sophia was gaining on him as he set off down the street. He was relieved when Sophia's mother yelled from the doorstep.

'Sweetie, it's not worth the risk. You get back here *right* now.'

Sophia looked dejected as she stopped pushing her chair and freewheeled to a gradual halt. Ryan felt relieved for about ten seconds, but just as he'd slowed down to a more comfortable jog his ears picked up the wail of police sirens.

36. DRIVE

Fay was a fast learner. She'd studied Ning and watched a bunch of YouTube videos about learning to drive, but getting the balance of clutch and accelerator pedals right was way harder than she'd imagined.

Frustration had whipped Fay into a fury when she finally got the right amount of pressure on the gas pedal and let the clutch up gently enough not to stall the engine. The van juddered, before setting off on the rutted gravel path between allotments.

As the engine raced, Fay pushed the clutch down and went for second gear. She hadn't got a feel for the gearbox and by the time she'd found second, a bump had knocked the van off course and she was heading towards a greenhouse.

She slammed the brake, but had yet to work out that the engine would stall if you didn't press the clutch pedal before stopping. The van came to a clattering halt, with a front wheel that had carved a rut through a line of cauliflowers.

'Shit!' Fay cursed.

An hour later she was doing better. Tyres crunched gravel as Fay switched deftly from second to third and corrected her steering when a bump threw her off course. The main paths through the allotment formed an uneven rectangle and she slowed for a tight corner, dipped the clutch and dropped back to second before accelerating away.

A bump she'd not previously encountered gave Fay a little jolt, but she smiled as she accelerated to twenty miles an hour and confidently selected third gear.

Two hours of intense concentration left Fay numb and groggy. She parked up by the shed, found a can of Red Bull inside and sucked it down as she squatted on her mattress playing with the maps app on her phone.

It was four miles from the allotments to an address in Finchley. Hagar tried to keep his living arrangements secret, but Fay had met a guy on the street who'd put her in touch with a heroin addict who claimed that she'd babysat Hagar's sons. Fay had paid three hundred pounds for the address, and knew she hadn't been ripped off, because Google Street View showed a black Mercedes she'd seen Craig driving parked out front.

Fay hadn't wanted anyone to see her practising with the van, so she put the headlights on for the first time as she stopped at the allotment's main gate, directly opposite the vast mound of three-pound-a-sack manure.

She had a key for the lock on the gate, but it had been in the shed for so long it had rusted badly and Fay had to fight to undo the lock and get the gate open. Once the van was on the outside, Fay closed the gate and felt queasy with nerves as she got back behind the wheel and pulled out on to the road.

She got into second gear OK, but then she accidentally selected first instead of third, making the engine race and the van lurch. A BMW coming up behind blasted its horn as the driver swung into the opposite carriageway.

The sat-nav spoke: *'Three hundred metres, straight ahead at roundabout, second exit.'*

Fay didn't like the idea of a roundabout, and she stopped at a red light, directly behind the BMW that had sped past a minute earlier. Two more cars rolled up behind and Fay was alarmed to find that the van started rolling backwards when she took her foot off the brake.

An alarmed driver behind blasted his horn as the van almost rolled back into him. Fay frantically braked, which stalled the engine, and she got moving just as the light went back to red. She didn't like the idea of starting on the hill again, so she jumped the light and clipped the middle of the roundabout before taking the second exit.

The rest of the journey was a similar mixture of anxious driving and near misses, but somehow she made four miles without crashing or getting stopped by the cops. Hagar's road sloped steeply downwards and Fay had to keep squeezing the brake as the van skimmed past, clearing the cars parked on either side by less than thirty centimetres.

'You have reached your destination.'

Fay sighed with relief as she stopped the van in front of number fifty-seven. Hagar's house was a grand Edwardian job, built in honey-coloured Bath stone with massive sash windows. The left side had a modern extension. This mirror-glass box rose two storeys, with a steeply sloped driveway leading down to a quadruple garage at its base.

There was no way of knowing who was home, but it was likely Hagar had a permanent security guard, so Fay moved quickly. After turning out the headlights, Fay walked around the van and opened the sliding side door.

The black bags of marijuana plants gave off a pungent smell as she reached inside and grabbed a metal can filled with petrol. After unscrewing the cap, Fay sploshed petrol about until all the bags were coated.

She gasped for air as she stepped back into the street and left the sliding door open as she got behind the wheel for one last ride. After picking up her phone, which she'd been using for navigation, from the passenger seat, and patting a denim pocket to locate a letter and a lighter, Fay let out the handbrake and started the engine.

The road's natural slope meant the van sped rapidly as it turned into Hagar's driveway. Fay lined up the vehicle at the top of the ramp, which led down a steep slope towards two broad garage doors. Leaving the engine running and the handbrake off, Fay lit a piece of rag stuffed into a petrol-filled Coke bottle as she jumped out of the cab.

The van picked up speed as Fay ran around the side. Once she was a few metres clear, she lobbed the petrol bomb through the van's open side and ducked instinctively. After a few anticlimactic seconds, a huge ball of fire erupted inside the van with enough force to throw open the back doors.

Fay wasn't happy to see the van veering slightly off course, but there was nothing she could do to correct it. As the freewheeling vehicle gathered speed, she crouched low and posted a letter through the front door. It contained a single sheet of paper with the words:

Get out of the Marijuana business.
Going for your cars is a final warning.
Next time, it'll be your kids.

Fay began a brisk walk out of the driveway, but couldn't resist looking back to see the van hitting the garage. It had veered off course more than she would have liked, but although the van smashed into the brick post between the two big garage doors – rather than punching through a metal door like she'd planned – it actually had enough momentum to smash through the bricks.

The garage doors squealed and crumpled as the van tore through. Flames lit up the garage interior and Fay briefly glimpsed the silhouette of an expensive-looking sports car. Over in the house, two dogs started barking and a light came on.

Fay cracked a wary smile as she swivelled on the balls of her feet and set off down the hill at full pelt.

*

The cops got to Ash's house three minutes after Ryan had scrambled out of the window. Luckily he'd been able to limp off into a housing estate full of alleys and elevated walkways and the cops showed no appetite to try and find him.

Ryan's guts ached where he'd been jabbed with the crutch and the heel of his right sock was soaked in blood. He got a night bus home and James dabbled with the idea of sending him to hospital to see if he'd cracked a rib, before deciding that his bruising was too low down.

After a shower, Ryan went to bed with gauze taped over a stomach wound and heavy strapping around his ankle. He was relieved that he no longer had to think about getting the package from Ash, but it was an uncomfortably warm night and aches and grazes meant that he only managed bursts of sleep between fights with duvet and pillows.

In the early hours of the morning, Ryan reached for a glass and found it empty. His torso glistened with sweat as he refilled and dropped in a couple of ice cubes. He was about to get back in bed when he noticed a light flashing on the little Nokia that Craig had given him.

Ryan picked up the phone and saw that he'd slept

through a message from an unrecognised number. It was written in capitals: ALL HANDS ON DECK. GET TO THE HANGOUT ASAP.

He jumped back out of bed. The window in the hallway gave him a view towards The Hangout. A man in a body warmer was running out of the door and there were several cars parked illegally on the grass behind the building.

'James,' Ryan yelled.

James didn't stir until Ryan jabbed his shoulder.

'Kerry, I'm too tired,' James moaned, as he rolled on to his back.

'Hey, lover boy,' Ryan said sharply.

'What?' James asked, sounding half dead as he sat up rubbing his eyes.

Ryan held up the Nokia. 'Message came through about half an hour ago. There's a whole bunch of cars and people up there.'

'What for?' James asked groggily.

'How should I know?'

'Have you spoken to Ning? She might know something.'

Ryan shook his head. 'I thought I'd speak to you first. Do you reckon I should go up there?'

'Probably,' James said. 'We need to know what's going on. You go put some clothes on. I'll give Ning a call.'

As Ryan scrambled into jeans and a hoodie, over at Nebraska House, Ning woke up and grabbed her mobile out of its charging stand.

'I've no idea what's happened,' Ning said, looking around her room as James explained. She flicked on a bedside lamp when she realised there was nobody asleep on the floor. 'Fay's gone. She's taken her shoes and phone. So Christ knows what she's up to, but I'll bet she's got something to do with it . . .'

37. BOSS

Ryan had dressed for trouble, wearing black boots, a stab vest plus an extendable baton clipped to his belt. As he strode through the courtyard towards The Hangout, keeping a wary eye out for dog turds, James' voice was coming through the com unit buried in his ear.

'I've logged into the London 999 dispatch system,' James said. 'Just under two hours ago, a major incident was reported in Finchley. Flaming van deliberately rammed into garage at 57 Hartwood Road, N3. That's Hagar's place.'

'The van Fay and Ning stole?' Ryan asked quietly.

'It doesn't say, but it's got to be,' James said. 'Five cars destroyed. Fire under control after significant damage to extension. No fatalities, one child taken to hospital as a precaution after smoke inhalation. Hartwood Road remains closed to through traffic.'

'Hagar's gonna be pissed,' Ryan said. 'I'd better shut up now, I'm going inside.'

Ryan was used to The Hangout being filled with people his own age, but now it was mostly men in their late teens and twenties. He recognised Warren and Craig. Some of Hagar's most senior lieutenants were at the back and Ryan felt a tingle down his back as he saw Hagar.

'Where you going, boy?' a big ginger-haired guy with an eye patch said, blocking Ryan in the doorway.

'I got Craig's message,' Ryan said.

The ginger dude looked suspicious until a guy Ryan had seen at the car-wash a few times shouted, 'Ryan's legit. Get over here, kid.'

Ryan walked over to the guy, who was called Max.

'What's up?' Ryan asked.

'Big-time shit hitting fan,' Max told Ryan. 'Eli's boys rammed Hagar's house. Hagar wasn't home, but his boy's in casualty.'

'Shit,' Ryan said.

At the other side of the room, Hagar and Craig stood between two pool tables. Craig was the bigger man and had a hand on Hagar's shoulder.

'Why rush into this?' Craig said soothingly. 'We know the girls stole that van.'

'My boy's in the hospital,' Hagar shouted angrily.

'As a precaution. He just breathed a little smoke. Judy said he's running around the emergency room, happy as Larry.'

'We know Eli bought the gear from the stash house

from Fay Hoyt,' Hagar said. 'He must have an insider. He must have found my grow house and got the girls to rob it.'

Craig shook his head, and his tone got tetchy. 'We don't *know* that for sure. We don't know anything.'

'Are you telling me that my security is so lax that a fifteen-year-old girl managed to find my grow house and my home address with no outside help? Who's supposed to be my chief of security?'

'I am,' Craig admitted.

Ryan knew that Warren had helped the girls find the grow house, and glanced over at a thoroughly uncomfortable expression on his face.

'Plenty of people don't like you, Hagar,' Craig said. 'We have sources. I'm just saying we should get a better picture of what really happened before doing anything rash.'

Hagar took a step back. 'I've made up my mind, Craig. Now are you with me or not?'

Hagar pointed towards the door, showing Craig where to go if he didn't snap into line.

Craig made a subservient nod. 'You're the boss,' he said, a touch reluctantly.

'OK, people. Get in close, listen up,' Hagar shouted.

Everyone had backed up to the edges of the room while Hagar and Craig were fighting. Now they peeled away, moving between and resting butts on the edge of pool tables.

'We've been attacked,' Hagar shouted. 'My home and family is where I draw the line. Eli has provoked us, so he'll be expecting us to come out on the street and hit his dealers. But that ponce isn't the only person with inside information. I've got a list of Eli's other assets. We're gonna hit the streets hard, but not in the places where he's expecting us.'

A few nervous laughs and a couple of whoops went through the assembled thugs.

'Four or five to a car,' Hagar ordered. 'There's a plentiful supply of tools and implements in the playgroup room. Each team gets three targets. And don't come back to me with excuses why you didn't take all of 'em out.'

*

Ning was desperate to know what Fay had been up to, but she couldn't mention any of the stuff she'd found out from James when she got through to her mobile.

'What's happening?' Ning asked. 'You OK?'

Fay sounded jubilant. 'I got hot and sweaty on your floor,' she said casually. 'So I rode up to the allotments on a night bus. Then I took care of the van and some other business.'

'What kind of business?' Ning asked.

'You were right,' Fay explained. 'The fight with Hagar is all mine. It wasn't fair dragging you and Warren into it.'

'What have you done, exactly? Where's the van?'

'I can't stick around and talk. I'm camped out watching The Hangout and people are starting to leave en masse.'

'It's the middle of the night,' Ning said. 'Who's there?'

'It looks like I was right about Hagar's temper being his weak spot.'

'You're not making any sense,' Ning said. 'I thought we were partners. What's going on? Why are you at The Hangout?'

Fay giggled. 'I just started a war, baby! Now I've got to clear my arse out of here in case someone sees me. You're not in school tomorrow, are you?'

'Term ended yesterday,' Ning said.

'Come up to the allotments in the morning,' Fay said. Her breathing seemed deeper and Ning suspected she'd started to walk. 'I'll explain everything. But leave it until ten-thirty, because I need my beauty sleep.'

'Why can't you just tell me now?' Ning asked irritably.

But Fay had hung up.

*

A chunky store clerk named Bijal sat on a stool behind the counter of Rapid 24 supermarket. It was 4:30 a.m. The store was empty, but her eyes strayed from a TV showing a *Friends* re-run as a knackered Volkswagen people carrier stopped on the courtyard out front.

The doors all opened at once. A skinny getaway driver. Three well-built men, including Hagar, plus teens Warren and Ryan. Not many places opened 24/7 and Bijal found nothing unusual in a carload of drunks pulling up. Usually they'd stock up on booze and cigarettes after visiting a nightclub.

But the men got Bijal's full attention when she saw

masked heads and a selection of baseball bats, nightsticks and the scary-looking dude with a white eye patch and bright orange hair. The door was only two metres from the TV. Bijal rushed to the other end of the counter, where an emergency switch could lock the door in a second.

Her palm hit the button, but at the same instant Hagar pushed the door. He felt the electronic bolts shoot outwards, but he was already half a step inside.

'That's not very welcoming, miss,' Hagar said jovially, as he approached the counter.

One of the other men vaulted the counter and slammed Bijal backwards into the cigarettes.

'You going for the alarm?' he shouted.

As Ryan came through the door, the thug slapped Bijal a couple of times, then knocked her down and trod on her stomach.

'Till's open,' Bijal shouted. 'Take the money.'

Bijal had been robbed before, but never by such a large crew. She expected the man to open the till and grab the money inside, but instead he hoiked the entire unit off the counter, tore the plug out of the wall and hurled it at the TV set.

As the TV smashed, the lights flickered. Hagar reached the shelves of booze and began swinging his baseball bat at bottles of wine and spirits. Ryan followed Warren to the back of the store, where the pair began to attack the dairy fridge.

The ceiling was low and Ryan got showered in hot glass as his bat caught a halogen bulb. A second later he got sprayed by exploding cream, as his nose caught the smell of wine and rum trickling across the floor towards his Nikes.

The shop wasn't too big, and within a minute the five-strong crew had smashed up every shelf.

'Ship out,' Hagar ordered. 'Drag the bitch into the street.'

As Ryan helped Hagar drag the screaming clerk out of the front door, Warren jumped back into the people carrier and the getaway driver began revving the engine.

Hagar dished out a couple more nasty kicks. 'You tell your boss Eli to get out of town. He's finished, you hear?'

'Who's Eli?' Bijal pleaded, cupping arms over her face for protection.

Ryan wasn't surprised by Bijal's response, because it wasn't like drug dealers went around introducing themselves to the employees of their legit businesses.

As Ryan slid into the car alongside Warren, the nutter with the eye patch was the last man out of the store, holding a packet of toilet rolls and a flaming lighter. The first stream of flaming tissue went all the way to the back of the shop and fizzled, but the second landed amidst shattered whisky bottles and sent fingers of blue flame in all directions across the shop floor.

'Fun, fun, fun!' Hagar shouted, as he jumped in the back, clumsily treading on Ryan's toes. 'Like olden days.'

The guy with the eye patch got in last and the front wheels squealed as they pulled off with the front passenger door still wide open. In the back, Ryan untangled himself from Hagar, who he now realised was holding the cash drawer.

'Chisel,' Hagar shouted. 'Get me a chisel or something.'

A guy crunched up in the backwards-facing rear row of seats passed Hagar a big flathead screwdriver. They'd driven half a mile and taken a couple of fast corners when the drawer made a satisfying clank, popping open on a coiled spring and a jangle of coins.

Hagar smiled as he ripped out the ten- and twenty-pound notes and threw them at Warren and Ryan.

'You two kids split that up. Call it a gift from your old uncle Hagar.'

38. TROLLEY

Ryan had built a mental picture of Hagar since first hearing his name on campus a couple of months earlier. He'd imagined someone fierce and sinister, who gave orders and left the dirty work to enforcers like Craig.

But this couldn't have been more wrong. Hagar sat in the back of the people carrier, bouncing around like a big kid, cracking jokes and telling stories about places as they drove past: the boarded-up cinema where he got his first proper snog, a shop where he and Craig used to steal fireworks when they were kids and a flat he'd purchased where the ceiling came down two weeks after he'd moved in.

'Building surveyor pointed to all these disclaimers in his contract. So me and Craig hung her out the window by her ankles and that lady wrote a cheque for my new ceiling lickety-split!'

Ryan had never spoken to Fay Hoyt, but James had kept him up to date on Ning's end of the mission and the more time he spent with Hagar, the more he realised that Fay had judged his personality perfectly.

Being a weeknight there weren't many places open, but they found a chicken shop. Hagar bought everyone chips, and soaked his own bag with five sachets of mayonnaise.

'I'm telling you boys, I'm loving this,' Hagar told Ryan and Warren, as he shovelled chips into his mouth. 'The higher up I've got, the less I've enjoyed the life.'

Ryan smiled. 'I'm about as low as you can get. You wanna swap places?'

Hagar whooped up a loud laugh as the big VW entered a tunnel. Then he laughed some more when the thug in the front passenger seat opened a bottle of Pepsi which erupted like a volcano.

They'd driven some miles off Hagar's turf. The tunnel brought them out in east London, with the skyscrapers at Canary Wharf lit up behind streets of newly built apartments. A second thug-stuffed people carrier – a Renault – awaited them in a rubbish collection area at the side of a swanky-looking fourteen-storey block.

'That's Eli's pad,' Hagar explained, as he pointed all the way up to the flashing red light on the roof.

Ryan and Warren shook a couple of hands as Hagar high-fived men getting out of the Renault. Once everyone had pulled on masks, the two teens made up the rear as a ten-strong posse headed through an unlocked metal gate, past a line of recycling bins and up some metal steps to a fire door.

The dude with the eye patch must have staked Eli's building out beforehand. He had exactly the right tool, which he slotted into the gap between two fire doors and jiggled about until it pushed against the metal bar on the inside.

A hot blast came from air-conditioning fans as Ryan stepped inside and caught the smell of chlorine. Another door took them into the rear of a moodily lit swimming pool. A wrinkled woman swam gracefully, until she noticed ten masked men, armed with bats and machetes, striding purposefully across the poolside tiles.

Carpeted stairs took them up another level, to a hotel-like lobby. A grey-haired concierge sat behind a granite counter, half asleep.

'Wakey-wakey!' Hagar said, as two thugs cut behind the countertop to make sure the concierge didn't hit an alarm. 'You've got the lift key, right? We need the fourteenth-floor penthouse.'

'I'm not supposed to,' the man said weakly.

Hagar pointed back at his crew, and someone else knocked a big bowl full of oranges and limes off the countertop.

'You gonna start a fight?' Hagar teased.

The concierge walked stiffly to the glass-doored lifts, one of which had a sign on saying it was in use only between 6 a.m. and midnight. The working lift took a few seconds to arrive and Hagar, five thugs and the concierge squeezed inside.

'You boys look like you need some exercise,' Hagar

said. 'See you up there, don't dawdle.'

Hagar might have been acting like a big kid, but Ryan noted that Warren and the three bulky men accepted the order to walk up fourteen floors without hesitation.

Two flights separated each level, and by the sixth floor the routine of eleven stairs followed by a 180-degree turn on a balcony started making everyone dizzy. Ryan was last through the door on the ground floor, but though his ankle still hurt from earlier, he was the only one who made it to the top without pausing for breath.

The fourteenth floor comprised a single penthouse. The concierge had unlocked for Hagar and the others and Ryan stepped through an elaborately carved double-height door.

'Took your time,' Hagar said brightly. 'Welcome to chez Eli! Where are the others?'

'Coming,' Ryan said breathlessly, as he took in the opulence.

After a marble lobby, the apartment opened out into a huge open space, with floor-to-ceiling glass on three sides and an impressive vista of barges making sedate progress along the River Thames.

A glass staircase led up to bedrooms and a balcony area on the floor above. The elderly concierge had been ordered to sit on a huge leather couch with his hands on his head, and Hagar held court as he grabbed a tall vase decorated with tabloid newspaper headlines and drawings of minor celebrities.

'Eli thinks he's sophisticated,' Hagar said, as he looked at lines of contemporary paintings along the single unglazed wall. 'Does this dog shit look like art to you? And he pays tens of thousands for this crap.'

Inevitably, Hagar let the vase smash at his feet.

'What you all standing around for?' he shouted. 'Let's trash this joint.'

As Warren and the others stumbled into the apartment in a breathless, sweaty lump, the rest of Hagar's crew moved into action, ripping paintings off the wall, smashing up furniture, blocking sinks and switching on taps full blast.

Ryan picked up a wooden sculpture and used it like a spear, punching a hole in a large Damien Hirst painting. Then he teamed up with Warren, stepping out on to the balcony and throwing potted plants into a tiny outdoor pool.

Trashing stuff was fun and the two boys were helpless with giggles as they stumbled back inside, their shirts and jeans dripping wet. The guy with the eye patch was trying to smash a glass dining-table using a cricket bat with nails hammered into it.

'Who wants a Rolex?' Hagar shouted, as he emerged from one of the upstairs bedrooms holding three diamond-crusted watches and a woman's jewellery box. He threw one of them down and two thugs almost cracked heads as they lunged for it.

As someone set off a sprinkler with a burning copy of *Wired* magazine and Warren tucked a nifty Sony laptop under his arm, Ryan was distracted by a crunch of metal outside. He stepped back on to the balcony, peered down over the railing and saw the VW people carrier he'd arrived in with a BMW coupé rammed into its side. There were two more cars. At least a dozen masked men were swarming into the lobby, while the getaway driver in the Renault had been dragged out and was taking a savage beating.

'Guys!' Ryan shouted, as he ran back inside. 'Eli's crew has arrived.'

'What?' Hagar shouted, as he stormed on to the balcony, followed by Warren and a couple of other men. 'Shit, they've got Curtis. Joe, call for backup. Everyone else, let's get downstairs and hit these pricks hard.'

Some of Hagar's crew were up for a fight, but Ryan didn't fancy it and Warren looked properly scared as masked men charged out of the apartment.

Another sprinkler went off, accompanied by a shrieking alarm as the first sprinkler successfully doused a flaming magazine rack and curtains. Ryan realised that he and Warren were the only ones left in the apartment as the concierge stumbled out, holding his mobile phone.

'He's gonna call the cops,' Warren said, as he went after him.

Ryan shrugged and pulled him back. 'Who cares? In a big building like this, the sprinklers will have already alerted the fire brigade and half the neighbourhood has probably dialled 999 by now.'

'Good point,' Warren said, before glancing around nervously. 'Eli's crew outnumber us. If they find us they'll smash every bone in our bodies. And some of Eli's crew have a rep for spraying acid in people's faces.'

Ryan was anxious too, but didn't want Warren to see it. 'I've got no intention of getting into a pitched battle. Let's head down a few flights. We can hide out on another floor until things cool off. Maybe even break into an empty apartment or something.'

Warren still sounded worried as he followed Ryan out, still holding the Sony laptop under his arm. 'Hagar will be pissed off if we chicken out.'

'Go down and fight if you want to,' Ryan said, as he opened the door on to the staircase and listened out for footsteps below. 'I'm sure I can think up an excuse . . . Sounds like it's all clear.'

Ryan began a charge downstairs. After six flights he stopped and Warren almost knocked into him.

'Sssh,' Ryan said, as he crept further down, with a baseball bat ready to swing. He couldn't decipher sounds that seemed close, but muffled.

'What is that?' Warren whispered. 'It doesn't sound like they're on the stairs.'

Ryan crept down two more flights. The fire stairs ran next to the lift shaft, and he placed an ear to the wall.

Then it all clicked into place. 'They're stuck in the lift,' Ryan said, as he thumped a hand against the wall. 'Someone must have pulled the fuse on them.'

Warren smiled uneasily. 'Who's in there? Our guys or theirs?'

'Don't know, don't care,' Ryan said.

As the two lads reached the eighth-floor landing, it sounded like a bunch of men were charging up from a couple of floors below. Ryan decided it was time to leave the staircase. He led Warren through a swing door, into a carpeted hallway with apartment doors on either side. Then the pair crouched low, so they couldn't be seen through the shatterproof glass.

Ryan didn't get up to see how many men went past, but it was either three or four. Warren moved back towards the door once they were past, but Ryan shook his head.

'It's probably still kicking off downstairs. Let's wait it out here.'

But Ryan's plan to sit tight was foiled after less than a minute. Gentle *prepare to evacuate* pips had been echoing through the building since the first sprinkler went off. But now something had properly caught ablaze and the fire alarm kicked in at full blast.

People began emerging from apartments, some in slippers and dressing gowns, while others emerged buttoning trousers and pushing arms through sweatshirts. Ryan ripped off his balaclava and Warren followed his lead.

The atmosphere among the evacuees seemed pretty relaxed. One guy held his drowsy-looking six-year-old by the hand, and joked with a neighbour that someone had probably burned their toast like last time.

'None of Eli's guys saw us,' Ryan said, putting his mouth up to Warren's ear so he could be heard over the alarm. 'This is our chance to sneak out. Two ordinary kids.'

A steady stream of people were moving down the fire

stairs, their pace dictated by an elderly couple half a flight ahead.

'You want a hand?' Ryan asked, as he saw a woman behind, struggling with a baby in one arm and a screaming toddler in the other.

Since the toddler needed attention, Ryan found himself walking down seven floors cradling a tiny sleeping baby. She made a perfect disguise, and the warm milky smell made Ryan feel strangely calm, and reminded him of when his littlest brother Theo was born.

At the bottom of the stairs, Ryan rocked the baby as he looked around warily. The fire alarm had caused the lift to drop mechanically, but there was no sign of whoever had been inside. The residents were calm in the lobby, but shocked when they saw the carnage out front.

The Renault people carrier had been rammed and its unconscious getaway driver was being treated on the ground by a fireman. The VW had been set on fire and its cavernous interior now oozed white fire foam.

Besides two fire engines, there was a motorcycle paramedic treating a badly beaten gang member. Two cop cars had just reached the scene and there was a dramatic pool of blood, and sticky foot prints trailing around the side of the building.

Ryan and Warren joined a mass of residents struggling to comprehend blood, wreckage and a plume of dense smoke coming through the open balcony of the top-floor penthouse. Once he'd passed the baby back to its mother, Ryan turned to Warren.

'The building supervisor might recognise our clothes,' he said. 'We need to get out of here.'

The two teenagers walked around the side of the building, down an alleyway with an identical tower on its other side. They passed two big dudes going the other way, one with a bloodied nose. They had to be from Eli's crew, but they kept their faces down, like their only concern was to not get arrested.

A fire crew was suiting up with breathing gear at the rear of the tower. Ryan led Warren on to a service road, walking fast, but not so fast as to look suspicious. After a few hundred metres they passed signs of a scuffle: a single size-twelve basketball boot, scattered coins and a smashed iPhone.

'That's Joe's boot,' Warren said, unable to resist the temptation of a two-pound coin.

'Which one was Joe?' Ryan asked.

'Ginger, with the eye patch.'

About fifty metres on they passed the machete he'd been carrying, now gory with blood.

'This is heavy shit,' Warren said.

Ryan hopped off the kerb and cut into the car park of a DIY store. Headlamps whizzed by on a busy road at its far side and he figured they'd be fairly safe once they'd made it through the traffic. The lot was empty, apart from three branded delivery vans. They were almost on the embankment up to the road when a shout came that made both lads jump.

'Warren!'

The boys stopped and swivelled. Ryan put one hand on his baton as he crouched down and looked under the truck.

'Hagar?' Ryan said, as he recognised the silhouette, and an enormous man lying flat on the ground behind him, making a soft moan.

'You boys injured?' Hagar asked.

'We're fine,' Ryan said, as stolen Rolexes on both Hagar's arms caught the headlights coming along the road.

'I've got a cut on my thigh, but it's not much. Frank's bleeding bad. Eli had this crazy Chinaman down there with a Samurai sword.'

Ryan stepped under the truck. There wasn't much light, but he could see blood streaming out of a wound on the back of Frank's head. Hagar had ripped off his T-shirt and Frank was holding it against his head, but Ryan pulled it straight off.

'What you doing?' Hagar asked.

'I did a first aid course,' Ryan explained, as he inspected a long gash in the man's head.

Fortunately Frank had a good length of hair and Ryan knew exactly what to do. He whimpered as Ryan used his finger to find the end of the cut.

'This is gonna hurt, but it'll stop the bleeding,' Ryan said, before turning back to Warren. 'We passed a shopping trolley stuck in the bushes back there. Go pull it out and see if it rolls.'

As Warren backed away, Ryan twisted a bundle of hairs from each side of the cut and knotted them together, sealing it up. He repeated this several times at two-centimetre intervals, his patient clenching with pain each time.

'I never would have thought of doing that,' Hagar said admiringly.

Ryan nodded. 'It's stronger than stitches. You know how hard it is when you try to pull a hair out?'

By the time Ryan had finished, Warren had pulled out the abandoned trolley and was running across the car park with it.

'Why don't you try making some more noise?' Hagar said furiously.

'Is it OK?' Ryan asked.

'Front wheels are kinda weird, but it's pushable.'

'I've sealed the cut as best I could,' Ryan explained. 'But he's lost a shitload of blood and he might not make it if he doesn't get proper care.'

Hagar nodded. 'The three of us should be able to lift him into the trolley. One of you boys will have to wheel him back over to the ambulance people.'

Warren didn't say a word, so Ryan stepped up. 'I guess that's down to me then,' he said.

Hagar gave him a friendly pat on the shoulder. 'Good lad. If the cops nab you, keep your trap shut and my legal people will be there before you know it.'

39. CASUALTY

There were two ambulance crews and at least four injuries. Amidst the chaos, nobody asked Ryan any questions and he rode to casualty in the back of an ambulance, keeping Frank calm while the professionals dealt with the unconscious getaway driver.

Ryan wasn't especially squeamish, but the getaway driver's arm was shattered, and something sharp had hit him in the face, leaving a gruesome wound around his eye socket.

Just driving past a hospital always reminded Ryan of his mum dying of cancer. Going inside one, seeing the signs pointing to X-ray and Chemotherapy and the familiar uniforms worn by nurses and porters stirred uncomfortable memories.

Ryan followed Frank's hospital trolley to a cubicle, while the driver got rushed to an intensive care bed.

After a few minutes waiting around, a nurse suggested he go to the waiting area. Three of Hagar's heavies stood by vending machines, while Craig spoke frantically into a cellphone.

'Hey,' Ryan said.

Craig gave orders as soon as he hung up. 'At least two of Eli's casualties have been brought in here, and some of his people are around. I'm heading off to take care of some business. I need you four to stay here and make sure they don't try to attack our wounded.'

Ryan fought sleep as he sat in a plastic chair for more than two hours. Tensions rose when a couple of Eli's boys came by and bought bottles of Lucozade from the vending machine, but they looked as tired as Ryan felt and it never escalated beyond a staring contest.

Ryan was gazing down at gum trodden into the floor tiles when Craig came back and slapped him on the knee.

'Rise and shine, kiddo,' Craig said, as Ryan rubbed his right eye. 'Walk with me.'

Ryan followed Craig through a hundred metres of corridors, eventually reaching the hospital's minor injuries unit. Hagar was there in a cubicle, sat in a wheelchair with his leg strapped up and a crutch resting across his lap.

'Guess who just called me?' Hagar asked.

'Eli,' Craig said.

Hagar looked surprised. 'How'd you know that? Did you speak to Eli first?'

'I know how the man's mind works,' Craig said.

'What did he have to say?'

'Says he didn't start no war and doesn't want this to escalate. He says Fay and that other girl are the ones who wrecked my garage, and that I should watch my CCTV footage if I don't believe him.'

'Have you checked the CCTV?'

'System's in a cupboard at the back of my garage. If the flames didn't melt it, the fire hoses won't have done it much good.'

'A techie might be able to get something out of it by remounting the hard drive in another unit,' Craig suggested.

Hagar shrugged. 'Eli doesn't know shit about my CCTV system, but he must know it wasn't one of his people for him to say that. It's possible he put them girls up to it. But why would Eli burn up the stolen crop, when he could make a mint putting it on the street?'

Craig nodded. 'There's no business sense in what happened tonight. Ramming your house is the action of someone who wants to piss you off on a personal level.'

'Fay Hoyt, the teen terror,' Hagar said dramatically. 'I should have known it's her. She knows I've got a short fuse and it's the kind of stunt her aunt or mother would have pulled.'

Craig looked uncomfortable. 'So where does this leave you and Eli? He must be pretty pissed that you burned his apartment up, and it won't take much for it to kick off over in casualty.'

Hagar smiled. 'Eli says he'll forgive me his interior

decoration bill, if I forgive him for buying the stolen cocaine from Fay.'

Craig looked relieved. 'I haven't done the sums, but that sounds fair. A war will cost us ten times that and the law will be all over us if things turn violent.'

'Eli and I are gonna hug it out on Friday,' Hagar said. 'In the meantime, he's promised to do everything in his power to track down Fay Hoyt.'

'Any leads?'

Hagar shrugged. 'We need to find those girls fast. Spread word that there's a price on their heads. Ten grand for Fay. Three for her accomplice.'

'Fay's always out sniffing for info on the street,' Craig said. 'With ten grand on her head, she'll be putting her neck in a noose every time she surfaces.'

Ryan realised he'd lucked out getting to hear this conversation and he was itching to get away and warn Ning.

'Why'd you bring the kid over?' Hagar asked.

'You said he was OK, and our regular guy's over in casualty with his eyeball hanging out,' Craig explained.

'Ahh, the pick-up,' Hagar said.

Craig laughed. 'Business doesn't stop, just because you throw a hissy fit and declare war.'

Although Craig was his subordinate, there was no indication that Hagar minded Craig's bluntness as he turned to Ryan.

'You up for a trip, boy?' he asked. 'Or is it past your bedtime?

*

It was a bright morning as Ning walked across the allotment holding a brown paper McDonald's bag.

'Bacon and egg McMuffin, orange juice,' she told Fay, as she stepped into the shed and passed it over.

Fay looked happy as she peered into the bag. 'Nothing for you?'

'Scoffed it on the way,' Ning said. 'So what happened last night? Why'd you sneak off?'

Ning knew from James and Ryan, but she'd blow her cover if she let on. Fay gave a rundown about the van, and watching the posse leave The Hangout.

'What happened after that?'

Fay shrugged. 'They all went off in cars. I had no way to follow them, but they must have been going after Eli's crew.'

'And why'd you sneak off?' Ning asked, sounding a little harsh.

'I'm sorry,' Fay said. 'You and Warren weren't comfortable, so I acted alone.'

'The three of us worked together to rob the grow house,' Ning said. 'What gives you the right to go and burn the proceeds?'

'I don't care about money,' Fay said. 'You and Warren can split my share of the money we made on the cocaine.'

Ning shook her head. 'It's not about the money. It's about us being a team.'

'We're not really a team, are we?' Fay said. 'I'm doing all this stuff because Hagar killed *my* aunt and *my* mother.'

Ning didn't say anything, but gave a sympathetic shrug as she settled in a folding chair. Fay took the top off her McMuffin and started eating the bacon.

'So what now?' Ning asked.

'Stay out of the way for a bit,' Fay said. 'Hopefully Eli and Hagar will be at each other's throats for a while. Maybe Eli will even save me the bother of bumping Hagar off.'

Ning had had a text from Ryan telling her that the war was off, but she couldn't tell Fay.

'How can you be so sure?' Ning asked.

'I can't,' Fay admitted. 'But my mum and my aunt both used to say Hagar's unpredictable, but the one thing you can rely on is his temper.'

Ning was tempted to remind Fay that her aunt and mother had both ultimately lost their battle with Hagar. But it would just upset Fay and put her on the defensive, so Ning went for a different tack.

'Have you spoken to Warren?'

'He was part of the posse that left The Hangout. I sent him a couple of texts but he hasn't replied.'

'School's out, we've got money,' Ning said. 'I reckon we should put some distance between ourselves and this neighbourhood until things calm down.'

Fay nodded. 'Nobody seems too bothered that I ran away from my foster-home. I called my social worker a couple of times, just so they don't think I'm dead and start a big investigation. And I don't suppose it'd be national news if you vanished either.'

'I could go back to Nebraska House and pick up my

stuff. Meet you at King's Cross in a couple of hours and take the first train going north.'

Fay shook her head. 'I'm not leaving town. Warren can't come with us. He's tight with his mum and his brother, so he can't just disappear.'

'Why would Warren want to come?' Ning asked. 'Hagar's crew can't suspect that he's involved with us. He was part of the posse, for Jesus' sake!'

Fay smiled and looked embarrassed. 'It's not Warren, it's me. I don't want to move away from him.'

Ning's lower jaw dropped. 'You mean you *really* like him?'

Fay laughed noisily and put a hand over her mouth. 'Yes of course I really like him. What do you think's been going on?'

Ning felt a touch awkward. 'Warren's our best source of information. He's a decent guy, but I thought it was more a friends-with-benefits kind of deal.'

Fay looked disappointed. 'Is that how you saw it? I thought there was a real spark between us.'

'Yeah, I suppose,' Ning said, losing her train of thought. 'Now I think about it. Just . . . I dunno.'

'So do you think Warren likes me?' Fay asked anxiously.

'I'm not exactly a world authority on blokes, but he does seem genuine.'

The two girls smiled at each other as Fay pushed hair off her face and went a bit red.

'If you're gonna stay in town, you've got to lie low,' Ning said.

Fay nodded. 'They'll be looking for us, as a pair. We probably shouldn't hang out.'

Ning felt a twinge of angst, because her mission was to stay close to Fay. 'I think we'll be OK,' Ning said. 'But we should only meet up in central London, not around here.'

'Makes sense,' Fay said. 'There's like ten million people in London. We just need to steer clear of Hagar's territory.'

40. CHATHAM

Ryan wound up at St Pancras Station at 6:15 in the morning, waiting for the first train to Chatham, thirty miles east of London. He was scared he'd fall asleep and miss his stop, so he looked up his arrival time on his phone and set an alarm.

At Chatham, commuters in work clothes crammed the opposite platform as Ryan crossed a footbridge and found Clark waiting in the ticket hall.

'Feeling strong?' Clark asked.

'I'm knackered,' Ryan admitted, as he began following Clark across the station car park to a high-sided truck painted with the logo of a removals firm – *Call us today for a quote. No job too large or small.*

'This'll give you some pep,' Clark said, handing over a dented steel flask as the pair settled into the cab.

Ryan unscrewed the lid and smelled strong black

coffee. He filled two tatty plastic mugs that Clark had rested on the dashboard.

'You like it sweet!' Ryan said, as the heavily sugared coffee hit his tongue. It wasn't to his taste, but he'd missed a night's sleep, so he hoped that a caffeine and sugar rush would blow off the cobwebs.

Clark swigged his coffee in two gulps, then reversed expertly out of a cramped space.

'Sounds like I missed all the fun and games in town last night,' Clark said, as he turned out of the station.

They started down a semi-rural road, with station traffic queuing in the opposite direction. Ryan kept yawning as he gave Clark a rundown of the previous night's events. He had to think carefully and leave out stuff that he'd picked up second-hand via James and Ning.

'Hagar's bloody temper!' Clark laughed. 'It'll be the death of him.'

'If he's so volatile, how did he get to become top dog?' Ryan asked.

Clark considered this for a couple of seconds. 'Hagar's temper means people fear him, but unlike most bosses, he hasn't got much of an ego. He's got a good crew around him, and he usually listens to what they say.'

'So what are we up to?' Ryan asked.

'Cleaning up shit,' was all Clark gave up. 'In broad bloody daylight.'

'Were we supposed to move the drugs last night?' Ryan asked.

Clark snorted and shook his head. 'Drugs, huh?'

Clark reached for the centre console and turned on local radio. Ryan began another question, but he got shushed.

'Traffic report's coming up on the hour.'

Ryan was annoyed that he'd given up all the gossip and got nothing out of Clark in return.

Twenty minutes after leaving the station, the truck pulled off-road. Everything in the cab juddered as they moved down a rutted path towards a large aluminium-sided shed. Although it looked shabby, Ryan noticed that some parts of the roof had been recently repaired.

Clark turned the truck back towards the main road, then reversed up to the building's main door.

'The countryside stinks,' Clark moaned, as he flung his door open.

Ryan had his best trainers on, and was grateful that the ground was baked hard, as he walked towards the shed. Clark opened up, and Ryan stepped in and looked curiously at metal stalls, linked up with perished rubber pipes, and the odd remnant of dried-out cow shit.

'Is this for milking?' Ryan asked.

Clark shrugged. 'There's not been a cow milked here in a decade.'

Further inside, the milking stalls had been ripped out, though perished rubber tubes still dangled from the ceiling. There was an acrid burnt smell, and scorch marks across the floor. To the left and right huge mounds of black bags were lined up against the wall.

'My eyes are watering,' Ryan croaked.

'You don't want to breathe too much of this in,'

Clark said, as he pointed at the black bags. 'All that lot needs to go in the back of the van.'

The first bag felt heavy, and as Ryan picked it up the bottom split and the contents spewed over the floor. He was surprised to see hundreds of shrivelled pieces of white plastic insulation, which had been cut in lengths of between one and two metres and the wire inside stripped out.

'It'd make my life a lot easier if they bought decent quality bags,' Clark explained. 'You've gotta support 'em from underneath or that'll happen every time.'

Clark showed Ryan the knack, taking three bags off the pile, cradling them in his arms and then waddling to the truck. Ryan's arms were shorter, so he could only manage two, and he wished he had something more than a T-shirt to wear as sharp ends of plastic strips dug into his arms.

As he walked back and forth to the truck, Ryan tried to understand what he was looking at. None of the bags were knotted, so whenever Clark faced the other way, he'd peek inside for some kind of clue.

But it was all just plastic insulation. Ryan guessed the insulated wire was being imported in bulk, but that some reels had drugs rather than wire encased within the plastic. The scorch marks on the floor and the smell must have been made when the plastic had melted off to release the drugs and metal inside.

Ryan's arm was bleeding by the time the sacks along one wall had diminished by a half. He noticed a powdery handprint around the top of one bag, and after a furtive glance to make sure Clark was still lugging a load up to the truck, he tore out the section of the bag with the handprint and tucked it into his pocket.

That was as exciting as it got, as Ryan made more than fifty trips, dealing with stench, cuts and his grazed ankle. When they'd moved a couple of hundred bags, Clark clambered in the back of the truck and started stacking the bags they'd thrown inside.

Beneath the last bags were large cardboard reels on which the wire had been coiled. Two reels fitted into a bin liner, but mostly they had just been stacked against the wall. There were two kinds of reel, one with a red label marked *Sonata X Loudspeaker Cable*, and a second with a blue label marked *Sonata Supreme Audiophile Cable*. Both products claimed to have been made in China.

Ryan was starting to realise that he had a few things to remember, such as his location, the names on the reels, the number plate of the removal van and one or two things Clark had said.

Clark was never more than twenty metres away, so Ryan couldn't risk snapping a picture. But his phone had a voice-activated recorder app, so he set it running and made some verbal notes.

It was past nine in the morning when Ryan and Clark each took a final armful of bags, lobbing them into the truck's crammed rear in a haze of triumph and exhaustion. Ryan's shirt and jeans were glued on with sweat and his arms speckled with small cuts as he found a standpipe on the outside of the shed and splashed himself with cool, slightly discoloured water.

Clark did an inspection of the former milking shed, and came out shaking his head. 'That's as clean as I can make it,' he told Ryan. 'But scorching the bloody floor like that, all for a few hundred quid's worth of metal . . .'

They stopped at a snack van in a lay-by and bought sausage and egg baps and weak tea in polystyrene cups. Then Clark drove on to a waste processing plant. The air around it had an evil-smelling haze, and clouds of seagulls fluttered around the back of rubbish trucks as they dumped loads at the base of a huge mound.

Clark's cargo was strictly off the books, so he drove in through an exit meant for staff parking, and handed two hundred in cash to the man who unlocked the gate.

'It's not good coming here at this time of day,' the tip worker complained. 'There's too many eyes.'

Clark shrugged as if to say, *what can you do*, before driving through the gate.

While dustcarts could tip their load, Clark and Ryan had to open up the rear of the removal van and throw out all the reels and bags of plastic insulation. Each time the mound got to fifty or so bags, a bulldozer would sweep across and push the whole lot into the main debris pile.

Ryan was conscious that one of his best pairs of trainers was squelching in juices spilled from a thousand rubbish bags, and just to make things absolutely perfect, Clark roared with laughter as a huge splat of seagull shit hit the back of his head.

'You're a good lad,' Clark told Ryan, when he

dropped him back off at Chatham Station. 'I'll tell Craig you're worth whatever they're paying you.'

Ryan realised that nobody had offered to pay him anything as he waited for the train home. It was past rush hour when he settled into a seat, short of a night's sleep and stinking of burnt plastic, BO and refuse.

He pushed a blackened hand down his jeans and pulled out a smartphone down to 9% battery.

'I can't fit all the strands together,' he told James. 'But I think we're close to working out how Hagar's crew brings drugs into the country.'

41. CREWDSON

The allotments were at their quietest on weekday mornings. Fay and Ning sat in front of the shed in folding chairs, catching the sun and occasionally disturbed by the high-speed trains shooting past at the allotment's far end.

'We could go see a movie,' Ning suggested.

'I need to buy sun cream,' Fay said. 'My skin's really fair. I'm gonna turn into a lobster.'

'You don't wanna see a movie?'

'Warren's gone to bed. We can all meet up and do something tonight,' Fay suggested.

Warren was a nice guy, but Fay falling for him meant Ning risked getting pushed out of the picture. As she wondered about finding a way to make Fay and Warren break up, Ning picked up a text from James, saying that he'd just heard from Ryan.

Fay had her eyes closed and Ning was tapping out a reply when she noticed two young men striding their way. Sun coming from behind made it hard to see details, but Ning was instantly suspicious because allotments were a pastime for the middle-aged and elderly.

'We've got company,' Ning said, as she gave Fay's knee a squeeze.

As Fay sat up straight, Ning realised it was Eli's deputy, Shawn. Ning made sure she had her backpack within reach. The situation was super awkward, because Ning knew Eli and Hagar had made up, but she couldn't tell Fay without breaking cover.

'Afternoon, ladies,' Shawn said, as he came within a couple of metres.

Fay squinted and held a hand over her brow. 'How'd you find us?' she asked.

Shawn laughed. 'I like to know all about the people I do business with,' he explained. 'I had you trailed after our first meet-up.'

'I don't know why you're here,' Fay said dismissively. 'You didn't want Hagar's shit, so I got rid of it.'

Shawn laughed. 'And in such spectacular fashion.'

'So what *are* you here for?'

Shawn laughed and spread his arms out wide. 'Hagar's put a bounty on you two ladies,' he explained. 'Although I expect my boss will waive the reward, as a gesture of goodwill.'

As Shawn and his buddy stopped walking, Ning saw three more guys closing from behind. She double-tapped her earlobe to activate her com, and sent James the text she'd been typing with the addition of SHAWN HERE NOW HOSTILE!!!

'And what if I don't want to come with you?' Fay spat, as she glanced around nervously.

'That's why I brought my friends,' Shawn said. 'This can be civilised, or you can come kicking and screaming. But you'll come.'

Fay and Ning glanced at one another. While nothing got said, it was clear neither of them wanted to go down without a fight.

Fay moved first, sending her plastic chair sideways as she sprang up. Ning dug her right hand in the dirt beside her chair and flicked a big clod up towards Shawn and his pal.

A natural runner, Fay sprang like a gazelle, deftly avoiding the lunging arm of Shawn's accomplice and vaulting a strawberry patch on the next allotment. Ning was slower, but strong. As Shawn shielded his face from the flying earth, she went on the attack, grabbing her lightweight chair and using it as a battering ram. Shawn doubled up as the plastic leg hit him in the groin.

While Fay disappeared towards the allotment's main gates, Ning charged in the other direction. A suntanned old-timer told Ning not to step in his broccoli and demanded to know *what the devil* was going on as she stumbled over his plot.

Ning was pissed off when she looked back. Shawn was still down, but the three guys who'd approached from behind were all on her case, presumably deterred from going after Fay by her sheer speed.

One of Ning's pursuers moved way faster than the others and closed relentlessly. Realising she'd be caught in seconds, Ning stopped running, grabbed a stick out of the ground and snapped it to make a sharp point. She spread out wide, and waited.

'See what you get,' Ning taunted.

But it wasn't just the sprinter's legs that were fast. As Ning swung with the stick, he ducked, then thrust forwards from a low position. He almost head-butted Ning in the chest, but she managed to turn. As she set off again, she felt the man's hand on her backpack and only broke free by letting it drop off her arm.

James' voice sounded on the com in Ning's ear. 'Talk to me. What's happening?'

Ning didn't get to answer because she'd cut across another plot and her trainer landed awkwardly in a furrow. She stumbled forward, keeping upright for a couple of steps but losing it when she crashed into a bamboo frame used for growing runner beans.

As Ning's body ploughed into freshly dug earth, the sprinter landed on top of her. She caught him with a nice elbow on the nose, but he had enormous shoulders and massive biceps that forced the air out of her lungs.

Ning continued to struggle as Shawn stumbled across the loose ground, then pointed a handgun at her head from less than a metre.

'Keep still, missy,' he shouted, clearly unhappy about getting a chair leg in the balls. 'Break her arm.'

'Ning, are you all right?' James asked, over the com.

'I've got your locator. I'm getting on my bike and I'm calling for backup.'

'Break her damned arm,' Shawn repeated, as blood from the guy on top of her's nose dripped on to Ning's T-shirt.

She'd fought her way out of all kinds of situations, but the guy was twice her weight and it was all muscle. Ning grunted and bucked as he squeezed her wrist, but he got her arm up behind her back and began pulling tight.

'No,' Ning sobbed. Then a scream, 'Somebody help me!'

'This'll teach you to hit me in the balls,' Shawn shouted, placing his boot on the back of Ning's head as her arm made a sickening crunch.

*

'James?' Ryan yelled, taking off his garbage-soaked trainers before walking into the kitchen of their flat.

James hadn't had time to send a message, but half-eaten marmalade toast and a laptop open at the kitchen table gave Ryan the impression that he'd left in a hurry. Ryan was torn: part of him wanted to get in bed and crash for a few hours, but he was also excited about all the stuff he'd found out in Chatham and he wanted to do some investigating.

Whichever he chose, Ryan needed to shower first. He stripped in front of the washing machine, lobbed everything including his trainers inside and put them on a hot wash with a big squirt of Dettol.

His body had lines of light and dark, where clothing

had protected him from dirt. The shower water ran slate grey as chunks of soot and dirt dropped out of his hair. The cool blast perked him up and he enjoyed feeling clean as he sat on the edge of his bed, rubbing antiseptic down his pock-marked arms. He put plasters over several cuts and replaced the dressing on his grazed ankle.

People forget rapidly, so CHERUB agents are trained to get everything in writing as soon as it's safe to do so. Ryan opened up a standard form on his laptop, typing a few paragraphs explaining what had happened overnight, then replaying the audio notes on his phone and making sure he hadn't forgotten anything.

Once he'd saved the note and e-mailed a copy to mission control on campus, Ryan opened up the special equipment box in James' bedroom and found a drug testing kit. Using tweezers, he picked white specks off the plastic bag with the handprint and dropped them into a pale green solution.

After swirling the test tube and letting it settle for half a minute, Ryan dipped a strip of test paper into the solution. Pale green indicated some level of cocaine, but the paper turned to the colour of spinach, indicating that his tiny sample was close to one hundred per cent pure.

Satisfied that he was on to the source of high purity cocaine he'd been sent on the mission to find, Ryan opened a web browser and did a Google search for *Sonata Loudspeaker Cable*. The search came back with the company's US website and he skimmed through the home page, reading that Sonata produced *reference quality loudspeaker cable at highly competitive prices.*

Ryan had never previously realised that cabling could make a hi-fi system sound better, and baulked when he saw that Sonata's top line Carbon X cable sold for a hundred dollars per yard.

Ryan's next click took him to a page listing Sonata's overseas suppliers. The UK distributor was a company called AV Master, based in Rochester. Ryan hadn't heard of Rochester until that morning, when his train stopped there five minutes before meeting Clark at Chatham.

For the next step, Ryan had to log into a secure browser. He yawned as he entered a long password, and swiped his left thumb on the laptop's fingerprint pad. Now he was in the CHERUB system, through which he could access databases run by British Intelligence, as well as other government agencies such as driver and vehicle registrations, company data and Revenue and Customs tax records.

Some of the databases took ages to respond, but within fifteen minutes Ryan had printed off a list of the directors of AV Master, along with ownership details for the removal truck. Apparently the removals firm had sold the truck at auction several years earlier and the vehicle seemed to have been purchased under a false name.

Ryan only had a low-level security clearance, so he couldn't access any records held by private companies such as banks, internet providers and mobile phone companies. He was tired and decided to take a nap and leave the background investigation to James. He was closing browser tabs when he noticed a familiar face on screen.

He was a director of the cable import company, AV Master, and Ryan knew it was important, but spent half a minute racking his brain before working out where he knew him from. The picture was at least a decade out of date and he had different hair, but Ryan finally twigged that it was the man who'd made his laminated membership pass the first time he'd visited The Hangout.

Ryan confirmed Barry's identity with a visit to The Hangout website. His full name was Barry Crewdson, manager of The Hangout centre in Kentish Town and deputy director of The Hangout London. Up to this point, Ryan had thought The Hangout was a community centre that had been infiltrated by drug dealers. But this started to change as he began studying the website and looking at government records for its senior staff and directors.

According to the website, the organisation had been founded in 1988 by Marie Crewdson, who'd been made Lady Crewdson by the Queen in 2004. The Hangout was a charity, with a network of thirty after-school clubs in England and Wales and centres for orphaned children in Iran and Pakistan. Lady Crewdson was chairperson of The Hangout and the other senior staff were mostly members of the Crewdson family.

The fact that the Crewdson family ran The Hangout

was no secret. Ryan quickly found newspaper interviews with various Crewdsons, mainly focused on child poverty and the work their community centres did with underprivileged kids.

In the pictures accompanying the articles, the Crewdsons were a sprawling, cheerful family who wore corduroy trousers and cable knit sweaters. They all seemed to have loads of kids, they all worked tirelessly for charity and every newspaper picture seemed to include a Labrador or a floppy sheepdog.

Having found the link between Barry and the company that was importing the drug-filled cables, Ryan started looking into government records and Google results for other members of the Crewdson family.

Lady Crewdson herself seemed pretty clean, though Ryan decided it was dodgy that the land registry showed that this saintly charity worker had paid six and a half million for a villa overlooking Regents Park. Besides AV Master, Barry Crewdson owned shares in a trans-European trucking company and a luggage importer. His brother and two sisters owned more companies, including a chain of scrap metal dealerships, betting shops, casinos, jewellery shops and a half a dozen property companies.

It all fitted together nicely. The Crewdsons were the last people you'd suspect. A wholesome sprawling family, who'd somehow come to make tens of millions of pounds while owning a network of companies that were ideally suited to transporting drugs and laundering drug money.

Ryan's lingering doubts got quashed when he got past reading upbeat pieces in the national press and unearthed shadier dealings on local blogs and the websites of local newspapers. A Hangout centre in north Wales had been branded a *hive of drug dealing* by a local councillor. A quantity of cocaine had been seized at a centre in Manchester. A Hangout mentor in East Sussex had been released on police bail following a drug squad investigation and Lady Crewdson herself had threatened to sue a journalist who'd claimed that a new Hangout centre in Cardiff had been funded by donations from a local drug baron.

The more Ryan tapped his mouse and clicked his keyboard, the dodgier the Crewdson family looked. He burst out laughing when he found that the former bowling club that had been Hagar's grow house was owned by Pegasus Properties, which was in turn owned by a Jersey-based company that had paid three hundred thousand pounds in dividends to Lady Crewdson's three granddaughters.

Ryan realised he'd hit on something huge, but after an hour online he got sick of waiting for James to get home, so he e-mailed all of his discoveries to mission control on campus and crashed out on his bed, hoping to catch up on some sleep.

42. CHASE

Ning felt weak as Shawn marched her up a steep flight of stairs, behind a Turkish social club. The rooms had been a dental surgery in a past life, and there was still a slight mintiness in the stale air.

Ning got a rickety chair in what had been a waiting room. The sprinter had sat behind her in the car, so Ning got her first proper view of him as he sat opposite. Dark-skinned, handsome, no older than twenty. His T-shirt bulged over massive arms and chest and in different circumstances Ning would have considered him hot.

'Goldfarb Dental Surgery,' Ning said, slurring her words as if she was on the edge of consciousness and knowing – or at least fairly optimistic – that James could hear over the com. 'Turkish social club. What you taking me here for? Is Eli Turkish?'

'Cut the yap,' Shawn said, as he pulled out his phone.

As Shawn dialled, two of the other three heavies were in the doorway. The third couldn't resist going into the dentist's room across the hall and messing around with the chair. Ning felt queasy every time she looked at her upper arm, with the broken bone supporting a huge dome of painfully bulging flesh, getting bigger all the time from internal bleeding.

She closed her eyes, hoping she'd faint and come around in a better place, but James' voice brought her back into the room. It seemed loud because the tiny speaker was inside her ear, but nobody else could hear it.

'Roger your location,' James said, as his motorbike rumbled in the background. 'I'm gonna pull over and look it up.'

Shawn on his mobile sounded like some comedy sidekick, getting slapped down for incompetence. When he ended the call with Eli, he acted like nothing had happened and took his anger out on his henchmen.

'Why did all four of you go after her?' Shawn shouted, as he pointed at Ning. 'Eli wants both girls and no excuses.'

'It was like that other girl had a rocket up her arse,' one of the guys said.

Another added, 'Usain Bolt or something . . .'

'You should be able to catch one schoolgirl between four of you,' Shawn spat.

One of the guys in the doorway didn't like Shawn's tone and faced him off. 'Maybe you'd have caught her, if you hadn't let a fifteen-year-old girl take you down.'

Shawn stepped up and went eyeball to eyeball. 'You think you're someone now, boy? I was working for Eli when you still had stabilisers on your bike.'

The guy facing Shawn off stood his ground. 'I know exactly who *you* are,' he sneered. 'Jumped-up errand boy, for the leader of a crew that's got no balls. We should be out on the street taking care of Hagar's crew, not worrying ourselves over a couple of schoolgirls.'

Ning perked up, hearing her captors fighting amongst themselves, and couldn't resist stirring it. 'He's got a point you know, Shawn.'

Shawn swivelled and scowled at Ning. 'You want me to break your other arm?'

Ning shrugged. 'I can't believe you *all* left with me,' she said, trying to sound as chipper as the pain allowed. 'When Fay saw you all leaving with me, she'll have gone straight back to the shed to pick up our gear. If one of you had stayed behind you'd have had a chance, but by now? She'll be on a train to somewhere far away.'

'Who asked you?' Shawn spat.

'She's right though,' the sprinter said, as he played with the wedge of bloody tissue stuffed up his right nostril.

'Jesus!' Shawn shouted, as he spun furiously and slammed his mobile phone at the wall. 'Why do I have to work with you idiots?'

The Samsung flip phone separated from its battery as it spun to a halt under the chair next to Ning. She used her good arm to pick it up and spoke in her most deadpan voice.

'I think you've broken it.'

Shawn's head was bright red and his eyes looked like they were about to shoot out of their sockets.

'You,' he said, pointing at the sprinter. 'Stay here, don't take your eye off her. The rest of you, put your heads together. Get out on the street and look for Fay Hoyt.'

'Look where, boss?' the one who'd been messing about in the dentist's chair asked.

Ning heard James over the com. 'We've located the club. We're less than two minutes away.'

She took note of *we're* and wondered if Ryan was his backup.

'Go back to the shed on the allotment,' Shawn ordered. 'Look for clues. Letters from relatives, old train tickets, that kind of shit. Fay's been living in that shed. There's got to be some indication of who she knows or where she's going.'

The three burly men sulked like kids who'd just been given a detention as they headed sourly towards the door.

'Five seconds,' James told Ning. 'Stun grenade.'

Ning glanced towards the window as the top of an aluminium ladder hit the wall outside. The man who shot up it wore a black riot helmet. He thrust a padded glove through the glass and lobbed a grey cylinder inside. As Shawn and his crew looked towards the noise, Ning dived across the waiting room chairs, wrapping her good arm over her eyes and keeping her mouth open so that the blast didn't make her eardrums pop.

As a sharp bang and bright blue flash erupted, something smashed the door in the club downstairs.

'Police. Everybody, down, down, down.'

Four cops in riot gear started running up the stairs. The one on the ladder kicked his way through the glass, followed by James, who was more cautious than the cops because he was in T-shirt, jeans and motorcycle helmet.

'On the ground!' cops shouted. 'Hands on your heads.'

Ning enjoyed seeing a huge riot cop body-slam Shawn.

'Kidnapping,' the cop told him. 'That's ten years, pal.'

James winced when the smoke cleared and he saw the state of Ning's arm. 'You OK?' he shouted.

'Just the arm,' Ning said.

'I won't bother waiting for an ambulance,' James said. 'I'll get one of the cop cars to take you to hospital and I'll follow on my bike.'

The chaos settled down to grunts and moans as the cops got everyone in cuffs and started reading them their rights. The muscular sprinter had put up the biggest fight and it took three officers to get his hands into position for cuffing.

As the breathless cops backed away, Ning noticed the weapon holstered to James' belt.

'Is there a cut on my back?' Ning asked. 'I think I can

feel blood.'

As James leaned forward to take a look, Ning snatched the Taser from his belt. Running on rage, she aimed it at the sprinter's back from less than a metre, and pressed the trigger. A metal barb shot out, punching through his T-shirt and delivering fifty thousand volts between the shoulder blades.

As James spun around, Ning gave a second squeeze on the trigger and yelled, 'That's for breaking my arm, you son of a bitch.'

'Whoa!' James yelled.

James had shown the cops his intelligence service ID, but they had no idea about CHERUB and he had to step in the way to stop the cops from arresting Ning too.

'She's good,' James shouted. Then more quietly to Ning as he snatched the Taser off her and gestured for the cops to back off, 'That's not cool!'

But although James was determined to prove himself as a mission controller, he still had a lot of empathy with the stuff that young CHERUB agents have to go through and he couldn't help seeing the funny side of what Ning had done.

'You're lucky there's so many cops around,' Ning yelled, as James pushed her backwards. 'Or I'd keep zapping until the battery ran out.'

43. MASSAGE

Three months later

'I love what you've done with this place,' Ryan said, as he stepped into James' quarters on CHERUB campus, straddling piles of dirty clothes and almost knocking a pile of well-thumbed motorbike magazines and a coffee mug off the edge of the kitchen cabinet.

'Have you met Kerry before?' James asked, glancing towards the attractive Asian woman on the sofa.

'I've seen you around,' Ryan said, as he reached across and shook her hand. 'James talked about you all the time when we were on the mission.'

'Good things I hope,' Kerry said.

'Slagging you off constantly,' Ryan joked. 'How long are you over from the States for?'

'Two weeks,' Kerry said. 'I'm attending an academic conference in Cambridge.'

'Cool,' Ryan said, as James walked behind the sofa and gave Kerry a kiss.

'Hope I'm not late,' Ning said, coming through the door. 'Traffic jam on the way back from physiotherapy. I brought popcorn. Chocolate or salty caramel... Kerry, hi!'

'How's the arm?' James asked.

'Weak and pale,' Ning said, as she held it out with a floppy wrist. 'Apparently it'll be at least six months before it's back to full strength. But hopefully I can go on some missions before then.'

Ning tripped on James' dirty running gear as Kerry stood up to kiss her on the cheek. 'Congrats!' Ning said. 'Show us the ring.'

'Ring?' Ryan said.

'How did you know?' Kerry asked, as she showed off her engagement finger. 'It's supposed to be under wraps.'

Ning shrugged. 'You know campus gossip. I think everyone knows.'

'Knows what?' Ryan asked.

'James popped the question,' Ning said. 'How can you *not* know that?'

Ryan shrugged. 'That's girly gossip. So when's the baby due?'

'Oh you're funny, Ryan,' James said. 'How about you sit your arse on my sofa before I kick it?'

'I would if it wasn't covered in porno mags and dirty clothes,' Ryan answered.

'He'd *better* improve his personal habits if he thinks

he's gonna marry me,' Kerry said.

'Have you set the day?' Ning asked, as she dropped on to the sofa next to Kerry.

'It won't be for a good while,' Kerry said.

'It's really because we're living apart,' James explained. 'I'm working here, she's still studying in America.'

'We've been going out since I was twelve, on and off,' Kerry said, as she smiled at James. 'He said it's time we really committed to each other. Long-distance relationships are hard, but this one's worth fighting for.'

'Now where's this bloody preview disk?' James asked.

'I don't know how you can live in this squalor,' Kerry said. 'You must waste half the day just trying to find stuff.'

'I know where things are, as long as people don't keep moving them,' James said.

After a couple of minutes, James worked out that the disk he was looking for had been in his DVD player all along and pressed play.

'So this is a preview of a BBC *Panorama* programme that's going out next Tuesday,' James said. 'It's all about the Crewdsons, The Hangout and the whole scandal.'

'The one I so brilliantly uncovered,' Ryan said, as James realised there was no room on the sofa and wheeled the office chair over from his desk.

'If your head gets any bigger, Ryan, you won't get it through the door,' Ning said.

'You and Ning should totally get it on,' James said.

Kerry nodded in agreement. 'There's definitely chemistry between you two.'

Ning scoffed. 'He's got his psycho girlfriend Grace, and I've got more sense.'

'Does Hagar get mentioned in this documentary?' Ryan asked, keen to change the subject.

James shook his head. 'Hagar seemed like the big cheese, but in the end he was just one of fifty street operators who sold gear for the Crewdsons. Fay and Ning trashed Hagar's grow house and his supply of coke and heroin went down the pan. One of the cops told me that Eli's still limping along, but Hagar's vanished.'

'I don't suppose he's short of a few quid, mind,' Ning said.

'I still can't believe that Barry guy was a drug kingpin,' Ryan said. 'Clarks shoes, ginger beard. He just seemed like a science teacher, or some other massive knob.'

'Isn't that exactly why the Crewdsons got away with it for so long?' Kerry asked.

'All right, it's playing,' James said, as he reached over the back of the sofa and grabbed a handful of popcorn. 'Everyone shut the hell up.'

*

Fay Hoyt gripped Warren around the waist as their bicycle came to a halt under a huge oak. She grabbed four neatly folded bath towels out of a saddlebag and cradled them in her arm as she gave Warren a long kiss on the lips.

'The nurse look is sexy,' Warren said, as he admired breasts packed inside a crisp white polo shirt, which went along with navy trousers and new white pumps.

'Kinky,' Fay teased, as she cradled the back of Warren's neck and blew gently inside his ear. 'I love you.'

'Stay on the bike then,' Warren said. 'We'll just keep on riding.'

'Nah,' Fay said, giving a slight smile as she took a single step backwards. 'I'll be fifteen minutes, tops.'

Fay looked back and blew a kiss as she started down a footpath between tall trees. She'd expected to feel more nervous, but low sun cutting through branches and golden leaves crunching underfoot gave her a sense of calm.

Alessandro's Health Resort nestled deep in woodland. A huge two-storey cabin, clad in Douglas fir beams, with steam rising off hot tubs on guest balconies and a car park stuffed with very expensive metal.

Fay slid a magnetic pass through a lock on a side door. For eight hundred pounds a night, the guests walked on marble and thick carpet, but Fay found herself in a windowless service corridor, its breeze-block walls lined with electrical ducts and exposed water pipes.

She moved briskly. A maintenance man with a bunch of keys the size of a football hanging off his belt didn't bat an eyelid as Fay walked past. She had every detail right, from the corporate logo embroidered on her trouser pocket to the ultra-plush towels on her arm.

Another swipe with the pass took Fay into the piped jazz and vanilla-scented air of the health spa's treatment area. A client had dripped her way along the marble tiles, but a cleaner would be along within a few moments to mop up.

The corridor forked. Fay glimpsed people in gym kit, drinking mocktails, as she took a left at a sign pointing to *Treatment Suites 11–19*. Fay knocked on the door of suite seventeen, and shuffled in without waiting for a response.

The man lying on a massage table was mixed race, early forties, a touch overweight. The massage therapist wore too much make-up and had the bulky shoulders of a tennis pro. She turned swiftly, and barked when she saw that Fay wore the uniform of Alessandro's junior staff, 'This room is in use. Come back to clean later.'

Fay put on an east-European accent and sounded sheepish. 'Are you Magdalena?'

'Yes.'

'There's a personal call for you at the front desk. I was asked that you must come, urgently.'

The therapist looked startled. 'Is it my mother? Why can't they transfer the call here?'

'I don't know,' Fay shrugged. 'It's my first day.'

Magdalena apologised to her client and wiped massage oil off her hands, before heading out of the room. The massage suites were lit with flickering LED candles and the atmosphere was kept humid. Sweat beaded on Fay's back as she stepped up to the massage table.

'It's Erasto, isn't it?' Fay said, dropping the accent.

The man was on his belly, with his face staring at the floor through a hole in the massage table.

'Do I know you?' he asked, propping himself on his

elbow and looking around.

'You used to prefer Hagar,' Fay said, as she studied a long pink scar over the man's heart. 'I heard about your little health scare. This place seems to be working out though. You're looking very trim.'

Hagar realised who he was sharing the room with and sat up straight. Fay knocked two of her four towels on to the floor, unveiling a silenced pistol.

'I'm afraid this health kick isn't going to work out for you, Erasto.'

'I've got money,' Hagar begged. 'I can make you rich . . .'

Hagar raised his hands as Fay aimed the gun. 'My mum taught me to shoot,' she said. Then in a sing-song voice, 'One through the heart, one through the head. Then you know he's really dead.'

Fay pulled the trigger twice. It was a good silencer, there was very little noise. She put the smoking gun back amidst the four towels and felt heat from its barrel as she headed out, opening the door with a kick so that she didn't leave DNA or fingerprints.

She walked briskly towards Warren and the bike. He baulked at the kiss she offered, grossed out by the tiny blood specks on her cheek and the matter-of-fact way she'd just made him an accessory to murder. But she put a hand on Warren's heart and it was insanely good feeling her warmth as he pedalled away.

'You and me are gonna grow old together,' Fay said softly.

Read on for a taste of *Rock War*,
the first in Robert Muchamore's
explosive new series!

Prologue

The stage is a vast altar, glowing under Texas moonlight. Video walls the size of apartment blocks advertise Rage Cola. Close to the stadium's fifty-yard line, a long-legged thirteen-year-old is precariously balanced on her big brother's shoulders. She's way too excited.

'JAY!' she screams, as her body sways. 'JAAAAAAAY I LOVE YOU!'

Nobody hears, because seventy thousand people are at it. It's noise so loud your ears tickle inside. Boys and girls, teens, students. There's a ripple of anticipation as a silhouette comes on stage, but it's a roadie with a cymbal stand. He bows grandly before stepping off.

'JET!' they chant. 'JET . . . JET . . . JET.'

Backstage the sound is muffled, like waves crashing against a sea wall. The only light is a green glow from emergency exit signs.

Jay is holding his queasy stomach. He's slim and easy on the eye. He wears Converse All Stars, ripped jeans and a dash of black eyeliner.

An immense roar comes out of the crowd as the video walls begin a thirty-second countdown film, sponsored by a cellphone maker. As Jay's eyes adjust to the light, he can see a twenty-metre-tall version of himself skateboarding downhill, chased by screaming Korean schoolgirls.

'THIRTEEN,' the crowd scream, as their feet stamp down the seconds. 'TWELVE, ELEVEN . . .'

On screen, the girls knock Jay off his skateboard. As he tumbles a smartphone flies out of his pocket and when the girls see it they lose all interest in Jay and stand in a semicircle admiring the phone instead.

'THREE . . . TWO . . . ONE . . .'

The four members of Jet emerge on stage, punching the air to screams and camera flashes.

Somehow, the cheering crowd always kills Jay's nerves. Thousands of bodies sway in the moonlight. Cheers and shouts blend into a low roar. He places his fingers on the fret board and loves the knowledge that moving one finger will send half a million watts of power out of speaker stacks the size of trucks.

And the crowd goes wild as the biggest band in the world starts to play.

1. Cheesy Crumbs

Camden, North London

There's that weird moment when you first wake up. The uneasy quarter second where a dream ends and you're not sure where you are. All being well, you work out you're in bed and you get to snuggle up and sleep another hour.

But Jay Thomas wasn't in bed. The thirteen-year-old had woken on a plastic chair in a school hall that reeked of burgers and hot dogs. There were chairs set out in rows, but bums in less than a quarter of them. A grumpy dinner lady squirted pink cleaning fluid on a metal serving counter at the side of the room, while a banner hung over the stage up front:

**Camden Schools Contemporary Music
Competition 2014**

Debris pelted the floor the instant Jay moved: puffed wheat snacks, speckled with cheesy orange flavouring. Crumbs fell off his clothes when he stood and another half bag had been crushed up and sprinkled in his spiky brown hair.

Jay played lead guitar in a group named Brontobyte. His three band mates cracked up as he flicked orange dust out of his hair, then bent over to de-crumb a Ramones T-shirt and ripped black jeans.

'You guys are *so* immature.'

But Jay didn't really mind. These guys had been his mates since forever and he'd have joined the fun if one of them had dozed off.

'Sweet dreams?' Brontobyte's chubby-cheeked vocalist, Salman, asked.

Jay yawned and picked orange gunk out of his earhole as he replied. 'I barely slept last night. Kai had his Xbox on until about one, and when I *finally* got to sleep the little knob head climbed up to my bunk and farted in my face.'

Salman took pity, but Tristan and Alfie both laughed.

Tristan was Brontobyte's drummer, and a big lad who fancied himself a bit of a stud. Tristan's younger brother Alfie wouldn't turn twelve for another three months. He was Brontobyte's bass player and the band's most talented musician, but the other three gave him a hard time because his voice was unbroken and there were no signs of puberty kicking in.

'I can't believe Jay gets owned by his younger brother,' Tristan snorted.

'Kai's the hardest kid in my year,' Alfie agreed. 'But Jay's, like, Mr Twig Arms, or something.'

Jay tutted and sounded stressed. 'Can we *please* change the subject?'

Tristan ignored the request. 'How many kids has your mum got now anyway, Jay?' he asked. 'It's about forty-seven, isn't it?'

Salman and Alfie laughed, but stifled their grins when they saw Jay looking upset.

'Tristan, cut it out,' Salman said.

'We all take the piss out of each other,' Tristan said. 'Jay's acting like a baby.'

'No, Tristan, *you* never know when to stop,' Salman said angrily.

Alfie tried to break the tension. 'I'm going for a drink,' he said. 'Anyone else want one?'

'Scotch on the rocks,' Salman said.

Jay sounded more cheerful as he joined the joke. 'Bottle of Bud and some heroin.'

'I'll see what I can do,' Alfie said, before heading off towards a table with jugs of orange squash and platters of cheapo biscuits.

The next act was taking the stage. In front of them three judges sat at school desks. There was a baldy with a mysterious scab on his head, a long-limbed Nigerian in a gele headdress and a man with a wispy grey beard and leather trousers. He sat with his legs astride the back of his chair to show that he was down with the kids.

By the time Alfie came back with four beakers of orange squash and jam rings tucked into his cheeks there were five boys lining up on stage. They were all fifteen or sixteen. Nice-looking lads, four black, one Asian, and all dressed in stripy T-shirts, chinos and slip-on shoes.

Salman was smirking. 'It's like they walked into Gap and bought *everything*.'

Jay snorted. 'Losers.'

'Yo, people!' a big lad in the middle of the line-up yelled. He was trying to act cool, but his eyes betrayed nerves. 'We're contestant seven. We're from George Orwell Academy and we're called Womb 101.'

There were a few claps from members of the audience, followed by a few awkward seconds as a fat-assed music teacher bent over fiddling with the CD player that had their backing track on it.

'You might know this song,' the big lad said. 'The original's by One Direction. It's called "What Makes You Beautiful".'

The four members of Brontobyte all looked at each other and groaned. Alfie summed up the mood.

'Frankly, I'd rather be kicked in the balls.'

As the backing track kicked in, Womb 101 sprang into an athletic dance routine, with four members moving back, and the big guy in the middle stepping up to a microphone. The dancing looked sharp, but everyone in the room really snapped to attention when a powerful lead vocal started.

The voice was higher than you'd expect from a big black guy, but he really nailed the sense of longing for the girl he was singing about. When the rest of Womb

101 joined in for the chorus the sound swamped the backing track, but they were all decent singers and their routine was tight.

As Womb 101 hit their stride, Jay's music teacher Mr Currie approached Brontobyte from behind. He'd only been teaching for a couple of years. Half the girls at Carleton Road School had a thing for his square jaw and gym-pumped bod.

He tapped in time as the singing and finger clicking continued. 'They're really uplifting, aren't they?'

The four boys looked back at their teacher with distaste.

'Boy bands should be machine-gunned,' Alfie said. 'They're singing to a backing track. How's that even music?'

'I bet they win as well,' Tristan said contemptuously. 'I saw their teacher nattering to the judges all through lunch.'

Mr Currie spoke firmly. 'Tristan, if Womb 101 win it will be because they're really talented. Have you any idea how much practice it takes to sing and dance like that?'

Up on stage, Womb 101 were doing the *nana-nana* chorus at the end of 'What Makes You Beautiful'. As the song closed, the lead singer moved to the back of the stage and did a full somersault, climaxing with his arms spread wide and two band mates kneeling on either side.

'Thank you,' the big guy shouted, as the stage lights caught beads of sweat trickling down his forehead.

There weren't enough people in the hall to call it an eruption, but there was loads of clapping and a bunch of parents stood up and cheered.

'Nice footwork, Andre!' a woman shouted.

Alfie and Tristan made retching sounds as Mr Currie walked off.

'Currie's got a point though,' Jay said. 'Boy bands are dreck, but they've all got good voices and they must have rehearsed that dance routine for weeks.'

Tristan shook his head and tutted. 'Jay, you *always* agree with what Mr Currie says. I know half the girls in our class fancy him, but I'm starting to think you do as well.'

Alfie stood up and shouted as Womb 101 jumped off the stage and began walking towards the back of the room to grab drinks. 'You suck!'

Jay backed up as two of Womb 101's backing singers steamed over, knocking empty plastic chairs out of the way. They didn't look hard on stage, prancing around singing about how great some girl's hair was, but the physical reality was two burly sixteen-year-olds from one of London's toughest schools.

The one who stared down Alfie was the Asian guy with a tear-you-in-half torso.

'What you say?' he demanded, as his chest muscles swelled. 'If I see *any* of you boys on my manor, you'd better run!'

The boy slammed his fist into his palm as the other one pointed at Alfie before drawing the finger across his throat and stepping backwards. Alfie looked like he'd filled his BHS briefs and didn't breathe until the big dudes were well clear.

'Are you mental?' Tristan hissed, as he gave Alfie a hard shoulder punch. 'Those guys are from Melon Lane estate. Everyone's psycho up there.'

Mr Currie had missed Alfie shouting *You suck*, but did see Tristan hitting his brother as he got back holding a polystyrene coffee cup.

'Hitting is *not* cool,' Mr Currie said. 'And I'm tired of the negativity from you guys. You're playing after this next lot, so you'd better go backstage and get your gear ready.'

The next group was an all-girl trio. They dressed punk, but managed to murder a Paramore track by making it sound like bad Madonna. Setting up Tristan's drum kit on stage took ages and the woman judge made Jay even more nervous when she looked at her watch and shook her elaborately hatted head.

After wasting another minute faffing around with a broken strap on Alfie's bass guitar the four members of Brontobyte nodded to each other, ready to play. When the boys rehearsed, Salman usually sang and played, but Alfie was a better musician, so for the competition he was on bass and Salman would just do vocals.

'Hi, everyone,' Salman said. 'We're contestant nine, from Carleton Road School. Our group is called Brontobyte and this is a song we wrote ourselves. It's called "Christine".'

A song I wrote, Jay thought, as he took a deep breath and positioned his fingers on the guitar.

They'd been in the school hall since ten that morning. Now it all came down to the next three minutes.

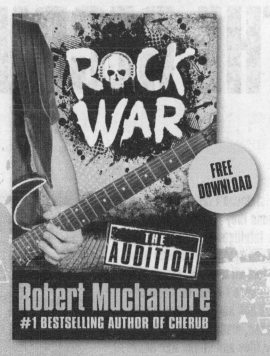

THE RECRUIT
Robert Muchamore

A terrorist doesn't let strangers in her
flat because they might be undercover
police or intelligence agents, but
her children bring their mates home
and they run all over the place. The
terrorist doesn't know that one of
these kids has bugged every room
in her house, made copies of all her
computer files and stolen her address
book. The kid works for CHERUB.

CHERUB agents are aged between ten
and seventeen. They live in the real
world, slipping under adult radar
and getting information that sends
criminals and terrorists to jail.

WWW.CHERUBCAMPUS.COM

Hodder
Children's
Books